D0416909
C2 000 004 849353

IN THE LIGHT OF MORNING

Also by Tim Pears

In the Place of Fallen Leaves
In a Land of Plenty
A Revolution of the Sun
Wake Up
Blenheim Orchard
Landed
Disputed Land

Tim Pears

IN THE LIGHT OF MORNING

WILLIAM HEINEMANN: LONDON

Published by William Heinemann 2014

2 4 6 8 10 9 7 5 3 1

First published in Great Britain in 2014 by
William Heinemann
Random House, 20 Vauxhall Bridge Road,
London SW1V 2SA

www.randomhouse.co.uk

Addresses for companies within The Random House Group Limited can be found at: www.randomhouse.co.uk/offices.htm

The Random House Group Limited Reg. No. 954009

A CIP catalogue record for this book is available from the British Library

ISBN 9780434022748

The Random House Group Limited supports the Forest Stewardship Council® (FSC®), the leading international forest-certification organisation. Our books carrying the FSC label are printed on FSC®-certified paper. FSC is the only forest-certification scheme supported by the leading environmental organisations, including Greenpeace. Our paper procurement policy can be found at www.randomhouse.co.uk/environment
http://www.randomhouse.co.uk/environment

Typeset by
GroupFMG using BookCloud

Printed and bound in Great Britain by
Clays Ltd, St Ives plc

To the memory of my father, Bill Pears, and all those who fought for the liberation of Yugoslavia (1941–45) and dreamed of a better world

'It is for your sake that I am dying.'

Slovene peasant Partisan,
calling to German firing squad, 1944

Contents

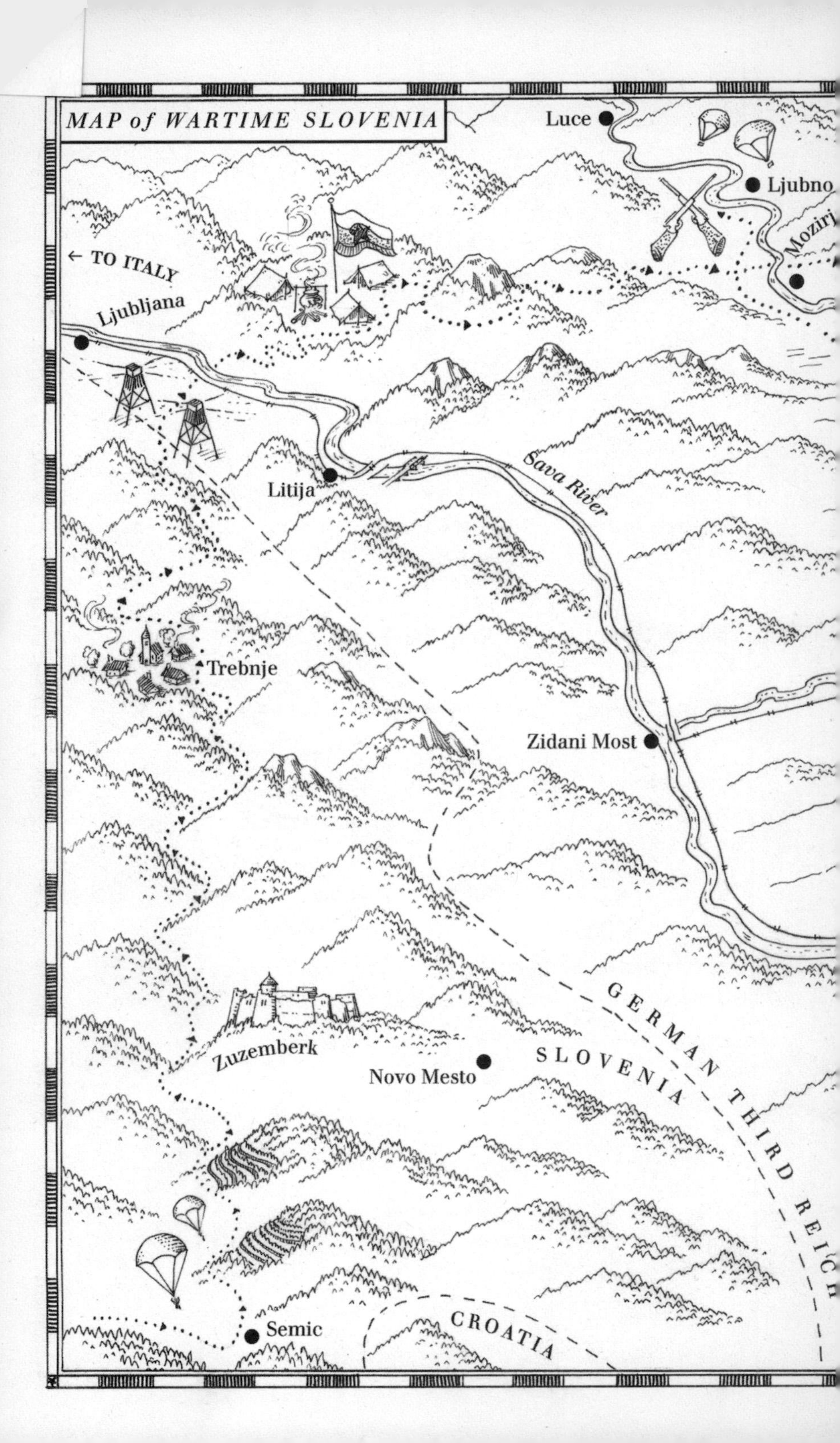
MAP of WARTIME SLOVENIA
Luce
Ljubno
Mozirj
← TO ITALY
Ljubljana
Litija
Sava River
Trebnje
Zidani Most
GERMAN THIRD REICH
SLOVENIA
Zuzemberk
Novo Mesto
Semic
CROATIA

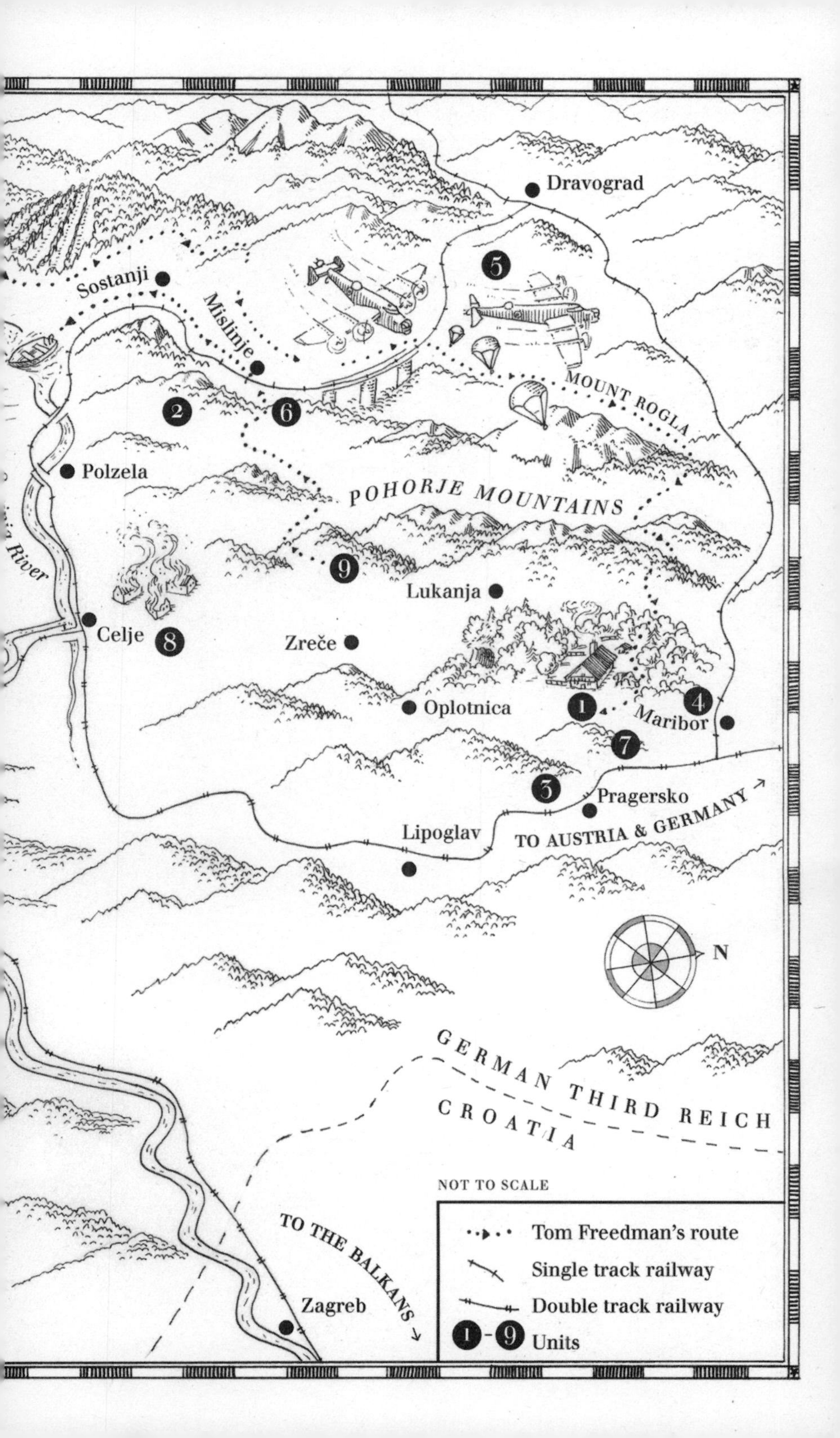

Dravograd
Sostanji
Mislinje
MOUNT ROGLA
Polzela
POHORJE MOUNTAINS
Lukanja
Celje
Zreče
Oplotnica
Maribor
Pragersko
Lipoglav
TO AUSTRIA & GERMANY
N
GERMAN THIRD REICH
CROATIA
NOT TO SCALE
TO THE BALKANS
Zagreb
Tom Freedman's route
Single track railway
Double track railway
1 - 9 Units

CHAPTER ONE

By Parachute to the Slovene Lands

May 15 1944

They stand on the sweltering tarmac in Brindisi, leaning into the wind of the Halifax engines. The air is thick and fumy with the sour-sweet smell of aero-petrol.

'Storms in the Med,' the navigator yells. 'Going to take you blokes up the spine of the country.'

Sid Dixon gives the man a thumbs-up. 'That's a relief, innit, sir?' he says to Tom. 'Least us won't be coming down in the drink.'

'Don't fancy a night swim?' Tom asks him.

'Can't swim, sir,' says Dixon.

'Are there no rivers in Devon?' Jack Farwell queries, pointing his cigar in a general direction north-west.

'They're for cows to cool down in, sir,' Sid tells him.

'What about the sea then, you country bumpkin?'

'Never seen the sea, sir. Not until this war.' Sid shakes his head. 'Still can't see the point of it.'

Farwell rolls his eyes in theatrical despair. Tom smiles. The badinage, he thinks, of nervous men.

The plane rumbles along the runway, roars and whines forward, gaining speed, then heaves itself into the air. It climbs laboriously; gradually levels off. The engines even down to a steady hum of efficiency.

It was balmy in the heel of Italy. They were told it would be cold in the plane, so Tom Freedman pulled on layers of clothes.

A vest, a shirt and two pullovers, scratchy and sweaty. An extra pair of thick woollen socks. They aren't enough. The plane is rising once more. There is rain and thunder, the peaks of the Apennines light up beside them – nature's mirror, Tom reckons, to what is happening far below, where the Allies and the Germans bomb each other's men to bits along the Gustav Line. The plane climbs ever higher, ever colder. The dispatcher gives them Sidcot flying suits, which they each clamber into, but still they sit there shivering, the three of them.

Major Jack Farwell, thirty-eight. A corpulent man, with thinning sandy hair. He looks at Tom and says something that is lost in the noise of the plane, then looks away. He only joined Tom on the language course in the last few days, and paid little attention. Jack was a Member of Parliament when he joined up. He went to the same school as the Head of the British Mission; signed up to this jaunt rather as he'd agree to a hunting expedition: looking forward to some sport. Downed his first gin of the day punctually at six and devoted the rest of the evening to boozy conviviality. Cards, gossip, argument. He yells again, frowning. This time Tom draws nearer.

'You look petrified, Freedman.'

'Are you not worried, Jack?' Tom asks.

Farwell looks at him askance. Jack's eyes are the palest blue imaginable, light and depthless. 'If anyone tells you they're not scared before a drop,' he says, 'they're either a liar or a bloody fool.' His acrid cigar breath.

'Are you scared?' Tom asks him.

'Me?' Jack says. 'Of course not.'

It is a joke, surely, but Jack is deadpan, there's not the slightest twinkle in his eye. Perhaps he is serious. They sit close enough for their flying suits to touch, but still they have to shout above the din. Jack has dry, lizard-like skin; white bushy eyebrows. 'What I want to tell you, Freedman,' he says, 'is that we don't have to like each other.'

Tom is taken aback. He had guessed that Farwell considers him bookish, dull; and that's about the sum of it. Lieutenant Tom Freedman is twenty-six. The first in his family to go to university. He was looking forward to his third year in the Honour School of Modern Languages, when war was declared. Apart from a brief bout of artillery training he has spent the war in libraries in country training schools, and in offices in Baker Street, helping to make sense of intelligence sent back from the field or of German transcripts intercepted.

'I'm sure you don't like me,' Jack continues, lurching close to Tom to make himself heard, 'any more than I like you.'

Tom wonders what he's done to earn Jack's antipathy; does not wish to acknowledge how mutual their feelings might be.

'You got to Oxford,' Jack says, 'because you deserved to. I went because my father did, and his before him. But that's not it. There's something shady about you, Freedman. You're not a man's man. But you're too bloody handsome. And quiet! You don't say enough, *that* must be what it is. You're the kind of cad, Freedman, who instead of talking to men prefers to listen to women. Let them witter their way into bed with you, is that it? I'll bet they eat you up, don't they, with those doe eyes and those soft lips? I'll bet they bloody well devour you. Well, I wouldn't trust you with my wife, but the point is that we're both British officers, Freedman, do you see? That is the point, man. And so I trust you with my life.'

What nonsense. How wrong could he be? Tom wonders how many drinks Farwell bagged before they left.

Jack Farwell reaches inside his flying suit and pulls a fresh cigar from his jacket pocket. He's pretty pleased with his little speech. 'Nice irony, eh, Tom?' he says, holding up one hand with the cigar, the other with his lighter, props to emphasise his point. 'Wouldn't trust you with my wife, yet trust you with my life.' He slaps Tom on the shoulder, as if out of gratitude for the minor role Tom has played in furnishing this profound couplet. Jack lights his cigar, inhales, blows out the pungent smoke in triumph. 'What we both have to do, of course, is to look after Dixon there.'

Tom can hardly imagine anyone less in need of care than their radio operator, Corporal Sid Dixon, who is leaning against a strut, looking around. A Devon farmer's boy, twenty-two. Short, wiry, tough. Dark-haired, brown-eyed. His sharp nose, and air of alertness, put Tom in mind of some keen bird of prey. Dixon signed up for this, 'to get back in to green valleys, sir. Couldn't stand all that sand.'

They are shivering. Dixon fumbles inside his jacket and locates a small flask of rum. He passes it with quivering fingers to Farwell, whose own hand shakes so much he can barely keep the rim of the flask to his lips. The sight is too comical: Tom is unable to stop himself from grinning. He realises his mouth must be a strained simian rictus over chattering teeth, the effect no doubt grotesque. Thus, he thinks – trembling, grimacing – we are taken to this remote theatre of war; this sideshow, as Jack Farwell resentfully dismisses it.

Night falls. The dark confers a stillness upon the scene, and seems to mute the roar of the engines, as if the men are no longer thundering through the sky but hovering in some higher dimension of space. Up in the cockpit the pilot appears as if he is made of stone.

Farwell demands a torch from the sergeant dispatcher and studies a map by its light. Sid Dixon lies back against his pack, closes his eyes, and within moments, to Tom's astonishment, is sleeping like a baby.

Tom tries to read, from his regulation pack New Testament, but cannot concentrate. He ponders their destination. His mind ratchets around information they've been given, the fragments of things he knows, in the dark unknowable void of what awaits him.

The Slovene Lands, or Slovenia, is a country the size of Wales. With fewer inhabitants. Even more varied terrain.

Slovenia is lapped by the sea in the south. The Julian Alps loom over it to the north.

Every Slovene has his smallholding; his vegetable plot, his fruit trees.

Over and over, Slovenia, in a repetitive mental stutter, revising cogent facts as if for an exam.

Slovenia is the most heavily wooded country in Europe. No, that can't be right, surely there are Scandinavian countries with more forest?

Slovenia has been slashed in two in a line from east to west. The south was occupied by the Italians – until their capitulation last September – but the north was annexed by Austria in 1941: it became part of the Third Reich. That is where Tom and the others are ultimately headed. They are destined for the vipers' nest.

Suddenly there is light shining in his eyes. 'What are you looking so worried for now, Freedman?'

Tom shields his eyes with his arm. Jack Farwell lowers the torch. 'You know what worries me?' he asks. 'What gut-rot are they going to give us down there? They tell us we're to avoid politics like the plague. Strict orders. Fine. I'll say nothing! But what kind of booze will the Reds provide? And what'll they make us smoke once my cigars run out?'

Jack does not expect or desire reassurance; without waiting for a reply, he resumes his study of the map. Tom glances over. Jack's finger rests on a spot in the Alps, between Slovenia and Austria: the Ljubljana Gap. He is like the Dutch boy, Tom thinks, with his finger in the dyke.

Jack says, without looking up from the map, 'I wouldn't worry if I were you, Freedman. We'll be lucky to survive the bloody jump.'

The dispatcher, a Royal Air Force sergeant, interrupts Tom's brooding. Dixon wakes and gives him a shot of rum.

'Wouldn't fancy your job,' Sid tells him, 'being stuck in this heap a metal.'

The sergeant, Scottish, red-faced, shoots back, 'Wouldnae fancy your job jumping out of it, pal.'

'I thought you lot had to?'

'Not us. It's the parachute packers got to jump, once a month, keep their minds on the job.' He has a sip of liquor. 'Here, have you heard the one about the plane full of German paratroopers over Greece?'

Dixon shakes his head.

'The dispatcher, right, he guides each parachutist to the door and pushes him oot. "*Achtung, achtung*. No time to mess about! Out with you cowardly *schwein*! Go! Go!"

'But one a these blighters resists. Kicks and screams, tries to jam his legs against the doorframe.

'"Out! *Schweinhund!* Zer is no place in ze German army for cowards!"'

The sergeant's German accent is vehement and absurd. Sid Dixon nods, smiling.

'Finally, the dispatcher gives him a kick up the arse and he flies oot the door.

'The parachutists still waiting to jump start to laugh.

'"So, you sink that vas funny, you *schwein*?"

'"Funny? *Ja*, sir," says one a them, as he jumps out. "Zat vas the pilot."'

Dixon chuckles. He and the sergeant each take another pull from the flask of rum. Tom lights cigarettes for the three of them.

Smoking, they become pensive once more. Tom tries again to concentrate, to keep fear of the unknown at bay by considering the known. The Balkan war, as it moves towards its no doubt bloody culmination, is shifting geographically. Armies are sliding northwards. Slovenia is assuming the greatest importance of the Yugoslav territories.

Reciting the facts is soothing, until Tom remembers he is not in a library but in this plane. The moment he has been dreading approaches. Three hours into the flight the sergeant dispatcher suggests they go aft to the rear of the fuselage. They waddle back, and it is only then that they realise how the height has been affecting them, for the short journey from the flight deck, along the catwalk, and into the bomb bay, is exhausting. The dispatcher helps them pull on their parachutes, and they sit down heavily, like three large slugs.

The altitude sickness is added to the queasiness in Tom's gut and makes his head throb and swim. The Halifax suddenly bucks and jumps. Caught in down-draughts, the aircraft begins to lurch and yaw. Then it is turning, circling.

'Skipper's seen the fires,' the sergeant informs them. They themselves can see nothing from the windowless bomb bay. 'Dropping to four thousand feet.' Wearing a body harness tied to the plane, the sergeant removes a wooden cover from a hole about four feet in diameter in the floor.

Large metal containers of explosives, guns and ammunition are attached to the undersides of the wings. They have been cut loose. The red warning light on the ceiling comes on as the pilot starts his second pass. They hear the engine power cut: the aircraft slows, rapidly loses altitude. Then the engines come back on full power, they feel the plane lunge forward, climb steeply, then bank in a sharp turn. The dispatcher moves two cargo containers with the mission's radio and batteries, backpacks, medical supplies to the edge of the hole, and clips the ends of static lines to rings on the parachutes for each one.

When the green light comes on the sergeant pushes out the containers. It will be our turn next, Tom can see. His mind is so woozy he wonders if he will faint. The static lines, having pulled open the container chutes as they fell away from the plane, rattle drily against the underside of the aircraft. The sergeant pulls them in as the plane circles again.

How uncanny it is, it strikes Tom, that I am here, in this clattering lump of leaden deadweight metal, in the night sky high above a strange country. How unlikely. How odd. His mind is detaching from him.

Sid says something, and Jack nods, but they seem, bizarrely, to be twenty or thirty feet away from Tom. They are like little copies of themselves, homunculi mocking him. He realises that he cannot focus on what is happening. Jack Farwell's reptilian face appears childlike, fragile, adrift, that of a despised, overweight schoolboy; Tom feels a sudden, immense pity for him. Sid Dixon looks back at him now, and smiles, as if he knows what is passing through Tom's mind for it passes through his, in union.

The sergeant hooks static lines to the parachutes strapped on Jack and Tom's backs. Perhaps these are really wings. Jack and Tom take their positions sitting on the edge of the hole across from each other. Its sides are some feet deep, to keep their legs from the plane's rushing slipstream. Sitting there on training jumps, his eyes fixed on the ground far below, Tom was often paralysed by fear, and had to be given a shove. Now he stares into a black night void below him. He is freezing cold, yet he can feel a neat line of sweat trickling down his spine.

Again the engines are throttled back and the flaps lowered, and again Tom's stomach is in his mouth as the plane seems to plummet hundreds of feet.

Tom glances across at Farwell: Jack gazes placidly into the dark. The coloured lamp is on again, red for *Action Stations*. Tom pulls on the end of the static line attached to the plane to make sure that it is tight. Then he reaches over his shoulder and tugs on the end attached to his parachute. The thought occurs to him that the crew are Axis spies, tipping parachuteless Allied soldiers out of planes. They want to kill him. Jesus Christ. The light is green for *Jump*.

'Go!' yells the dispatcher, and Jack Farwell, as senior officer, disappears. A moment later the sergeant repeats his command. Tom closes his eyes, grits his teeth, and shakes his head. 'No,' he whispers. He feels the sergeant's boot between his shoulder blades.

Tom plummets into a whirlpool of cold wind. It rips and tears at his clothing. He is tossed and buffeted. He is both a dead weight dropping and a tumbling speck of fluff. Mountains, stars, clouds whirl around him. He catches a single glimpse of the big plane, going away over his right shoulder, before he is yanked up by the shoulders, and held in the secure grip of the harness. The swaying canopy of the parachute cuts a dark circle out of the sky above. Relief washes through every exultant pore of his flesh.

In the distance far below he can now see the fires marking the drop area. The noise of the aircraft engines dies away, and so too does the wind. There is no sound except for the rustle of air against the silk parachute. Tom hangs, motionless in the black night. The ground rises towards him. The earth tilts fast on its axis. The fires disappear from view around the crest of a hill.

In training they had been instructed never to anticipate landing, especially at night: reflexes are conditioned to the speed of a jump off a rock, and you expect to hit the ground a fraction of a second earlier than it actually happens. Legs are broken by this misjudgement. Instead keep your legs together, knees slightly bent, arms on the risers of the chute; relax, and roll with your fall when you reach terra firma.

Tom sees what he takes to be a pool of water some distance away, reflecting stars. Just as he is trying to make out other features of the landscape below, he hits the ground.

May 16

Tom has survived the drop. No broken bones. As he unbuckles the parachute he becomes aware of whooping and yelling in the darkness. Suddenly, he is seized by two sweat-smelly, rough-shaven young men. They hug him, and kiss him, then take him one by each arm and lead him he knows not where. There is a faint yellow light. A window. A peasant house. Jack Farwell is already there. Tom is given a shot of liquor that scalds his throat, but does not clear his head.

'*Slivovka*, they call it,' Jack says, grimacing. 'A rough plum brandy. I've an awful feeling we'd better get used to it, Freedman.'

Sid Dixon is brought in. They are given more glasses of *slivovka* by men who propose noisy toasts. To Tito! To Churchill! Jack appears to have learned not a word of Slovene. Tom translates as best he can, though hardly well, his first day on the spot, throat burning, brain throbbing. Does Farwell expect him to hang on his shoulder and act as his interpreter? Of course he does.

While their arrival is celebrated in this manner, other members of the Partisan detachment bring in the containers scattered around the drop zone, and divide up the contents. Tom staggers outside. As he stands pissing against a tree he looks across and can make out a couple of fighters cutting a silk parachute into strips.

In the first light of morning they leave the house and enter a world taking shape before them, green meadows in high valleys speckled with wild flowers. Crocuses grow right up to the snow's edge. Birds awaken and fill the thin air with their song.

The supplies are loaded on farm wagons that are pulled away by oxen along white chalk roads. The Englishmen are led on a shorter route, accompanied by half a dozen men in assorted clothes, the only sign of a uniform a red star sewn into whatever headgear each sports. Around them are mountains.

Tom turns to Sid Dixon behind him. 'So this is where we are,' he says. 'This is where we shall be.'

Dixon nods. 'It'll do me, sir.'

The meadows are surrounded by dark pine forest. The outer tips of each sombre tree's branches are a light, luminous green. In a pasture stands a twin-towered gateway facing the forest like the entrance to a great castle that has vanished. There comes the sound of bells, a flock of sheep ahead. Loath to pause their grazing, the greedy beasts scatter at the last moment to let the single file of men through. A young shepherd watches, never takes his eyes off them. They pass a tall stone tower with a conical roof, a fairy-tale tower. Tom sees Rapunzel, Rumpelstiltskin, Sleeping Beauty. They are being led not towards war but away from it, into an entrancing idyll. His head is thumping, his throat is dry, he has a terrible thirst but they do not stop.

Instead, three of the Partisans take the packs off the backs of the Englishmen, put them on their own, and up the pace.

They walk past white peasant houses with red tiled roofs. Children pause to gape at them: if greeted they wave back, shyly, or turn away. Women do not see them. An old man limps across from a barn to waylay them but the Partisans do not tarry and the old man fails to intercept the crocodile formation of ragged soldiers. He beseeches and complains with the tongue of a toothless mouth, lips working over his gums like a baby. Dixon breaks rank, runs across to hand the dotard a cigarette, then trots back to catch up with his companions.

To Tom's surprise they do not stop: the march seems like a stroll to the Partisans, it costs them less effort than it does the Englishmen to haul their weight across the rolling surface of the earth. Neither do they speak, for while the foremost man in particular scrutinises the way ahead, the others too remain in a state of high alert. Jack Farwell, crimson-faced, breathes heavily, he takes off his jacket and ties its arms around his waist; ties his pullover around his neck. He looks like a kidnapped cricket umpire. Sweat darkens the armpits of his shirt, but he does not complain.

They descend into a boggy, marshy valley that is cool and dank. Tom listens, and realises the high-pitched calls of alpine birds have faded away. They approach the entrance of a cave out of which a brownish stream flows. As they pass he sees the slimy stream is made of frogs jumping and sliding over each other, hundreds and hundreds of common frogs, emerging from their winter home, out into the open.

They climb again, through a strange wild garden full of orchids. Above them are flashes of gold in the morning sun: the dipping flight of yellow wagtails. Tom feels nauseous from thirst and headache and tiredness but they do not stop. They emerge into still higher meadows. His gaze lowers from the mountains to the ground and he sees it is alive: the grass is seething. He blinks, wipes sweat from his eyes. There are black beetles on the stalks, and grasshoppers green as chlorophyll.

They stop at a place where water comes out of the hill from a spout of rock. The Partisans bid them take it in turns to fill their bellies with the cool rust-coloured water that leaves a taste of metal on the tongue. When their turn comes the Slovenes grunt with pleasure.

'The best mineral water in Yugoslavia,' one of them proclaims, rubbing his stomach in a circular motion, and Tom translates. 'Very good for the liver.'

They walk between peaks in another meadow where the petals of wild flowers take off and fly in the air from one to another, flower dancing to flower. Drawing closer, Tom sees they are not petals but butterflies, blurs of crimson, yellow, violet. Electric-blue dragonflies, too, and other insects, vibrant and buzzing with a gorgeous satiation of spring.

They descend steeply into a snug valley, and move towards a village. As they approach, the Partisans take up their weapons, though they barely slow and do not stop. At a certain distance it becomes apparent there are no roofs on the houses, or on the church. A smell of charcoal comes to Tom's nostrils.

Every building is open to the sky, blackened by fire. The village is deserted. Houses are pockmarked with bullet holes. On a blank wall a half-washed-out inscription, *Il Duce ha sempre ragione*. Across it scrawled in red paint, *Smrt fašizem – Svoboda Naroda*. Death to fascism – freedom to the people. *Zivio Tito*.

Again they climb, into wooded hills, the ground is chalk and flint beneath their aching feet and the trees are beech now. Once, they pass a tiny stone forester's hut, like the home of a troll. The smooth younger beech trunks reach from the earth like the slender limbs of young women, as if this were a place in nature where vegetable aspired to animal. Tom is reminded of strolling in the Chilterns with the family dogs. He has a memory of drinking bitter: yeasty and leaving the taste of hops to linger on the tongue. These beech forests, though, unroll on and on through the afternoon, with no tarmacadamed lanes to cross, no country pub in which to slake one's thirst with a pint of warm beer. No, there is nothing here but ridge after ridge of beech trees across an endless corrugated escarpment.

Tom remembers his mother on those walks, how the dogs went sniffing after their own adventures but kept coming back to her; to check they hadn't lost her. When his attention returns to his surroundings, he finds that the trees have turned from beech to pine. The scent of sap mixes with the smell of needles mulching underfoot, and they walk without cease for two more hours.

And then at last, just as the light is fading in the woods, they are precipitously descending and begin to glimpse through the trees an open vista. As they come out of the forest the Partisans relax, light cigarettes, ease out of the single-file formation, let the pace slow, a little, as they walk down off the hills. They drop through orchards of fruit trees, the highest still with pink and white blossom, petals falling upon them as they descend, now – the Englishmen are assured – in safe territory.

They are greeted by the senior British liaison officer, Captain Wilson. He puts Jack and Tom up in a peasant hovel that serves as British Mission in a hamlet half a mile from the small town of Semic, home of the Slovene Partisan Headquarters. They have walked for fifteen hours; they have not slept for forty-eight. Sid Dixon does not want to rest until his radio equipment arrives; the officers do not wait.

We are here, Tom thinks, as he puts his head down. *We have made it.*

May 17

Breakfast consists of tea and porridge, on which Tom pours fresh creamy milk, still warm from the cow's udder.

'We're well supplied now,' Wilson says. 'Here, that is. Not where you're going, I'm afraid.'

The small room is furnished with a table and four chairs. Kit bags, files and attaché cases are piled in corners. When the table has been cleared Farwell and Wilson lay out their maps. 'So here's the Ljubljana Gap,' Jack says. 'Cut through the Alps.'

'A double-track railway line runs through it,' Wilson says, stuffing his pipe with black tobacco. 'It was built by the Habsburgs to connect Vienna with Trieste, their port in the Adriatic.'

'You want to listen to this, Freedman,' Farwell says, as if Tom were not already intent on every word.

'You're being sent into the German-occupied zone – they call it Styria, the Jugs call it Stajerska – to supply Slovene Partisans with the means to attack rail lines running to and from the Gap.'

'To block the movement of German troops to the Italian front?' Tom asks.

'Very good, Lieutenant,' Wilson says.

'Or,' Farwell adds, 'as we prevail in Italy, to stop them retreating to deploy elsewhere.'

'You'll move around,' Wilson says, waving his pipe at the map, 'coordinating drops of explosives.'

'How much ease of movement will there be?' Tom asks.

Wilson lights his pipe. The smell is less of tobacco than of a garden fire. 'The total strength of the Liberation Front in the Fourth Zone,' he says, 'is, as far as I can gather through the fog of their exaggerations, some two thousand men. They're in small companies or tiny groups, *odred*s, scattered across three thousand square miles of mountains and valleys. Most are poorly armed. They've attacked the odd road convoy, retreated into the woods. Been living hand to mouth, most of them, reliant on peasants who are terrified of reprisal.'

'And what do they face up there?' Jack Farwell asks.

Wilson does not look up to meet Jack's gaze but continues to peer at the map. 'A force of thirty-five thousand, if you add together the Germans and their Slovene Home Guard quislings.'

Tom catches Jack's eye. Jack frowns, his lips tighten. 'I rather like long odds,' he says. 'At the racetrack, the longer the better.' He lights a cigarette, takes a deep drag, lets out a long plume of smoke. 'In war one's a little less fond of such a gamble.' He lifts his shoulders. 'Well, gentlemen, we'd better get going.'

'Not right away, I'm afraid,' Wilson says. He tells them that a German offensive is in progress in the Fourth Zone, and it's not possible to take them there for the moment.

'Don't they know,' Jack snaps, 'what's going on at Monte Cassino?'

Tom finds Sid Dixon, so they can report their safe arrival. First the message must be enciphered. This was the part of his recent training Tom had most enjoyed, using the Worked Out Key system: from a thick paper pad he takes out a page of letters set out at random; the base in Bari will have an identical copy of this page to decipher the message. Above the letters Tom writes the letters of his message, making of each one a pair.

Now he takes a small square of silk which has the alphabet across the top and down the side, and in the middle a random jumble of letters. He finds the first letter of the first pair along the line at the top of the silk, and the second letter down the side, and finds the random letter at their intersection in the middle. This is the first letter of his message, which he writes on a fresh piece of paper. Tom continues. It is painstaking, concentrated work that suits his studious temperament. At one point something causes his attention to waver: he looks up and sees Jack watching him, shaking his head.

'Do you want to check these?' Tom asks.

'Good heavens, no,' Jack replies. 'I have complete trust in you, Freedman. You remind me of my Cassie doing the *Times* crossword puzzle. Plodding work. Admirable!'

When the message is complete, Tom gives it to Sid Dixon, who makes radio contact with base and then taps out the Morse code with nicotined fingers on his brass key.

Captain Wilson obtains an audience with the Partisan military leadership, and takes Jack Farwell in to Semic. Curious to explore the town himself, Tom follows after them, stiff from yesterday's march. He passes squat wooden houses, surrounded by orchards with different varieties of tree, and open ground on which animals are tethered to stakes in the grass. A cow and goats graze. A boy leads a pig by a long rope, the end attached to a ring in its nose. A jeep passes Tom on the rough road. Clouds intermittently block the bright sun, but the morning is warm. Two children, a boy and a girl, stand and watch him: they are so immobile it is as if they believe that, should they be able to contain the least twitch of movement, they may remain invisible to him. Even when he has walked twenty yards past them and glances back he sees that they have not shifted an inch. Yet they do not look as though they are straining to achieve this effect: their shy country stillness is natural, effortless.

There are, among the orchards, vegetable plots from which green shoots and leaves are burgeoning. In one, a thin woman bends and hoes between lines, with swift rhythmic repetition.

Tom makes his way towards the pewterish bulbous top of a church tower. The houses are built of stone now, painted pastel colours, with red tiled roofs. They stand closer together; their orchards and gardens have shrunk. Horse chestnuts stand at the sides of the road, graceful candelabras of pink and white blossoms rise from their green-leaved branches. Wild asparagus grows at the verge.

Chained dogs emit low snarls of welcome. Tom admires the overhang of a wooden porch, finely proportioned yet by its marks rough-hewn. He inspects an icon of the Virgin Mary in a wall niche, her shoulders dolorously rounded and her eyes cast downward. '*For he that is mighty hath magnified me,*' Tom whispers to himself. '*He hath scattered the proud in the imagination of their hearts.*'

There is one dog unchained: a scrawny black mongrel, whose legs look too long for his terrier-like body, walks with a high-stepping gait, as if he's on his way to market. He pauses, observes Tom with an air of snooty appraisal. When he has seen enough to satisfy his curiosity he turns and resumes his progress.

There is little sign of artillery or military vehicles. This is not a garrison town but a large country village that has found itself at the centre of events. Two men in uniform trot past on sturdy ponies. A peasant woman walks beside an old nag drawing a tiny cart. As it overtakes him, Tom sees the bed of the cart is filled with jars of something, he cannot tell what. A white-haired man is clearing the road up ahead with a shovel and wheelbarrow. The town's street cleaner? As Tom gets closer he sees the only refuse the man is collecting is horse dung. The dense globules of digested grass are halfway back to mud already; they will soon be dug into the old man's garden. Tom overtakes him, inhales the sharp sweet odour of the ruminant's ordure. The day is warm, the air thin and clear. There is a buzzing of insects in the background.

Around the square in the centre of the village, clusters of oddly uniformed men, and a few women, bristle with intent, speaking to each other loudly and decisively. Tom tries shyly to eavesdrop, but understands little of what the jabbering soldiers say. Ignoring him, they come to mysterious decisions, part from one another at purposeful speed. One jumps onto a motorbike, kicks the stand away and pushes off in a single flurry of movement; he veers off out of the square in a plume of dust. The smell of petroleum is different from that in England; less chemical.

The army and the townspeople appear to coexist, in parallel. Like those childish notions of ghosts, Tom thinks, who linger beside us but in an alternative dimension, unseen except in queer atmospheric conditions. Soldiers and civilians, trying to ignore each other.

Around noon, in a birch grove on the east side of the village, Tom comes across a group of a dozen British officers and men. They sit dazed and stupefied in the grass, eyes closed or gazing into space like long-demented men. He gets talking to them. They are escaped prisoners of war who have slogged down through Austria and Stajerska, over the mountains, evading German patrols. Half of them wear ragged civilian clothing; most of their boots are broken; the men are in bad shape, with sores and abrasions that will not heal because of their poor diet. They are waiting to be escorted further, into Croatia and on to the Adriatic coast.

A young Slovene appears with a gaggle of children bearing food: bread, cheese, three bottles of thin red wine, which they pass around. The youth introduces himself to Tom. Pero has guided the Brits along the last leg of their journey here. He is a Slovene student from a town called Celje. He has a Scottish mother, he says, explaining his fine English. He is being assigned to Tom's group as their courier and interpreter. He is a tall, willowy youth with a broad peasant's face yet fine features, giving the impression of both solidity and subtlety; his movements are quick and keen.

'Come, I want to show you,' he says. Bowing, he takes Tom deferentially by the elbow. Glancing back, Tom's eyes meet those of one of the exhausted British officers, who manages a wry smile and rolls his eyes.

As they walk Pero speaks, rapidly, of his wish to hike one day across the Scottish Highlands. 'To visit the site of my ancestors' crofts,' he tells Tom. 'Before they were turned out. I want to gaze at the architecture of Edinburgh.' The boy's eyes are wide and shining, as if the prospect lies before him now. 'The Athens of the North,' he says, conclusively. He has taken on his mother's nostalgia for the home of her birth.

'It is so good you have come, our Allies, Russia's allies. We are all so happy you are here, you know.'

'We are glad to help,' Tom assures him.

They stop before a line of graffiti. Freshly written in white chalk on a grey wall are words Pero translates: *The people shall write their own destiny*.

'This is what we are doing here,' he says. 'Our great Slovene poet, Ivan Cankar, wrote those words forty years ago, and we are making his prophecy come true today.'

Tom, impressed but non-plussed at this earnest enthusiasm, is not sure what to say. Pero removes the cap from his head, lays it flat on his palm, gestures to the red star sewn upon it.

'Of course, the people have to be led by an avant-garde ideologically capable of setting out a government, and of building a truly democratic society.' Pero takes Tom's arm as he speaks. 'I'm sure you know that foreign rulers have referred to the Slovenes as a nation of servants.'

Tom knows, to his regret, no such thing, nor much else at all about the place he's come to. He thinks of how Napoleon had derided the English as a nation of shopkeepers. Well, that was before Waterloo, was it not? But something from a long-lost history lesson suggests to him that Napoleon was popular in these parts. Had he got down here? Surely not. Across the Alps?

'Yes, we are servants,' Pero tells him proudly. 'We are servants of the people!'

May 18

Jack Farwell was kept waiting yesterday. 'They tried to fob me off,' he reiterates, with irate incredulity, at breakfast. He is not a man to stand for such treatment. Having eaten, Jack is about to return to the Partisan Headquarters to pursue his cause there when a Partisan major comes to their house and introduces himself. He is heading for the Fourth Zone himself and has been ordered to accompany them on their journey north; he is to be responsible for their safety. Tom translates as best he can into English.

'Our safety?' Jack asks, looking the man up and down. 'You're the one sent to keep an eye on us, are you? Well, it's good to know we're to leave eventually.' Although they are of equal rank, Jack barges past him, and out of the house.

Embarrassed by Jack's rudeness, Tom wishes to apologise. He wonders if this would be classed as insubordination. The major, meanwhile, watches Farwell walk away; his expression remains blank, revealing neither annoyance nor amusement.

'Please come in, sir,' Tom says. 'Let me offer you a cup of tea. Though I've an awful feeling we've just finished the milk.'

The major turns his attention to Tom: there is a moment's piercing contemplation, and what Tom experiences as some kind of electric jolt of recognition. The major's blank face cracks open in a wry smile. Perhaps the recognition was one of humour; that they might be meeting on the same plane of ironic amusement. 'I should love to,' he says. 'And do not worry about the milk. It is an odd British taste anyhow. I take my tea black.'

The major's name is Jovan Vaskovicˇ. He asks about their journey here. Tom tells it as a series of blunders only enormous luck carried them through.

'I would like to jump from a plane,' Jovan says. 'I doubt if I will ever have the chance.' His brown eyes are the colour of hazelnut shells that have just turned from green to fawn; the skin crinkles at the edges of his eyes. His face is lined, crooked, well lived-in.

Jovan meets Sid Dixon, sees the radio they are to take with them. 'My men will protect this machine with their lives,' he promises Sid.

'I should like to show you something,' Jovan tells Tom, who readily agrees. They walk along a gravel road out of Semic, away from the hills into a flattish, uneven landscape. Rows of vegetation ankle- or knee-high in the fields. Copses of birch trees and scrub. Green stalks of bracken, the pale ends of their curled fronds droop modestly before they burgeon wide. Today the air is cooler, and the sky is streaked with dull clouds.

'The medical supplies we receive from your planes are very good,' Jovan says. 'But we do not have enough.'

'Then we must get you more,' Tom says.

'Also, the wrong medicines. Sometimes we think they are sent as a joke.'

'A joke?' Tom repeats. 'Having met them recently, I don't think the blokes in Stores have a sense of humour.'

Jovan nods, smiling. Again their eyes meet, and there is that feeling, for Tom, of contact at the surface revealing a deeper meeting, too. 'Last month,' Jovan says, 'we received a parachute container full of atrobin.'

'I should know what that is,' Tom confesses. 'My father is a pharmacist. But I'm not sure I do.'

'Atrobin is an excellent drug,' Jovan nods, 'for curing malaria. Very effective. But there's been little malaria in Slovenia for a few thousand years, I believe.'

'I'm merely a lieutenant,' Tom tells Jovan. 'But I'll do what I can.'

'How long have you been doing this work?' Jovan asks him.

Tom wonders if Jovan is being polite: is it obvious? He feels it must be apparent in everything he says and does. 'Since nineteen forty. My tutor at Oxford joined intelligence, and asked for me to join him. We interpreted information, and also helped agents preparing to go into occupied Europe. But this is my first time in the field.'

A pair of army trucks pass them in a cloud of white dust. As it settles, quiet returns to the landscape like water recomposing its surface after a disturbance. In the distance across the plain a white wispy column of smoke rises. They reach a small village. An old woman is planting something in a stone basin outside a house. Jovan stops and asks Tom, 'Which of these houses do you think is the hospital?'

'The hospital?' Tom looks around. Did he hear right? '*Bolnišnica*?'

'I was asked the same thing a week ago,' Jovan says. 'Standing where you are now. I did not know the answer.'

A girl walks out of a house, and across a patch of grass. She looks over, takes in the two men, pays them no heed; disappears into another house. 'Neither do I,' Tom admits.

Jovan spreads his arms. 'They all are,' he says, and resumes walking. 'Each house is a different ward. This whole village has become a hospital. The inhabitants have moved into the barns.' He turns and points at a house. 'That house is the maternity unit. The one over there, I believe, is the bakery. And there the children wash blood out of the bandages, with ash if they have no water. Come.'

They reach a stucco-fronted house. Jovan opens the dark wooden front door. Tom follows, into a short dim hallway. A door opens, and a man steps into the passage wearing an apron like a decorator, covered in paint. Or rather a butcher, Tom realises, for it is blood. With the man comes an aroma of alcohol. He passes them and steps outside. Jovan leads Tom into a room. On rough trestles lie what look like open coffins. Eight of them in the room, the heads of four against each of two opposite walls; just enough room between them for one person to stand. On each boxed-bed lies a wounded man. Some have limbs in splints. All lie silent, stoic. Again the stink of liquor, combined with a faint sweet smell of putrefaction. A girl of fourteen or fifteen comes into the room, and goes to a patient in the corner. Jovan leads the way back out.

'The men,' Tom says.

'They've gone into the woods,' Jovan says. 'They are with the Partisans. The girls run the village, as you see,' he says. 'They have been quicker to adapt than their mothers.' As they walk back towards Semic, Jovan tells him of a Partisan choir of wounded soldiers, who sing in hospitals, and on the front line.

'Will this area remain safe?' Tom asks him.

Jovan shrugs. 'Nothing is certain. There are Home Guards – collaborators – garrisoned all around this district, Bela Krajina. The Germans prod them into launching counter-offensives. Our people retreat into the hills. The Home Guard take back a slice of the plain. Most of them stick close to their village, as Partisans do if they can. Whether a man joined us or the Home Guard seems to have depended upon whether the priest of his village had socialist leanings or was anti-communist.'

Tom asks him more but Jovan explains that he himself only arrived here in Slovenia two weeks ago. It is a comforting thought that Jovan may be as surprised as Tom by what they encounter. He is a Serb, he says, not from Serbia but from Herzegovina. He's been in the National Liberation Front from the beginning, in 1941. He wears baggy black corduroy trousers and on his head a black *Titovka*, the military side-cap adopted by the Partisans. His appearance strikes Tom as a cross between an army soldier and a pirate.

'And you, Tom?' Jovan asks.

'Me?'

'In England. Mother of Parliaments. Where you got your civil war out of the way three hundred years ago. Do you make yourself busy, Tom, at election times?'

Tom shakes his head. 'I am not much of a political animal.'

Jovan smiles, with an inquisitive frown. 'So it is true that Englishmen keep their cards close to their ribs? Do you not have dreams? The desire to build a better world?'

'My dreams were academic ones. The world I wished to enter already existed. It didn't occur to me to improve it.' Tom looks away. He is glad they are walking, he can avoid Jovan's gaze, for he knows how callow he must appear. *I sound like Candide.*

'The good thing is, we are to work together,' Jovan reassures him.

'We are here to help your Slovene Partisans attack rail lines.'

'There is nothing else?'

'"We have no secrets from our allies", as Jack says. Major Farwell.'

Jovan nods. 'Our soldiers need no encouragement,' he says. 'They just need weapons and explosives. Give us the arms and *matériel* and we will do the job.'

When Tom shakes Jovan's hand, looking into his brown eyes, he feels a throb in his palm: as if, like some Masonic signal, Jovan has imparted it deliberately. Tom realises that Jovan's angular face is actually, now he has become accustomed to it, younger than he'd thought. He is probably no more than five years older than Tom; it is just that those years have been more fully lived. Jovan is so sure of victory. The confidence is in his handshake. Tom is reluctant to let go, but Jovan loosens his grip, and the two men part.

'Where the bloody hell have you been?' Farwell demands. He affects to being always in a huff.

Tom begins to tell him of the village hospital and medical needs. 'They use schnapps as an anaesthetic,' he says.

'Never mind,' Farwell cuts him off, waving his hand, shaking his head. 'Don't want to hear it. Bloody bad luck for a soldier to talk about hospitals. I've explained to the Jugs it's intolerable for us to remain here. Our men are fighting their way up through Italy; we need to cut off the Kraut supply lines. I told them if they're scared to escort us we've got our own compasses, we'll make our own way. That shook 'em. They've agreed to go the day after tomorrow.'

Be glad to see the back of us, Jack, Tom thinks.

Farwell frowns. 'I've agreed to address some bloody meeting tomorrow night. Quid pro quo. Up to the job of interpreting, Freedman?'

May 20

The commander and the commissar of the Slovene Partisans have invited Wilson, Jack Farwell and Tom to dinner with them and their senior staff. In the schoolhouse, the largest room in the village, they sit at a long table on which has been laid a vast spread: platters of sausage, ham, bully beef and potatoes. Most of the food, Wilson says, is from supplies that the Allies dropped by parachute – and the first toast of the evening is a sardonic 'grace' by the commissar, thanks for the food to whoever on high delivered it.

The food is washed down with much local wine. The meal is interrupted by a series of toasts, including one from Wilson to the Polish troops who, he announces, have taken the town of Cassino. Cake is served, heavy and thick with fruit.

At one point Jack Farwell rises and, to Tom's astonishment, instead of requesting that he interpret, proceeds to deliver a brief, fiery speech in Slovene. Had Jack found Pero, ordered him to translate and written it down, phonetically? Together the Allies and the National Liberation Front will defeat the Germans, Jack declares, and fascism will be wiped from this earth forever. He delivers the simple speech with drama and force, and when he sits down he is given a great ovation.

The commander has been in Stajerska – the annexed northern half of Slovenia – recently, and he is keen for them to appreciate how different life there is from this liberated territory in the south. There, German control is total. They will camp in the forest and move at night. They will be hungry. Patrols will hunt them. Jovan, sitting opposite Tom, nods solemnly to him in affirmation of this cheerful message, and Tom feels the threat of it lessened by his friend's insouciance. Further courses are brought, and toasts raised. Eat, and drink, for tomorrow…

The commissar explains to them, in a most reasonable tone, that the great Red Army will liberate Europe, and if only their capitalist bourgeois allies would do a fraction in the west of what the Russians are doing in the east, fascism would be defeated in a week. Will a second, western front never come? He says this with a resigned shrug of apparent pity for their decadent weakness. Jack Farwell rises red-faced to the bait and says what a blasted shame it was that the Nazis and the Reds had been in bed with each other for so long. Wilson tries to calm him down, but there is no stopping him, and he does so only when the table and chairs are cleared away.

Partisan men and a few women now flood into the hall. Sid Dixon is among them. An accordion is played, and dancing commences, men with revolvers still strapped to their waists, the Partisankas with grenades swinging from their belts. They wear a fine motley of uniforms: German, British, Italian, Slovene Home Guard. Some in their own Yugoslav uniform, showing a Soviet influence on design – high collars, tight across the chest – but cut, surely, from British blankets? When Tom shares this observation, the commissar tells him that the National Liberation Front fought largely barefoot for the first years of the war, and if the Allies really supported them they would drop more shoes and boots.

A little later Jovan quietly explains to Tom that Yugoslav village youth – who made up most of the Partisans – would naturally go barefoot all summer; that it was only their officers from the city who presumed this natural state to be a deprivation.

Of course, he added, it became a deprivation in winter. Then the young soldiers suffered frostbite, gangrene, the amputation of toes.

'From my village,' Jovan tells him, 'before the war, women walked to Dubrovnik in their rough canvas sandals. At a point outside the city they put on their good pair of shoes, and placed the old sandals in holes in the stone walls by the roadside, to collect on the way home.'

The Slovenes dance in squares and circles, interchanging partners, swinging each other around. The male and female soldiers perspire freely in their uniforms, their sweat smells of meat and liquor. Rousing songs are sung, loudly. The atmosphere, between tough young men and women, is chaste, childishly friendly. You might expect war to bring about a loosening of the restraints upon sexual behaviour; Tom had seen enough of the soldiers' wives and sweethearts he'd worked with in intelligence back home, and was glad now to be without one himself. But here, Jovan informs him, sex in the mixed Partisan army has been prohibited for the duration, on pain of death. If a female Partisan becomes pregnant, she and the man involved are summarily shot.

Farwell, Wilson and the senior Partisan officers, including Jovan, slip away. Tom stays, leaning against the wood-planked wall. As he has leaned against others, many times, in England. He is too lanky, has two left feet, and if he danced with a perfumed girl in his sweaty grip he invariably fell out of step with the tune. It was better to hold up the wall, to nurse a warm beer through the evening. But here it seems the few girls expect nothing, and the men dance with each other. Surrendering to an impetuous burst of drunken enthusiasm, Tom throws himself in to the dancing. He jumps and claps and yells a 'Hey!' when the Slovenes do. He swings a hefty Partisanka round, loses his balance, the walls reel and the floorboards rise up to greet him. Men pick him up, laughing their approval, patting him on the back. He dances more, arms interlocked on the shoulders of men on either side. It doesn't matter if he fouls up but mostly he gets it spot on, for the choreography is ingeniously simple: up and down, or side to side. He feels like one of the rugby crowd at college, drunken louts he despised, and understands all of a sudden what fun they were having.

Later on, Sid Dixon takes up the accordion from which he coaxes a wheezy tune, to which he teaches the Slovenes 'Knees Up, Mother Brown'. As Sid sings each verse, thirty Partisans wait, with mounting excitement, for the chorus, whereupon they launch themselves into as lively a performance of the ridiculous dance as can ever have been seen in England. *Knees up, knees up, never get the breeze up, Knees up Mother Brown.* Tom wishes they had a camera to record it for a *Pathé* newsreel.

Sid moves on to the 'Okey Cokey', and he and Tom show their hosts how to put their left hand in, their left hand out. The Slovenes mimic instantly. In out, in out, shake it all about. And when Sid Dixon injects a variation featuring a goose-stepping Hitler – his finger suggesting a moustache, a sieg-heiling outstretched arm – it seems to Tom that whatever might lie ahead, they have already done a fair bit for Anglo-Yugoslav relations.

May 23

Their passage north remains impossible. Jack Farwell fumes. Captain Wilson tries to distract him with a visit to the small section of Partisan artillery, Italian 75mm mountain guns. Sid Dixon plays cards under a lean-to in the garden with the British Mission's Slovene bodyguards, hands of poker for shots of plum brandy, the quality of their bluffing deteriorating through the afternoon.

Jovan pays a visit. He is armed, with a sub-machine gun. 'I have a gift for you,' he informs Tom. 'It is Italian.' A Beretta Modello 38A. 9mm. It has a lovely wooden butt and stock, looks and feels far more comfortable than Tom's Sten. Heavier, too – some ten pounds in weight, he reckons – but not burdensome. The magazine jams into the breech from below, and there are two triggers. 'One for single shots,' Jovan tells him, 'the other for automatic fire.'

They go into the orchard, where Tom empties the magazine into the trunk of a dead tree. He can't shoot without scrunching up his eyes and ears. The noise brings Sid and the bodyguards staggering around the house from the garden. Seeing there is no danger, and shielding their eyes from the bright daylight, they stumble back to their cards.

Tom slings the Beretta over his shoulder. He has not yet got used to the idea of owning a murderous weapon – but how beautiful it is. And Jovan has given it to him, not to Jack. 'Thank you,' he says.

Jovan smiles, nods. 'The Italians may not have been the best soldiers, Tom,' he says, 'but they had both the smartest uniforms and the finest weapons.'

For Tom Freedman, these are days of language acquisition. He studies his book of Slovene vocabulary, mercifully less extensive than English. He listens to people speaking and goes over his own pronunciation with Pero. Abundant inflections, odd places in a sentence where stress falls, or is absent, become rapidly familiar to him. People address each other with the familiar singular, *Ti*, or polite, plural, *Vi*, just as in French.

The lack of definite or indefinite articles; grammatical gender signified by the ending of a noun; the passive form – 'he went in the house' becomes 'house was being gone into by him' – these lose their oddity. Tom gives the language as it emerges from the mouths of men his quiet attention and after a certain point it begins to offer itself to him. And he speaks it, tentatively, haltingly, at first. People struggle to understand him. They frown and grimace in response.

'You are doing very well,' Jovan tells him, one evening, as they walk in the fruit orchards around Semic. 'We speak a sort of mixture of south Slavic languages. Serbo-Croat-Slovene. That is how I more or less understand them, and they me, though some of the younger Slovenes resent anything other than what they see as a pure Slovene spoken on their soil. In this part of their country the Italians have suppressed the language for twenty years now. In the north the Germans have resumed a suppression practised intermittently for centuries.'

'I think it's fascinating, Jovan,' Tom says, his eyes bright. 'I can't wait to tell my tutor. He wrote a brilliant monograph on how language fosters a people's sense of themselves, particularly a minority, whose language and human rights were suppressed. His examples were Breton, Basque and Welsh, which are related. It's a tremendously exciting area for research, and I doubt very much whether anyone's been here.' He nods to himself. 'Perhaps I might come back afterwards.'

Tom looks up. He sees Jovan smiling at him, and feels suddenly self-conscious. He shakes his head. 'I'm sorry,' he says, blushing. 'I was back in the cloistered world I come from. I miss it, rather, but it's small, I know. And long ago.'

'No, no,' Jovan says. 'I like your enthusiasm. Actually, I was also involved with words, you can say. I published half a dozen short stories in Belgrade magazines before the war.'

He offers a cigarette, which Tom accepts out of politeness, expecting it to be rough and tarry. It is excellent: smooth and with a delicate but distinct flavour.

'You like it,' Jovan says, pleased. 'Morava. It's Serbian.' They each inhale, hold the smoke in their lungs, savour it on their palates, before exhaling slowly. 'It is not the best Yugoslav tobacco, though, which comes from my part of the world: Herzegovinian tobacco was prized at the courts of both Vienna and Istanbul.'

CHAPTER TWO

Into the Third Reich

May 26

A route has been decided. The British trio, along with Jovan and a small armed escort, strike out for the north, led by Pero, the young courier. The radio and two heavy batteries are hauled in packs by Partisans. Jack Farwell, Sid Dixon and Tom Freedman each carry a rucksack, stuffed with his kit. Major Farwell wears his field uniform, with peaked cap and Sam Browne belt and strap. Tom has purloined a felt cap from Wilson. Sid Dixon, much bothered by perspiration on the march from the drop point, has a green kerchief tied around his neck.

'Glad to see you wearing proper country yokels' attire,' Jack ribs him.

'Sorry, sir, didn't realise we was going to be on parade.'

'To be expected from the ranks, I suppose,' Jack tells Tom. 'At least *you* haven't borrowed a commie cap off your Red friend.'

Tom blushes. Jack has already discerned his and Jovan's friendship. He wants to say something in response, but he's never been much good at such banter; he suspects Jack employs it to cover his nerves, to pretend they're simply a group of carefree hikers setting off on a jaunt.

They walk through lush pastures stained yellow with patches of buttercups that have flowered overnight, a beautiful rash on the skin of the earth. After a while the amblers coalesce into a single file, sharpening as they thread their way forward from the safe area around Semic through green lustrous valleys, becoming more like soldiers as they do so: solemn, alert. Passing by nettles, Tom notices for the first time in his life the musky scent they give off. It seems he is less the single unified personality he'd thought of himself as, than a wireless receiver of signals that he's gradually becoming attuned to.

The Partisans are armed with German rifles – some captured here in Slovenia, most in north Africa and dropped by Allied planes. Jovan carries a Schmeisser machine pistol.

They pass a section of single-track rail line. It is being repaired by men under Partisan armed guard. Jack pauses when he realises from their dirty uniforms that they are German prisoners: he finds this amusing, considering what his team aim to do further north. 'No doubt the Hun will use forced labour to repair whatever *we* manage to destroy,' he proclaims.

Thin, pale cows graze in a leisurely, deliberate manner, as if to make clear to anyone watching that it will take more than war to make them hurry. On some south-facing hillsides are vineyards. The small, twisted plants look like they've been on their terraces for a thousand years. Green buds push improbably out of the gnarled joints.

Walking through a wood, they come across a hollow full of sheep, where they surprise two uniformed men lounging by a tree. At the sight of Tom's group, the men break into a run. Jovan runs after them, shouting, '*Ustavi ali bomo ustrelil!*' He lifts the strap of his rifle over his shoulder, but before he can raise it, another soldier has taken aim. There are three loud cracks. One of the fleeing men halts and throws his arms in the air. The other staggers, and rests a hand against the trunk of a beech tree. He appears to ponder his predicament a moment before coming to a decision: to sink to the ground, and then roll on to his back. Tom stumbles over after Jovan. The wounded young man has a downy moustache, the sort that is barely worth shaving. He is gasping for breath, staring up through the leaves of the tree above him. A bullet that entered his back has come out of his chest.

The day is warm but the other youth is shivering. He seems to be trying to swallow but cannot do so, his Adam's apple shifts weirdly at his throat. Jovan looks at him angrily. 'Why did you run?' he demands. The youth can only shake his head.

The boy on the ground stops panting.

'Where do you live?' Jovan asks. The youth points a trembling arm. 'Go,' Jovan tells him. He gestures to the dead boy. 'Get some help to take him home.'

By the sheep they find two rifles with cartridge belts, leaning against a tree. The young members of the Home Guard had been milking the ewes. The Partisans offer their English guests the milk. Tom's shaking hands will not hold the bucket still. He tries to drink, milk spills down his front. The Partisans, laughing, take the pail from him and pass it round amongst themselves. When it is finished, they set off again.

So that is it, Tom ponders, as, walking, his breathing gradually returns to his control; *that is what death looks like*. A vital youth becomes a carcass, in seconds, and it's all over.

'It's shit, innit, sir?' Sid Dixon is walking beside him. 'Some kid. Younger'n my little brother.' For a moment Tom thinks that Dixon has come to offer him his support, and is touched, and indignant, but then he looks across and sees that Sid is trembling slightly as he walks. Tom reaches over and puts his hand on the corporal's shoulder.

'Bloody awful,' he says. 'I can't imagine that a person could ever get used to it.'

They climb up from the valley floor to skirt the town of Zuzemberk. Jack Farwell asks who's down there. The town holds a skulking garrison of Slovene Home Guard – *domobranstvo* – Pero tells them: locals recruited by Germans to defend the church and conservative institutions against the evil of communism, an appeal that found a response among the traditional Catholic Slovenes. Jovan gives Jack his field glasses to study the castle overlooking the Krka river. A medieval fortress with seven bastilles, only one of which still has its coned roof.

'We set the castle on fire while the Italians occupied Zuzemberk,' Pero explains. 'After they left it was reclaimed by the Home Guard. There are a few Germans there with them, as well,' he says. 'The Home Guard venture out by day, if they are feeling very brave, and retreat before nightfall.'

Jovan says nothing. He too seems shaken by the shooting of the young shepherd, though he is tight-lipped, less upset than angry. Tom walks beside him, and asks if he is all right.

'I cannot stand unnecessary death,' Jovan tells him, quietly.

They walk on and see no trace of occupation or battle. Sleepy villages, livestock grazing. A dog barks in the distance: at them, Tom feels, as if it is aware of intruders in its land. A man hammers a post into the ground. Only once does Tom hear the sound of a motor engine, a distant whine that at first he'd thought to be an insect. He recalls being told in training that the inhabitants of countries under occupation keep their heads down and get on with their lives with as little alteration of routine or comfort or safety as possible. A small number rebel. A small number collaborate. When an occupier is weakened, Tom remembers, and begins to show signs of withdrawal, then the people invariably rise up to chase him out. They just need a little encouragement.

They stop at dusk at a farmhouse, eat lamb stew mopped up with heavy bread, down glasses of a rough red wine. One of the Partisans asks the Englishmen when the second front will open.

'Soon, actually,' Jack Farwell says, with the air of someone privy to inside information. 'Very soon.'

Another Partisan, a stocky young peasant, opens his mouth, as if to speak. To Tom's surprise, out comes not speech but song. He has a fine voice, high and melodious, almost feminine. '*Tece mi tece*,' he sings. 'Flow, river, flow.' The others listen carefully, occasionally nodding at the words, as if he were explaining something they'd not fully understood before. Sometimes others join in, perhaps during a chorus, Tom can hardly tell. He is dropping off where he sits, eyelids closing and blinking open. They are led like drowsy beasts to a barn, lie one beside another in the straw, and sleep.

May 27

At first light they set off. The Englishmen, their muscles aching, walk stiff as old men. You feel it most, Tom notices, in your buttocks. Gradually your sinews elasticate. He can feel pain in places, parts of him, he'd not known existed. Pain gives him knowledge, a map forming, realms of muscle like a rippling, burning matrix that is his body, himself.

It is a little warmer than the day before. One or two of the Partisans wear items of clothing the Englishmen have given them, packs lighter for their generosity. Each man carries a blanket, and an Italian waterproof sheet.

Soon they skirt another garrison town, Trbnje. Jovan pauses to study it. He passes Tom his field glasses while he makes notes. There are streets with terraced houses painted in bright colours, similar to those in Semic. Tom can see neither soldiers nor guns. Only some old men – generals? – clad in no apparent uniform, studying something; battle plans, perhaps; the movement of troops. One of them steps forward and positions an artillery piece here; another – predicting their enemy's response? – moves a body of men there.

Jack takes the glasses, fiddles with the focus. 'Ah,' he exclaims. 'Wouldn't mind a game of chess myself.'

Outside peasant farms stand neat woodpiles, the trunks and branches precision cut before being split with an axe, so that the face of each stack is flat as a section of dry stone wall. In an orchard a wooden ladder leans against an apple tree, as it must have leaned since autumn.

They hitch a lift for their packs on a peasant wagon, for a couple of miles along a track. Sid scratches the ox behind its ears, then walks beside it, in companionable proximity. The drover does the favour with no sign of curiosity or satisfaction: when they veer off into the woods Tom watches him roll on along the track with not a backward glance.

They pass by a small, derelict castle, so covered with ivy that it looks like it is being dragged underground. Sid pauses to light a cigarette and Jovan immediately tells Jack Farwell to order him to put it out.

'The smoke can drift,' he says. 'An enemy might not see us but may sniff the cigarette.'

Pero, the guide, walks thirty yards ahead of the next man. However vigilant his attention, Tom assumes, he might meet an enemy patrol, by chance, at any moment.

In the pine forest Tom waits for Jack to reach him. 'Can you hear voices?' he asks.

'Where?'

Tom is unsure. He struggles to convince himself it is only wind in the leaves; branches scraping against each other with a sound like someone singing.

Would he notice so much around him if he were not alert to danger in the first place? He becomes aware of something at the far left of his field of vision, and turns. Deep in the forest, there is a figure watching. He draws his Beretta from behind his back and raises the butt to his shoulder. He holds his breath and aims.

'*Stoj!*' a voice exclaims. A hand grabs and lowers the barrel of Tom's rifle. He looks and sees the figure drop onto all-fours and lope off into the shadows. Tom stares after it, breathing hard.

'It is bad luck to kill a bear,' Pero says. 'Very bad. They leave us alone, we leave them alone.'

They stay that night in a farmhouse. After a thin stew and a hunk of coarse bread, they are given scrambled eggs, followed by honey and cream.

'Make the most of it,' Jovan tells the Englishmen.

Sid Dixon sets up his wireless, and relays news: the Allies are advancing on Rome. But Marshal Tito's HQ in Drvar in Bosnia – to which there are British, American and Russian Missions attached – has been attacked by German forces.

The Partisans crowd round, asking for details, desperate to know more. All are worried for Comrade Tito; their faces betray an intimate, selfless concern.

May 29

They walk all morning and reach a village just short of the border, where they rest, and eat. They have reached the northern extent of the area in which the Partisans can move, with relative safety, in daylight.

'From now on,' Jovan informs the Englishmen, 'we are to travel only by night.'

The half-dozen soldiers who'd escorted them have slipped away. They are joined now by a new, much larger group, including some with British Bren light machine guns. A fresh guide is to lead them.

'If we run into a German ambush or patrol,' Jovan says, 'you must let our Partisans engage them, and guide us around the obstacle.' Their priority – with which, Tom notes, Jack fortunately agrees – is to get themselves and their radio safely into the Fourth Zone.

They wait in the middle of the safe village. Jack smokes a cigarette, stubs it out, lights another. 'Which do you prefer, Freedman,' he asks, 'partridge or pheasant?'

'I'm not sure I've ever eaten partridge,' Tom confesses.

'Not to eat, man,' Jack says. 'I mean: to shoot.'

'I'm not much of a hunter, to be honest, Jack.'

'What, not at all?' Jack asks. 'Not even foxes?'

'I never seen a hunt,' Sid Dixon joins in. 'We don't have 'em round where we are,' he says. 'Our little hills and valleys is too crooked. You wouldn't get much of a ride round our way, sir.'

'What do you do about foxes?' Jack asks him.

'Leave 'em alone, mostly. You get the odd one's a nuisance. There's a couple of dogs in our village to deal with they.'

At dusk they set off in single file towards the border. Moonlight imbues the forest with a silvery gloom. The only sound is the crackle of their boots on brittle twigs. After ten miles, shortly after midnight, they pause. A new guide appears; the first one turns back. They press on. Within a mile they reach the edge of the forest, and look out.

The physical frontier is a double barbed-wire fence, with a cleared area a hundred metres wide either side sewn with anti-personnel mines. Sporadic watchtowers house lookouts. An advance party has already cleared a narrow path through the minefield, removing each mine by hand, and cut the wire. The Englishmen are each told to follow the man in front precisely, and they set off, crouching to minimise their silhouettes, packs bumping against their backs. The night is cold but Tom can feel sweat sliding down his skin. How narrow exactly is this tightrope of a path between the landmines? He's seen amputees. He imagines the explosion, his toes, a foot, ankle blown to bits, the meat and the blood and the gristle of his own flesh. He must not funk it. He concentrates fiercely on the Partisan in front of him, trying to see in the moonlight the outline of earth he has placed his feet upon, his eyesight keen and nocturnal.

They cross the frontier. Just before they enter forest on the northern side Tom glances to his left. A smudge of white on the horizon: clearly visible, what he presumes must be, ten or twenty miles to the west, the lights of Ljubljana.

The moon sets, and the forest is pitch black. Tom listens for the sound of the man ahead, and blindly follows him, a sightless pilgrim. They scramble up wooded ridges, splash through streams, stumble down scree. At some dark unidentifiable place they meet another new courier, who takes them forward across the double-track railroad connecting Vienna with Italy: the very target, further north, of their intended attacks.

Beyond the rail tracks lies the wide flowing Sava. The soldiers of the Partisan escort return to their village south of the frontier. The courier, Jovan, Pero and the Englishmen are ferried across the river, one at a time, each with equipment, in a tiny rowing boat. As Tom, the last man, comes over the first light of dawn is beginning to illuminate the scene – the ferryman's oars dipping into the water, the shape of the boat girdling him – but in a ghostly, partial way, as if the night will not easily let go of its black ubiquity, until Tom realises that the river is covered in mist. When he reaches the far bank there is a new patrol ready to escort them on.

They dash across an empty road and with relief enter forest beyond, climbing steadily up into the mountains. After some hours of hiking they reach the patrol's farmhouse headquarters: there these new arrivals in the Third Reich lie down, exhausted, and sleep.

June 6

Days and nights have passed, walking in the dark, waiting; eating, marching on.

When permitted to sleep, Tom slips swiftly into exhausted unconsciousness. On the hard ground, whether in peasants' houses or in the forest, his weight makes his hip or shoulder ache: the pain registers somewhere in his dreaming brain but is not enough to pull him out of the depths of sleep.

When they wake, a farmer's wife feeds them bread and broth. Neither she nor her husband look in their direction.

'It's bad enough to help Partisans,' Jovan tells Tom. 'To help you, foreign soldiers, that is very dangerous for them. They are simple people: I believe they hope that if they have not seen you, no one can prove you were here.'

In the hot afternoon Sid Dixon rolls up his trouser legs to make them into shorts. Jack Farwell pretends to be blinded by the glare.

'Good God, Corporal, have those legs ever seen daylight before?'

'Should a seen me in the desert, sir,' Sid replies. 'Proper darkie, I was.'

As darkness falls they set off with a young courier. They move forward in silence, at a fast pace. Tom walks the stiffness out of his limbs. For a while he feels strong, but worries he'll flag before too long. He regrets the active service he's missed out on; sports lessons he bunked off at school. He is impressed that Jack Farwell, more than ten years older than Sid Dixon or himself, has not yet grumbled.

Tom bumps abruptly into the Partisan in front of him. Can feel the breath of the man behind him. They grasp their weapons then stand still, on guard, making no noise; so as to hear the enemy. Something has been spotted, or heard, or sensed, up ahead. The courier slips back past Tom. They turn around. The rear of the line becomes the front. They retrace their steps, and take a different, more circuitous route.

If there is a hill, however steep, they never track around but are forced up it – breathless, lungs heaving, sweating profusely – and descend the other side, knees taking the strain.

Later on in the night it happens again, the whisper of a German patrol; again they double back, resume. The threat is intangible; their response feels like a nocturnal, adult version of childhood games he recalls from Scouts. Or the Great Game, revived, transposed from the north-west frontier to the Balkans, the Khyber Pass to the Ljubljana Gap. Tom is not an aching, sweating foot soldier, with not the foggiest idea where he is, but a representative of the British Empire. His companions are, what? Like the Pathan Musselmans in the British Indian Army... They walk in silence, each tired mind a world unto itself.

They are met in the darkness by a new courier, a girl this time, who, fresh and unencumbered, resumes without pause at a hard pace. Jack Farwell now objects, but Jovan says they have to make their destination before daybreak. Tom wonders whether Jovan is assessing them, their physical resolve, so he will know what they are capable of when truly tested? Jack Farwell struggles on.

June 9

The days progress one into another. They reach tiny farmhouses high in the mountains. Food is mutton stew, if they are lucky, or more often a watery bean soup. Dark, heavy bread. White wine. Waking in the afternoon squashed together in a room, or a hayloft. The stink of sweating feet, of unwashed socks. Ablutions. Jack and Tom shaving in a pigs trough; Sid Dixon lets his beard grow.

'You still look like a yokel,' Jack tells him, 'but now it's from the last century.'

The nights are dark, lit fitfully by flashes of far-off gunfire and by signal rockets. The mountains are hostile, pitted with gullies and trackless rock. As they climb higher, each of the Englishmen feels some nausea. At one point their path is cut into the side of a rock face. Tom shuffles forward, crabwise, feeling his way against the cold rock, vertigo making him shrink and cower. Jack Farwell enjoys Tom's grave discomfort. 'Just as well it's dark, Freedman,' he jeers. 'You can't see the sheer drop.'

'You don't think I'm cut out for this, do you?' Tom asks him when they pause to rest.

'What I think counts for nothing,' Jack says. 'You're precisely the sort they go for now. The back-room boys don't really trust impulsive types like me. Reflective, that's the word, that's what they prefer these days.'

Tom is not sure how to take Jack's comments, though he knows he's being needled.

'With me, what you see is what there is,' Jack continues. 'You may not like it. I don't give a damn.' He takes a puff on his cigar then hurls it down the rocky incline. 'That's the last of them,' he says. He puts an arm on Tom's shoulder. 'Might do well to steer clear of me the next day or two, old chap.'

In the afternoon Sid Dixon sends messages to Italy, and receives others back. Tito and his staff, and the foreign Missions, are safe. The US Fifth Army has entered Rome. Then he switches to the short-wave Forces programme. Those three familiar short notes and one long one; the Beethoven Fifth; the BBC. An announcement. Sid lifts his headphones. 'The second front!' he yells. 'It's begun!' Tom translates: four thousand ships are taking troops and guns across the Channel; the RAF is bombing German coastal defences. Before Jovan can stop them, two of the Partisans shoot their guns in the air. Others hug the English soldiers. A couple start chanting something.

Jack Farwell is beaming. 'Well, old boy,' he says to Tom, 'it's started. The push from the west.' He lights a cigarette, takes one puff, grimaces and throws it away. 'I say, Freedman, what are those boys yelling? Up the Arsenal?'

'*Nasa je Trst!*' Tom tells him. 'Trieste is ours!'

'Well, why not?' Jack nods. 'Let the blighters yell.'

Later, while they eat, Jovan makes the men who'd let loose their rifles stand guard for their indiscipline. Jovan is an outsider to the rest of these Slovene Partisans. Tom hears them refer to him as 'the Spaniard'. He asks Jovan why.

'My father was a merchant in Herzegovina. I was sent to Belgrade to study law.' There, Jovan explains, he was drawn into the milieu of progressive student clubs; by the time he graduated, in 1937, he had been imprisoned twice for his membership of the outlawed Communist Party. The party sent him to Spain, where he fought for the Republicans in the Civil War. Upon their defeat he escaped to France, and spent the next two years in an internment camp, along with a number of other Yugoslav communists. To Tom's disappointment, Jack joins them.

'Those two years,' Jovan continues, 'we developed a twin conviction: that revolution is first and foremost a national affair; but that communism is international or it is nothing.'

'"International" meaning everyone does as Uncle Joe tells them?' Farwell asks.

Tom winces at Jack's rudeness, but Jovan only smiles. 'We trust the representatives of the British Empire,' he says, 'will teach us helpful lessons in colonial freedoms.'

'Indeed we will, Major,' Jack responds. 'We've given civilisation to half the benighted peoples of this world. Something to be damned proud of, I'd say. We'll be glad to help you out as well.'

Jovan is far removed from the kind of dogmatist Tom had imagined; his amusement makes Farwell, splenetic apologist for parliamentary democracy, appear the demagogue. In 1940 he returned from the camps in France, through conspiratorial party channels, to Belgrade. A number of the Partisan army divisional commanders, and generals, he says, are Spanish veterans. Jovan has been with the Liberation Front since the surrender of April 1941, and Axis occupation. First those frustrating months of waiting, until the Soviet–Axis pact was torn up with Operation Barbarossa, the German invasion of the Soviet Union. Then the rising in Serbia in the summer.

'It is also true,' Jovan admits, 'that they *prefer* to think of me as a Spaniard than a Serb. All the Serbs they saw in Slovenia were either business sharks or military officers giving orders.'

They walk on through another night. Tom becomes an automaton, walking. Each member of the patrol has by now informed his English guests how beautiful Slovenia is; the most enchanting region in the Kingdom of Yugoslavia, by far. While they walk across it in darkness. Now and then Farwell will mutter to Dixon, 'Beautiful country, Corporal,' followed by sardonic chuckles.

June 10

They wait, in the forest.

The resistance headquarters is constantly on the move in this annexed country, as are all the assorted Partisan patrols and platoons scattered amongst the mountains and forests. All rely on couriers, who try to keep track of the shifting paths and ever-altering positions.

Pero began his Partisan career, he tells Tom proudly, as a boy courier, running lines across an area around his family farm. 'I have carried many messages between our headquarters in the south and here in the Fourth Zone. I have guided one group of walking wounded to a hidden hospital. And the escaped Allied prisoners of war and downed airmen you met, who are heading for evacuation to Italy.' The courier system, he says, is a wartime expression of Balkan hospitality: a traveller will not be let go by his host until escorted onward and delivered into safe hands in the next village. 'It is our tradition,' Pero says, with a modest shrug, as if they might prefer to live less honourably if they had the choice, but their ancestors have left them none.

No courier knows the identity of more than one comrade, Pero explains, in either direction. The contact points between segments of the line are changed every few days. There are certain post boxes – a hole in a tree trunk or rock – where messages can be left without two people having to meet. 'One of our couriers was a woman with a baby,' Pero says, eyes wide at the gall of it. 'She hid messages in the baby's nappy.'

They sit tight in the woods. It seems a link in the chain has been broken, and they wait for its mending. Cast adrift of these tenuous necklaces of boys and girls draped across the forested mountains, they are just an isolated band, easy prey. Tom reads, from the only book he has with him, his New Testament. He reads of those who wished to join Jesus and his disciples. 'Lord, let me first say farewell to those at my home.' But Jesus said to him, 'No one who puts his hand to the plough and looks back is fit for the kingdom of God.'

It is, he thinks, all or nothing. Jack sees what he is reading.

'Good for you, Freedman,' he says. 'I'm glad one of us is keeping in with the top brass. Back home, Cassie goes to church for both of us.'

Darkness falls. Suddenly there is a call, some commotion, and the man on lookout brings in a young boy: their next courier has found them.

Contact regained, their march resumes in moonlight. Above the forest they follow their own moonshadows. They scramble across a steep bank of scree, loose rocks clanking and thudding below them, and up onto a long ridge. Tom watches his feet plod, one after the other; a hundred times, a thousand times. Then something attracts his attention: a small brightness, on the ground. There. And then again, a few yards further on, to the left, a light on the ground. It is in water, a puddle at the side of the track.

Something clicks in Tom's brain and he tips his head back. The sky is adazzle with bright white jewels. He has never in his life seen half as many stars. It's a wonder they can all fit in the sky. He could reach out and scoop a handful, let them trickle sparkling through his fingers. The man behind him curses. Tom takes a deep breath, and resumes walking, trotting to catch up with the man in front.

They are back in pine woods. After a while Tom becomes aware of a blueness being breathed into the silvered air; plants slowly assume colour, it seems to seep into them; and his muscles are presented with a new challenge: beside the path grow wild strawberries. Tom bends to pick one. The taste of it makes his head swoon. He had forgotten food could be so delicious. He picks another. As he straightens, the discomfort in his back, lifting the forty-pound load in his pack, is immense. Ahead of him he can see others bend to pick a strawberry too, stooping as they walk. He wishes Jovan would let them pause, but understands by now that there is no chance that they will, in daylight, still short of that night's destination. He bends and plucks one more: strains to regain upright posture. The small berries are red, and ripe, enticingly growing all along either side of the path. Tom decides he has with great reluctance to forego the pleasure. He can see those ahead of him coming to the same sorry conclusion. They carry on, their shoulders slumped, heads bowed.

That evening, after the day's sleep, just as they prepare to resume, a courier arrives with a message informing them that they are only an hour from Fourth Zone HQ and requesting that they wait until morning, so that they can be greeted with due and proper ceremony.

June 13

They find the headquarters in a forest encampment: a force of some hundred men, a number of whom are lined up, bearing a tattered flag – Tom recognises the pre-war blue, white and red Yugoslav national flag, but now it also has a red star imposed upon it. The soldiers wear a scrappy mixture of ragged German uniforms and civilian clothes: each man bears a different weapon. Some look home-made: simple open bolt, blowback operated guns or sub-machine guns fashioned from nine-millimetre steel tubing. Tom wonders at their parts: what rudimentary ratchets and recoil springs can be inside? The men look to him like a company of tramps, weather-beaten men of the road, vagabonds in the forest. Is this the army they have toiled so far across hostile terrain to join?

Jack Farwell accompanies the commander down the motley line, returning the salute with a rigid formality, just as if he were beside the King himself, inspecting the Coldstream Guards. He then addresses them with exactly the same words with which he'd toasted the Slovene headquarters staff in Semic three weeks earlier; and arouses a similarly enthusiastic response. They wave guns, shake hands, beam at him. There are drinks and toasts.

It is evening. They are eating stew cooked up by two women in a large iron vat over an open fire. Tom wonders who carries the cauldron when they move. How much must it weigh? He watches Jovan eating: he consumes his food with speedy relish, enjoying every mouthful and then forgetting the meal instantly, for it has done its job. Tom is still eating. He carries his mess tin over to Jovan and sits beside him before he can get up and walk away.

'What's to be your role here, Jovan?' Tom asks.

'I have been sent to Slovenia to be the political commissar here, in the Fourth Zone,' Jovan tells him. 'I perform my duty, where it leads me.' He talks to Tom of his youth. Jovan's family, Serb merchants from western Herzegovina, could afford to support him all year round in Belgrade. Most families could not. More than a thousand students at Belgrade University lived for most of the year in the villages of Herzegovina, Bosnia, Montenegro, cutting the grass or tending the sheep with book in hand. They came to Belgrade to sit their exams, and took back to the villages the ideas they encountered at the University. 'It took more than forty hours on narrow-gauged trains, with long halts in Sarajevo and Mostar, to reach my father's village.'

It must have been like the earliest days of steam in England, Tom imagines, a hundred years earlier, when people were terrified by trains that moved at twenty miles per hour.

'In the summer of nineteen thirty-six, after I took my Final examinations,' Jovan tells Tom, 'I travelled around Herzegovina with a small group of fellow communist students. We walked from one village to the next, tramping for hours over the burning limestone rocks, nothing to drink for hours. We met teachers and students, and talked with them. The seeds of revolution, you see, Tom, have been sewn in the minds of many people. Even of the peasants struggling to survive in that stony wilderness.'

Tom thinks of his own student days, studying Molière, Goethe, in the upper reading room of the Radcliffe Camera, far away from the world below. And what did he ever do in the vacation? With how much more intent, and meaning, has Jovan lived?

Tom thinks of Christ telling the wealthy man who said he had observed the commandments what else he must do to inherit eternal life. 'Give away all you have and follow me,' Jesus said. The man was crestfallen. 'It is easier for a camel to pass through the eye of a needle,' Jesus said, 'than for a rich man to enter the kingdom of God.'

'In those rocky places,' Jovan continues, shaking his head, 'where there is no earth, no mud, only a thin skin of red soil between stony walls. Such poverty, Tom, it was hard to believe. We resolved to be rid of it.'

If the wealthy man will not give away what he has, then it shall be taken from him, Tom surmises. Well, and why not? He looks at Jovan: the inner fire burning has given a glow to his crooked, handsome face.

June 14

A planning meeting has been convened. The conference room consists of logs in a clearing. The Fourth Zone commander, present commissar and staff officer of the Fourth Zone are there, along with company leaders. Jack Farwell, Tom, Jovan. Ten-year-old Yugoslav maps are laid out and studied for targets: railways in Stajerska that have not yet been attacked, for want of explosives. The commander declares that once, at least, they should have the element of surprise. It must not be wasted.

Company leaders now begin to demand that they, and their small group, be given a target here, or here, on the map, each extolling the merits of his own fighters, miners, engineers. The eagerness of the Partisans for authentic military action becomes apparent. 'We will blow these bastards out of here,' one of the commanders proclaims.

Farwell had been anticipating the necessity of persuasion but finds himself instead engaged in arguing for realistic ambition. At one point he catches Tom's eye. 'I say, Freedman,' he beams, 'I can't say I was too impressed to be sent to this sideshow. But damn it all, look at them: these boys are up for a scrap.'

CHAPTER THREE

Attack on the Viaduct

June 15

A radio message was sent, and the reply is received the following morning: 'Four Halifaxes tonight.'

They are in a mountain range called the Pohorje. At its highest point, Rogla, is a large flat meadow surrounded by forest, God-given for their supply drop that night: fire signals can only be seen from the air; pilots can come in low without fear of higher mountains around. All the Partisans in the Pohorje massif, around five hundred men, are congregating there.

Through the afternoon they join the headquarters, ragged bands of men, and a few women. Rough, ill-educated, tough country people. Each with a haversack, some with weapons. They have been fetched from caves, forest glades, mountain huts, led here by young couriers.

Oxen have been butchered. The cooks work without pause, and the hungry Partisans wait in silent gratitude, then eat their fill. Afterwards they lie and doze.

At dusk it is time to go. The Englishmen hear no orders given, yet sounds of rustling, clanking and knocking ripple through the trees all around them as the guerrilla soldiers stir from their slumber, gather their possessions, move.

They are all in the meadow hours before the time of arrival, listening out for the sound of aircraft in the night. Every few minutes someone thinks he hears something, everyone else strains even harder, but it is nothing. A wind-borne mirage of sound, a trick of the mind.

An hour after the designated time a sound comes that they all hear. It grows louder… then fades away to silence. Then is audible once more. The commander orders the fires lit. The drone becomes a roar and then there is only the big bomber flying directly overhead. Jack Farwell flashes their identification signal and the pilot responds.

The Halifax circles, and begins dropping its load on the return run: first, large metal containers under the wings and then, on subsequent passes, padded bundles pushed out of the hold. They can hear the rustle of the silk parachutes in the darkness above them before they appear. And when they do, each one is a fresh surprise: it seems to materialise as if out of another dimension.

The first plane completes its drop, and is followed by three more. In the meadow, hundreds of Partisans rush about, unharnessing parachutes as they land, carrying off containers. In addition to the military supplies, large bags of white flour are dropped without parachutes. Each bag has been placed inside a much larger sack, to collect the flour when the inner bag inevitably breaks on impact. These plummet from the sky and thump on the ground, in amongst the Partisans, as if some playful giant were tossing them down. A direct hit will squash a man like a fly.

It appears to Jack and Tom, watching with the commanders, like utter chaos, whoever is to hand collecting whatever lies nearest to them. But by dawn the meadow is cleared, supplies sorted and dispersed to temporarily secure hiding. The drop includes medical supplies, and a pedal generator for Sid Dixon's radio batteries. There are also toothbrushes, soap, clothes, sweets, tobacco. Most of the guns and ammunition for the Partisans are German and Italian, to keep in line with those they already have, captured from the enemy or handed over by surrendering Italians. There are also a few British Bren guns.

After the soldiers have slept, those who need to be are armed with the new weapons. Jovan takes Tom and Jack around the wood. The Partisans are cleaning their rifles; taking them apart and putting them back together if they are new. Again it is as if an order has been given, so universal appears the habit. They lavish attention on the task, but some become aware of the Englishmen and nod and smile, their appreciation evident. The Allied planes have brought them the tools to do the job.

June 17

Two targets have been chosen. Tonight they will attack. Jack Farwell is to go with one large detachment to a tunnel some miles south. Tom and Jovan will accompany a second detachment to a railway viaduct further north.

Sid Dixon will stay behind on the Pohorje, with a skeleton headquarters staff. He has made friends among the Partisans without, it seems to Tom, learning a word of the language; and he has discovered a batch of Indian tea leaves among the supplies dropped, of which he has procured a couple of pounds. 'Good luck, sir,' he says, raising a mug of char to Tom.

'Here is the sabotage you have come for,' Jovan says. 'I hope you approve of our methods.'

'In artillery training, when I first joined the army, blowing things up was not exactly my speciality,' Tom admits. 'But I did like setting off Polish rail charges. Two small sticks of plastic explosive we attached to a single line of track. The wheels of the locomotive we wanted to stop crushed the charges, and set off the detonators; only about a metre of rail was taken out, but it could be just about enough to derail the train. We had a bit of fun playing with them on an old siding in Berkshire. A subtle explosive, if one could say such a thing.' Tom nods at the memory. 'Rather satisfying, actually.'

Jovan frowns. 'I am not sure, Tom,' he says, 'that it will be quite like that here.'

*

Soon after dark they set off down the mountain, two hundred men and women each with fifty pounds of plastic explosive in his or her knapsack; some bear weapons; others carry shovels and picks. They walk in silence; but this is quite different from the long trudges of these last weeks: Tom discerns a peculiar energy in the gait of the soldiers along the column, as they close in upon their first large-scale military operation.

It is a beautiful night. A half-moon, the sky almost cloudless. It now feels quite natural to Tom to be awake, outside, on the move when the world is sleeping.

All of a sudden the column comes to a halt. Jovan tells Tom they are less than a mile from the target. The soldiers lower their rucksacks to the ground, and sit down, while half a dozen men slip ahead to dispatch the guards on the viaduct. After a while one comes back, to give the all-clear.

They now descend to the railway line, walk to the viaduct and scramble down the embankment. Three free-standing stone columns bear the weight of the middle of the bridge across the dry gulley: massive granite pillars, each at least twelve by twenty feet. Each porter deposits his or her explosives, then is sorted into new, smaller units to set up blockades and ambushes north and south along the line and an adjoining road: there are known to be German garrisons in all directions, the nearest a mile away.

Men with picks and shovels begin to attack the rocky ground around the pillars so that they can bury the explosive, giving it far greater power than if it were merely laid on the surface. At first the men, in an effort to minimise the sound of their labours, chip delicately at the stones, but this has little effect and their officers order them to use full force. Standing some feet away, the noise of a dozen navvies banging and shovelling, of metal on stone, rings out in the night; it seems certain to Tom to wake all the Germans in Slovenia. This is not subterfuge, but a suicidal cacophony. Sparks are struck. Time slows down. The men make little impression in five minutes: Tom checks his watch in agitation and sees only one minute has ticked by. He follows Jovan from one pillar to another to view progress. The men take it in turns: two swing their picks, then the others dig. In between they lean on their shovels, panting, sweat visible on their faces in the moonlight.

After an hour of digging, the holes are sufficient; Tom watches the two Partisan miners put into each of them three thousand pounds of plastic explosives. These are connected with primer-cord, detonators are fixed, everything taped up, wires laid, before rocks are placed back into the holes on top of the explosives.

The wires are run up the embankment and along the tracks a safe distance. Jovan whispers to Tom that he doesn't understand why the German guard on the viaduct has not been replaced. When they reconnoitred, it was checked, apparently, throughout the night, yet here they are performing this interminable noisy sabotage without interruption or challenge. The event takes on in Tom's mind an air of unsettling improbability. It is as if at any moment reality will erupt in obliterating attack, the Partisans victims of some elaborate quisling entrapment.

The miners connect the electric wires to a plunger, and one of them yells out a countdown. '*Deset! Devet! Osem! Sedem!*' In between the man's declarations is total silence. '*Šest! Pet! Štiri!*' Tom takes a last look at the granite viaduct, monumental in the silvery night. '*Tri! Dva! Ena!*' He looks across, and sees one of the miners depress the plunger with an emphatic flourish. A second later comes what sounds like the loudest and most terrifying clap of thunder Tom has ever heard. It reverberates up and down the mountain valley for several seconds. Stones are thrown up into the air by the explosion. He notices that he is not the only one flinching; the men crouch down and cover their heads, and even at that distance Tom feels pinprick shards peppering the backs of his hands.

He follows the miners at a run to the viaduct. All three columns and arches have been destroyed: where the bridge stood is a gap of fifty yards. Sundered railway tracks stretch from each end into the gap, twisted and broken. Tom cannot quite work out his response. He hears Jovan's voice beside him, feels his arm around his shoulders.

'It is very beautiful, Tom, is it not?'

Tom smiles. 'Yes, Jovan,' he says. 'That's exactly what it is.'

They run back along the track and into the forest up the paths by which they came, a small rearguard left behind to cover their retreat; though they do not need to, and soon rejoin the main body of troops, with not a shot fired.

June 19

Jack Farwell's group return to the Pohorje similarly unscathed, their attack on the tunnel also a success. There were sentries at either end, but, on coming under fire, all had surrendered. Jack himself, so he claimed, had found holes in the side walls of the tunnel expressly made to plant explosives, and there the Partisans laid their charges.

'The Austrians put the holes in when they built it, so they could block the line if they needed to, to keep the barbarians out. Now we've blocked it for them.' He tips his cap in a northerly direction. 'Most welcome, Adolf, old boy.'

The Partisan commander is certain the Germans will come looking for them now, will come pouring across the massif, but he is loath to quit the best supply drop point imaginable. So sentries are posted, dotted at vantage points around the hills, and messages transmitted to Italy: send us more explosives.

June 21

The Partisans are camped in the woods all around the fringe of the massif. Meat is stewing in pots; in improvised ovens, bread is baking. Jovan escorts Tom around the encampment. A barber cuts hair. A dentist is checking teeth: his only remedy for pain is to pull them; his skill is to do so swiftly and cleanly. A man walks away hunched, resentful, holding a darkening bandage to his mouth. A doctor holds a clinic under a linden tree, his instruments laid out along a branch. 'When we had no medicine, the normal ailments of life disappeared,' he tells Tom. 'Now you have given us medicine, look!' He gestures towards the line of sorry-looking Partisans waiting to see him. 'Now they are all falling ill, and drag themselves to see me.'

The doctor inserts stethoscope earpieces and places the diaphragm on a patient's chest. There is something comical about the consulting-room procedure taking place outdoors; Tom pulls on Jovan's sleeve, and they move on. Morale is high. It makes Tom think of some great Scout jamboree more than a war of resistance against occupation.

'For those like me,' Jovan tells him, 'of course it was more, it was a revolution from the beginning. Slovenia, though, is a nation of smallholders. What would be the appeal of communism for them? People accept the truth of the revolutionary movement not because they believe in it as we do, but because it has offered the only way out of this mortal crisis.' They sit on the ground. They each smoke a Player's untipped, from among the supplies dropped. Jovan frowns through the smoke. 'It became a civil war because other groups sided with the enemy. Once the Chetniks agreed not to attack the Germans or the Italians, it was a small step to accept food from them; a further small step to accept weapons, to use against us. If the Chetniks had fought against the occupation, we would not be so strong. They have betrayed their people, and helped us.'

When Tom returns to their tent, Dixon tells him they have received a radio message: four Dakotas are coming tonight with further supplies.

June 22

Another glorious night of chaos in the meadow. Parachutes falling, flour thumping. Explosives, weapons, food, warmly received. A second radio and, to Tom's amazement, a man drifting to earth: he turns out to be a second wireless operator, Morris, sent to join them; no word of his arrival had been given, as far as Tom knows, and he has deciphered all the incoming radio messages. Jack is less surprised, although this is in keeping with the image of insouciance he likes to give off. Tom saw plenty of such types in Oxford: Jack affects to have seen it all.

There are also two containers of entirely left-footed boots. Responses vary wildly: some, taking Jack Farwell's lead, laugh with facetious delight at this bureaucratic incompetence; the Fourth Zone commissar and others scowl at the deliberate slight, attempt to interpret its intended meaning. 'The Red Army would never insult us like this,' he says.

'No,' Jack tells Tom. 'The Soviets have avoided insulting the Jugs by never giving them anything.'

Ian Morris is a cockney corporal. He emerges from his tent after a few hours' sleep and takes a look around the forest. Sid Dixon is already up, boiling a kettle. 'I thought the next place I'd see'd be Rome,' Morris says, mournfully. 'I can see all the trees I want in Richmond Park.' He paces around the clearing.

'Sugar?'

The two men discuss signal codes, call times, wireless reception. 'Weird thing is, you begin to make out the different operators at base,' Dixon says. 'I don't know how. From the speed they tap at, I suppose.'

Morris takes his first gulp of tea, then leaps up and spits it on the ground. 'Urgh,' he exclaims. 'What the 'eck's that?'

Sid Dixon grins. 'Goat's milk,' he says. 'You'll get used to it.'

Scouts report that, on orders from the German district commander, a dozen men from the garrison nearest to the viaduct have been shot. A courier brings up a copy of the German-language paper published in Maribor, in which the rail attacks are blamed on Allied saboteurs. A large reward is offered for their capture. Tom feels oddly different after reading it. No longer anonymous figures passing through the landscape, ghost soldiers, now the Englishmen's presence is known; they are identifiable, tangible targets. From now on, he understands, they will be hunted. And there is a new hunter.

'The *Crna Roka*,' Jovan tells him. The Black Hand. At their mention Tom notices Pero, sitting close by, wince. Jovan's face darkens.

'Who are they?' Tom asks.

'The worst section of the Home Guard,' Jovan explains. 'Made up of criminals and thugs. There are rumours that they have moved to Maribor, just north of here. Their purpose is to hunt down Partisans, and our sympathisers, and kill them as brutally as they can.' He looks at Tom. 'Do not be so worried,' he says. 'They are cowards. We will be quite safe from them with the headquarters staff. It is only small units, families or individuals that they dare to attack.'

June 27

Tom is shaving one morning when he hears gunfire. Couriers come running, to give reports and receive orders. A German patrol has stumbled upon a Partisan unit; a skirmish ensued; enemy reinforcements have been brought to the mountain, and now encircle it. They are held off until dark, whereupon the command is given to break out: they must somehow sneak through the enemy lines. But the enemy knows that is what they will try to do. Just as they set off, the heavens open: a summer storm, an absolute corker. Bright electric filaments of lightning streak out of the clouds, biting the earth. Then the sky darkens, and there is drumming rain. *The voice of thy thunder was in the heavens: the lightnings lightened the world: the earth trembled and shook*. It is impossible to see or hear anything. Following couriers who know these mountains they shuffle forward in single file, an endless caterpillar, holding on to the man in front, and make a slow, orderly procession. The enemy are presumably sheltering in whatever bivouacs they can muster, hoping the Yugoslavs won't bump into them. The only sound is the rain on leaves, oilskins, the bubbling earth; if there is firing further away than a dozen yards, they cannot hear it. The Partisans and their English guests stumble along, in a kind of nature-imposed truce.

They reach adjoining mountain heights as day breaks. The rain eases off. Thick grey clouds lift from just above their shoulders, and become a thinner, paler grey. The timing is miraculous.

'You see,' Jovan tells a group of soldiers close by them, 'when the people's actions are right and just, even nature is on our side.' The more simple-minded among the Partisans readily agree. He repeats what he said to Tom, for whom Jovan can claim ironic intention. Yet Jovan's natural persuasiveness is such that even Tom feels a response to some deep longing for meaning; for supernatural agency working on their behalf; that the righteous have a destiny, for which they shall be spared.

The sun comes out. They can feel the temperature rising from one moment to the next, as steam lifts from their clothing. They lie down and kip where they are, leaning against their rucksacks. In the afternoon food is passed around, slabs of cold meat and bread.

Jack sits down with Tom. They have packed and repacked their rucksacks. Tom smokes.

'When we came here, I don't mind admitting,' Farwell says, 'I thought: You bastards, sidelining me in these endless bloody mountains, with these savages. But the odd thing is, Freedman, if we can knock out these railway lines, we might even have some impact on this war.'

'You really think so?' Tom asks.

Jack peers at him, with his translucent blue eyes. 'There's no need to be so bloody earnest about it, man,' he says. 'It may not be a large impact. It may make no difference at all. Let us do what we must, and be damned.'

Jack's bluff confidence is oddly protective. He is able to take decisions and live with them unburdened by anxious thoughts of what alternative course he should have taken. He carries responsibility lightly. However different they are, Tom wonders if in time he might learn this gift of leadership from him.

CHAPTER FOUR

Supplying Units Attacking Railway Tracks

June 28

At nightfall they head west, part of a large body of Partisans. At intervals during the night a platoon of thirty soldiers, or a unit of half a dozen, peels off on one side or the other and melts into the forest.

Tom watches them go and then, suddenly, he finds himself in a small group that Pero is leading south off the path. Tom does not understand. He runs back to the column and along it until he finds Jack Farwell, and tells him what is happening.

'Yes, you need to go with them,' Jack confirms. 'Dixon, too. Change of plan. You'll need to take on a bit more responsibility now.'

'But what's going on?' Tom demands. 'I'm supposed to be assisting you. I'm not supposed to make decisions.'

The Partisans shuffle past them in the dark. The night is cool, and Tom can feel ice down his spine, though he is sweating.

'Don't worry, Freedman. You're a liaison officer. All you need to do is get base to drop supplies where the Jugs ask you to. And once you receive a reply, tell the Jugs what time they're due to arrive. It shouldn't be difficult.'

Tom is bewildered by this sudden turn of events. 'But I'm only a lieutenant,' he says.

Jack laughs. 'We'll wangle a promotion, if that's what you're after.'

'No, no,' Tom tries to explain, but Jack is not listening.

'Captain Freedman, yes, I can see that sounds better,' he says.

Tom tries to calm himself. 'Is there nothing else I should know?' he asks.

Jack looks away. 'Nothing for you to worry about,' he says. 'Do a good job.' He turns and walks away. Tom trots back down the line, until he hears a voice.

'Oi, sir. We're down here.'

Tom joins Sid, and Pero, and a small number of others. To Tom's surprise, and relief, Jovan is among them. They stand on a slope below the main path and listen to the sounds of breathing, of boots on stones, rustling clothes and equipment, which fade to a whisper, and then are gone.

Following Pero, they walk in single file. The night is cool. Tom does a head count: there are ten of them altogether. They have lost the protection of the large, headquarters contingent. He recalls the account of the *Crna Roka*, the Black Hand, and feels once more vulnerable.

At daybreak they come to a farmhouse on its own in the hills. An old man with thick white hair is outside studying the clouded sky. They were not expected but he appears unsurprised, and ushers them inside. They crowd into the kitchen, where the old man's daughter-in-law is already up. She sets about finding them food.

It is still dim in the kitchen. The woman knows her way around in the murk but for the visitors' benefit the old man lights lamps made from large, raw potatoes, hollowed out and filled with soft lard. The Partisans watch as the old man tries to light the wick he'd placed in the lard, using twigs flamed from the stove, burning his fingers, for the lard is barely flammable. But the old man perseveres, unflustered by the strangers' eyes upon him, focused in his self-appointed task, until a smelly, flickering light illuminates the faces around the room. Then the old man leaves, with Jovan.

The smell of burning lard joins those of fireplace smoke and body odour. Tom studies his companions who bunch up on trestles around the table. The six new Partisans sit in silence.

'These people,' Pero says to Tom, and Sid, 'are your bodyguard.' He introduces them. There are two women. One has a young peasant's broad-boned, gentle features. 'This is Francika.' She blushes when she hears her name spoken, but keeps eye contact. She has freckles across the bridge of her nose and cheeks; and there is something odd about her eyes. Is she cross-eyed? Very slightly, perhaps, in one eye. The other woman – 'Marija' – is older, darker, sharper, more intent somehow; and even in her unkempt uniform, weary, unwashed, retains some faint air of sophistication.

'*Me veseli*,' she says, nodding formally to Tom and Sid in turn.

There are two men, twenty or thirty years apart, both small, compact, with the same green eyes. 'Franjo', the older, turns shyly away; the younger, 'Nikola', nods to the Englishmen, beaming. They are surely father and son, but they look more like identical twins, one of whom has slipped out of chronological kilter with the other.

There is a big silent bear of a man – 'Stipe' – and a rough-looking vagabond who peers around the simple room, it strikes Tom, as if searching for something worth stealing.

Suddenly this man shoots a hand across to Tom, who takes it. 'Marko Golob,' the man whispers. 'You may have heard of me.'

Tom nods non-committally. The man still holds his hand, fixes him with his gaze. 'I am a famous fighter,' he says. 'Ask anyone.'

'Marko was one of the original Partisans,' Pero agrees, 'who took to the woods in the first days of the annexation.'

'I was a shepherd. Now I am a soldier. Ask anyone,' Marko advises the Englishmen. 'They know who I am, I've fought with most of them. I just like to do things my own way, that's all.'

A great pot of stew is placed upon the table, and fresh brown bread from which they each tear a hunk. A miraculous meal, bread and stew the loaves and fishes that peasant women of this country produce, somehow.

As they eat, Jovan returns with the old man and his wife. She carries a pail of fresh milk. The man speaks and Tom gathers that his son is far away – with the Partisans? Or in a labour camp? It isn't clear. Children appear in the room. Twins the age of twelve or thirteen, Tom thinks; the girl goes over to help her mother, the boy stands in the doorway, head bowed shyly but watching what he can from the corner of his eye. Pero winks at him. A younger girl enters and within a short while is sitting on Francika's lap.

The woman gives them milk that has soured into yoghurt, served with a spoonful of honey. In this crowded, smelly kitchen it is another intimate miracle, remarkably delicious.

Tom murmurs his appreciation.

'*Kislo mleko,*' the darker Partisan woman, Marija, tells him. 'Enjoy it. I have been in the woods for almost one year. This is very unusual. And,' she adds, nodding towards their hostess, 'of rare quality. I never tasted better, even in Belgrade.'

'Of course not,' Marko says abruptly, as if admonishing her for some insult by omission. 'Slovene women are the best cooks in Yugoslavia.'

'Surely,' says Francika, 'you mean in all of Europe?'

'In Europe?' Marko counters. 'My brother went to America to make his fortune, but he came home. You know why? He missed our mother's food.'

The young Partisan, Nikola, seated next to his father, asks, 'Is that true?' his green eyes widening.

'Oh yes,' Marko says with a definite, emphatic nod, thin lips tightening over rotten or missing teeth. 'Yes, indeed.'

'I believe it,' Nikola says. 'I believe it.' Franjo pats his son on the back, and nods agreement.

The boy in the doorway, meanwhile, has made his way over to Pero, and is studying his pistol in wonder.

Jovan stands up. Everyone else stops talking and looks towards him. He thanks the woman for her food, the old man for his generosity, all the family for their hospitality. He explains that none of them can leave their house today. 'And now, if you will allow us,' he says, 'we must sleep.'

The boy leads them to a barn, which they share with two hugely pregnant cows. The Partisans lie down in the straw and sleep. The air they breathe is flavoured by the smell of the cows blowing off periodically through the day.

June 29

In the afternoon they emerge from deep sleep, uncurling from the straw, and troop over to the house. The boy is trying to herd a pig that is somewhat larger than he is out of an enclosure. The big Partisan, Stipe, walks over. The sow runs hither and thither, avoiding the boy. The way her ears flap and her tail bobs makes it look as if she is playing a game. Perhaps she is; Tom knows little of such creatures. Stipe goes in, past the boy. He corners the sow and lifts her up, and carries her out of the enclosure. She must be about as heavy as Stipe is.

Stipe's physical presence is greatly reassuring. He is not tall, but massive. His neck is thick, his shoulders are very wide. He has a great barrel chest, and his legs are like tree trunks. It is as if his body has been squashed, so as to compress the physical power therein. He is not in fact that short, no smaller than Sid Dixon, yet he has the strength of some warrior troll or ogre. Tom is glad the man is on their side.

Francika is already in the house, helping the mother. She urges them to sit. They eat bread with dripping.

There is time this afternoon to regenerate their radio batteries. In Italy, a Briggs engine had been considered. But gasoline might not always be available, and even the midget engine was noisy. So what they have is a pedal dynamo. This particular model, Sid reckons, was captured from Germans in the Western Desert. It has a saddle and pedals, like a bicycle, and when ridden makes a noise like an enormous egg-whisk. Eight hours' cycling are required to charge one battery. They take it in turns to pedal.

The youngsters, Pero then Nikola, ride like sprinters in a race. 'They could be in the *Tour de France*, sir,' Sid says. 'Riding for their country.'

Once Sid and then Nikola's father, Franjo, have had a go, Tom opts to take a turn. He can feel immediately the increased power of his legs, since he'd last ridden a bike, all those years ago in Oxford: he pedals furiously, sweating, gasping, until he is spent, and receives a loud round of applause.

Those not cycling clean their weapons. Brown-haired Marija argues with Stipe over how to reassemble the MG34 light machine gun that he carries. Using a wood-handled spike borrowed from the farm, and a strip of leather, Marko repairs one of his boots as best he can, talking himself through the task. The son of the farm family helps them when he is allowed to, taking an eager turn on the dynamo.

Tom offers Jovan a cigarette. He had hoped Jovan would offer him encouragement, or reassurance, but instead Jovan has been taciturn since they broke off from the headquarters staff. 'May I offer you a word of advice from a Partisan officer?' he says. 'Avoid undignified spectacles, like this pedal machine.' He gestures towards the dynamo with his chin. 'You think the soldiers will like you for it. Perhaps you are right. But they will not respect you, and this is more important.'

They smoke in silence for a minute or two. 'You were not expecting this mission either,' Tom ventures.

'I should be with the command, of course!' Jovan replies instantly. 'I should be with your major, incidentally, to keep an eye on him. The Fourth Zone staff may be good soldiers, but they are naive.' Jovan emits a bitter laugh that has no feel of humour in it. 'Or perhaps the commissar is not so naive: he knows how to keep his job a little longer.' He spits a strand of tobacco on the ground. 'To hell with them,' Jovan says, and suddenly, as if shrugging a cloak off his shoulders, his mood shifts. He smiles and puts an arm around Tom. 'I am sorry, Tom, it is not your fault. Come, let us plan our campaign. Pero!' he yells. 'Bring the maps!'

Jovan, Tom and Pero study waxed road maps laid out on the grass. The main railway line is on the eastern side of the Pohorje range, between Celje and Maribor; while on the western side, between Celje and Dravograd, is a winding, single-track line.

'There are ten Partisan units scattered across these mountains,' Jovan explains. 'If we start at the top of the main line and work south, getting explosives to blow it every few miles, the Germans will catch us very quickly. Our passage must be unpredictable.'

'I know many of these mountains,' Pero says. 'We will criss-cross them.' He sketches out a route, a zigzag path, from one unit to another.

'How far apart are the railway lines?' Tom asks.

'Between thirty and eighty kilometres,' Pero tells him.

'As the crow flies,' Tom says.

'Yes,' Jovan agrees. 'And we are not crows. We have a lot of hard walking ahead of us.'

'We are one day away from the first unit,' Pero says. 'What they have been able to do so far is very little. But with British explosives…'

With the wireless batteries recharged, they listen to the news. US troops have liberated Cherbourg. Big, terrible bombs have been landing in England, from God knows where. With the map coordinates Pero gives him, Tom enciphers a message. Dixon radios for a drop. Tom watches him delicately tapping out the keys with his thick farm labourer's fingers. Confirmation comes back: delivery in two nights' time, at the appointed coordinates.

Towards dusk they pack up and move off. The family gathers to watch them leave. The woman gives them bread and potatoes to take with them. The old man kisses each man among the soldiers. The boy walks beside Pero as far as the forest. The sky is pink. Tom can smell wild garlic. He turns back: only the two girls are still watching. The women and the old man have resumed their chores; have forgotten us, Tom surmises, have returned to the present moment they inhabit. The boy does not want to go back.

'Soon you will be able to join up,' Pero tells him. 'Go home now. We will return.'

'You are the British commanding officer now,' Jovan tells Tom. 'This is your mission.'

'I suppose so,' Tom agrees. He nods, realising how much he wants Jovan to regard him as worthy of the role. 'Yes, it is. I am ready.'

Jovan takes his hand, and clasps it. 'All for one and one for all.'

Tom smiles. 'You are adopting Dumas as an early Marxist?'

'Why not?' Jovan agrees. 'I was always Aramis, when we played musketeers as children. You?'

'D'Artagnan.'

They tramp into the night. A pheasant is disturbed: its throttled cry as it rises, expression of its panic. Tom walks behind Jovan, who is first behind Pero the guide. Stipe lugs the light machine gun, Marija has a bandolier of ammunition slung over her shoulder. Father and son Franjo and Nikola stay close together, followed by Sid Dixon, and Francika. Marko the half-toothless, unshaven, rough fighter, whom Tom occasionally hears muttering to himself, brings up the rear.

The First Unit

June 30

They bivouac in the forest and fall asleep at dawn, exhausted. Tom wakes at noon to find himself resting against the trunk of a tree, alone. He staggers up, scans the wood, sees he has rolled twenty yards down the gentle slope they'd lain on. The Slovenes, accustomed to these slant conditions, have wedged themselves in place with rocks or broken branches.

A dull, cloudy day. They boil the potatoes and eat them seasoned with wild garlic. In the afternoon they walk through the forest. At one point intermittent trees have a two-foot high white band around them, at knee height. Fifteen or twenty trees are so marked, as if a remote woodsman has daubed them with white paint, marking them out for felling. But as he passes close by one, Tom sees that the bark has been eaten away and resin bled – to poultice the wound? The resin turned white as it dried. Marko behind Tom must see him studying the trees. 'A forest,' he tells Tom, 'is not a forest without deer.'

They meet up with the first unit: a twenty-strong gang of fighters. Marko and Pero each know one of the men. Two planes are due. The drop point is a grazing pasture between hills. They build bonfires. A soft rain falls. Darkness comes early. They light the fires with difficulty. Jovan orders them into position. They hear the first plane arrive over the valley. Far above the mist and rain Tom can hear it circling. The mists thicken and thin like smoke. One moment they think the planes might get through, then it is so thick and raindrops are falling from the boughs around them and the leafy tops above seem lost in a veil of rain. The fighters keep dragging more damp wood to keep the fires burning, which smoke and hiss. For half an hour the planes circle in the moonlit sky above, while those on the ground can only watch the clouds and wonder.

The longer they take the more chance there is of a German patrol hearing. Eight Partisans are posted out around the drop zone as lookouts. At any moment they may all have to cut and run.

Then a brave and bloody-minded pilot finds his way through a crack in the clouds, down between the craggy mountain peaks. Into the valley the plane appears, and then out flutter the parachutes, down come the free drops. Almost on the first one's tail follows the second plane. Once a parachute fails to open and the heavy container comes whistling down to earth like a Roman candle, and with an almighty bang buries itself deep in the soft earth.

Those members of the unit not acting as sentries sort the supplies, and then the members of Tom and Jovan's *odred* help them carry everything to a hut a couple of hard climbing miles up into the mountains.

Jovan and the unit leader confer, while Francika heats a kettle of stream water and then cooks food for all, rough ground meal moistened with hot water and patted into rubbery balls. *Zganci*. Today they are lucky, for Francika sprinkles the *zganci* with a few crumbles of pork rind that look and taste like bacon.

They bid farewell to the newly supplied unit, who will attack the main line tomorrow, and walk a few miles before making camp. In the first light of dawn Jovan chooses a resting place and they lie down on their oilskins. Before Tom closes his eyes he sees ahead of him in the forest a long tree fallen, its passage checked by the branch of another tree. A perpendicular line across a phalanx of horizontals, the pattern reminds him of the rough timber Christ carried up to Calvary. He closes his eyes to pray. Perhaps it is tiredness, the exhaustion that is becoming his regular physical condition, but he cannot think of anything to say, no pleas for the living or the dead. 'Thank you,' Tom whispers. Who to? God? What for? That Jovan is with them? And why gratitude is the sentiment that comes forth, he does not know.

The birds sing their early-morning songs. Tom's drowsy brain turns them into lullabies, as he sinks into sleep.

The Second Unit

July 1

Tom is woken by someone knocking on the door. For a moment, dream gives fluid way to memory. A man, a builder, was knocking on the walls of his parents' home. Tapping the plaster with a wooden hammer, like a doctor checking the health of the house. To the boy that Tom was it looked like odd, mysterious adult behaviour he couldn't quite explain.

Wait. Wake. He is not at home but in the middle of a faraway country. He looks around. The trees are shrouded in a thin mist. The knocking continues. The speculative-sounding tap, tap-tap, of a woodpecker in the forest.

Marija is already up. Tom watches her gathering kindling for a fire. She wears a battle-dress blouse and an old pair of plus-four trousers which she's buckled about her ankles. She is a dark and strongly built woman of about thirty, with deep-blue, almost violet eyes. Her hair shines in the sun poking through the leaves. Unlike others', lank and greasy, her hair looks as though she has just washed and brushed it. Her hands, too, Tom has noticed, are often more clean than anyone else's.

When she sees Tom is awake she invites him to help her eye and cut potatoes. After he's performed his perfunctory ablutions he comes and sits beside her. He works slowly, carefully extracting blemishes, wasting little. Marija uses her knife twice as fast, cutting thick strips of skin away as she peels. He is sure she must waste precious food, but she seems to have no choice. Others begin to stir around them. Stipe sits nearby.

'I have been to London,' Marija informs Tom. 'For a week I stayed in the Mayfair Hotel.'

Her violet eyes, Tom thinks, are fierce, and sad. 'You must have been rich to stay there.'

'My husband was. He is a Serb. We lived in Belgrade. When the Germans came he was afraid, because I am Jewish. He left me and went to hide out in his family's village.'

Tom shakes his head. Marija nods in Jovan's direction. 'Not all Serbs are warriors like that one,' she says. Jovan stands some yards away, studying a map. Tom glances towards him, and sees a fleeting smile suggest he overheard.

'Even if all of them think they are,' Marija says.

Tom's Slovene is improving each day: he understands almost everything people say, even though each of them, except for the father and son, has a different accent from each other, and for many things use entirely different words. The further north they're from, the more German has entered their vocabulary.

Right through his school and university days, Tom's teachers had often commented on his gift for languages: such a good linguist for so reticent a youth. His brain soaked up vocabulary, retained it in his memory, he merely had to concentrate to find the words he'd read or heard. The same would happen at school in other subjects – History, Geography, Maths – but only briefly. Intense revision before an exam held numbers, dates, items of information; soon afterwards they slipped through his mental net and were gone.

Again, now, it is as if Tom's brain already holds a matrix for each language he's so far encountered. The rules of grammar, syntax, conjugation: his brain whirs like a fruit machine, the oddities of the language slot into place. There is not only singular and plural in Slovenian, for example, but also dual, where precisely two of something are being discussed, with noun forms specific to two. When it is two people being spoken of, such as Jovan and Marija, the linguistic structure seems to suggest partnership; romance.

It remains less easy for Tom to make himself understood, his rendition of words is pitiful: sometimes he says something and the other person gapes at him as if he has burped. Though the Slovenes are laconic, and shy, they savour vowels in their mouths, along journeys from one consonant to the next. In English it is a virtue to clip syllables, and whole words, as short as possible. There are countless place names, for example, like Worcester or Bicester, with syllables entirely omitted. When Marija speaks to him, by contrast, every syllable is an opportunity for oral expressiveness: a simple letter of the written word can contain two, even three, changes of direction on Marija's tongue. The place they are in, the Pohorje, becomes in her voice, *Poya-haw-ria*.

'How did you come to join the Partisans?' he asks her.

'I left Belgrade, and came back to Ljubljana. My parents were no longer there. I stayed with my cousin, a doctor. After the Italians left and the Germans took over, in the autumn of last year, my cousin was arrested and taken away. Jews are used as hostage fodder; for reprisal executions. I knew they would find me soon. I took to the woods.'

Tom has grown leaner. He takes advantage of this lull: he unloops his trouser belt and with the tip of his penknife cuts a new hole. 'And now,' he says, 'you carry the ammunition for Stipe and his gun?'

Marija laughs out loud. Stipe, whittling a twig with a black-handled jack-knife, sits close enough to overhear, and frowns. 'I carry the gun for her,' he says, in a deep voice that rumbles out of his barrel chest.

'Our machine gunner was killed, we were left alone with the gun, I had to use it,' Marija said. 'It was the first time I had ever fired anything. In my life! We discovered that I could do it very well.'

'She is the best shot I have seen,' said Stipe. 'At two hundred metres she can put a burst through a saucepan lid.'

'Yes,' Marko, who has joined them, agrees. 'You would be surprised, Englishmen. This woman is a crackshot.'

Tom translates for Sid, who puts on a worried expression. 'I thought there was something scary about her, sir.'

They eat the boiled potatoes. Francika passes around some more *zganci*. Stipe puts down his whittling. He is dark, saturnine, glowering in repose, yet once animated he lightens, appears to shed weight, to lose his forbidding countenance.

'And you?' Tom asks him. 'When did you join?'

'The Germans came to my village one morning,' Stipe replies. 'They believed we had helped to feed Partisans, to give them information. There were many trucks, with much space in them. I slipped into the fields, and watched from a distance as they burned our houses. I had nothing left, what could I do? The Germans are the best recruiters for their enemies.'

Stipe shakes his head at a memory. 'After they had gone I went back into the village. The poorest houses had failed to catch alight. The women who owned them decided it would be best to burn them, since whoever emerges to govern the country is likely to pay the cost of rebuilding the village. They tried to set fire to their own houses, but they couldn't do it. The fires wouldn't take.'

Stipe walks away, picking his teeth with the stump of the peg he had whittled. Tom notices that Pero has gone. Off in search of a courier, Jovan explains, for they are entering an area Pero doesn't know.

Sid Dixon sets up his wireless. 'I've got a problem, sir,' he tells Tom. 'With static and atmospherics. Can't get a signal.'

It seems never to be in the field quite how it was in training. Here there are always snags and pitfalls. They spend most of the day roaming the forest, trying to find a radio signal. Marija becomes involved. She tells Nikola to carry the aerial up a tree. 'Higher,' she yells. 'Climb, boy. As high as the wire will go.'

The day passes in waiting. Jovan tells them they will stay in the same place in the forest that night, with a guard who is changed each hour.

They lie on the ground. Jovan, a yard or two away, reaches out and pats Tom on the shoulder. Tom grasps Jovan's hand, and squeezes it. They nod to each other. Tom smiles. Words, he realises, are superfluous; their companionship does not need them. Jovan loosens his grip, and turns over to sleep.

At some point in the night rain starts falling; silently at first.

July 2

Warm rain falls through the trees. The Partisans sleep in their oilskins, close together under an outstretched parachute, and wake with mosquito bites. Sid Dixon's face is swollen. Marko says something that makes the others laugh. Tom translates. 'He says you look like you've been sparring with Joe Louis.'

Sid nods in rueful acknowledgement. Marko gives him a comradely slap on the shoulder.

Tom himself has hardly been bothered by the mosquitoes. I must have cold blood, he tells himself; though protection from insects is something to be grateful for. His clothes are damp, he feels grubby: a hot bath, a bed with clean sheets, fresh underwear, seem like the highest luxuries imaginable.

Pero returns, with a girl who tonight will lead them towards the second unit, high in the mountains.

Another meal of *zganci*, which Sid admits to Tom he's had enough of now to satisfy his curiosity. Pero asks Jovan to tell them all a story from the early days of the war.

'They may not want to hear these tales,' Jovan says.

'Yes,' Marija declares. 'Of course we do. We Slovenes love stories; even Serb ones.'

And so Jovan nods, and after a moment's reflection says, 'After the capitulation, we members of the Party left Belgrade. We returned to our villages, to initiate the struggle there. But there was nothing to be done in my home in Herzegovina: the Ustasha fascists were established, and everyone knew everyone,

I would have lasted no time at all. So I joined friends and we travelled to Montenegro. Comrade Tito had given orders to carry out only small guerrilla attacks against the Italians there, but do you know what happened? The people rose up! We offered to lead them but they ran ahead of us.'

Stipe nods approvingly. 'Did you throw the Italians into the sea?'

'In the beginning all fought together,' Jovan continues. 'Royal Army officers commanded our units. Clan leaders fought with their villagers. It was a peasant army spread too thin: the Italians sent more troops, and counter-attacked.'

'Tell them about the Albanians!' Pero interjects.

Jovan shakes his head at Pero's enthusiasm. 'Outside Kolašin the Italians were flanked by Albanians, who ran like dogs through the woods. They were glad to resume fighting with Montenegrins, as they had under the Ottoman Empire. They shot wildly and as they ran they yelled, "You peasant rats, we're coming to kill you, you Christian runts!"'

Jovan frowns. 'We were forced to retreat. We gave up the towns we'd won. People withdrew into their clans. The Chetniks began to think about self-preservation instead of national pride.'

Marko spits onto the forest floor. 'We will fight until these bastards have left our country, don't you worry about us.'

'A free Slovenia in a free Yugoslavia,' Pero declares.

Francika has passed round the green stems of a plant, which the soldiers chew. Tom and Sid copy them, dumb human ruminants. The plant tastes grassy, and green, and leaves an aftertaste of soil.

Sid leans over to Tom. 'Can you ask her, sir,' he says, nodding to Francika, 'how she came to be with the Partisans?'

'I was not political at all,' Francika explains. She is twenty-three years old, and a widow. Her husband was a village shopkeeper.

He had no interest in politics, either. All they wanted was to make a living from their shop, to enjoy the respect of their neighbours, to have a family. 'A German officer was killed,' she says. 'Two years ago. A hundred men from our valley were taken at random and executed in revenge. My husband was one of them. I joined the movement in rage, in despair.' She looks at Sid. 'I loved my husband, so very much, but now I find I have sometimes almost forgotten him. Here, with these people, I found a kind of home.'

Tom has noticed that Francika is always ready to help: mending clothing, loading up packs, preparing camp. She is methodical, pedantic, she repeats things to make sure the listener has taken note, yet they do not seem to find this irritating. Though calm, unhurried, she is always ready when it is time to move. Jovan tells Tom that, if something were to happen to him, Francika would take over the leadership of this group. 'There would be a moment's discussion,' he predicts, 'then all would agree. Even Marija.'

But for now Jovan is the unquestioned leader. He is self-controlled, unruffled, used to imposing his authority with few words. He's not been with this group any longer than Tom, yet commands their instinctive respect. His orders are thoughtful, clear and certain. His voice is even in tone. Like Marija, he seems able to maintain a neatness in his appearance despite the primitive conditions and constant movement. After the initial fury at his banishment from headquarters, he seems to have reconciled himself to this minor mission.

The two of them are drawn naturally together, Jovan as glad as Tom to have someone with whom to talk on equal terms. It amuses Jovan to posit Tom as a representative of the British establishment. 'Why do you support the Yugoslav royalty? Even now you still expect Marshal Tito to form a government with Petar.

Let Petar stay with your royal family in Buckingham Palace! Let them play cricket on the lawn.'

'Croquet,' Tom says, smiling.

'Whatever they want,' Jovan says, 'I don't mind,' and then in English, in the manner of Clark Gable, 'I don't give a damn.' Tom is drawn to Jovan, as he recalls he was drawn, once, to an older boy at school whom he hero-worshipped.

Jovan's discipline is imposed by small measures. He insists that his men shave at least every third day; tells them that they will be mistaken otherwise for Chetniks, who have vowed not to shave their beards until the Germans are gone – and the communists wiped out. Sid Dixon, when he learns this, begins to shave again. 'To be honest, Major Farwell was right, sir,' he tells Tom. 'I was beginning to look just like my old granddad.'

They set off late in the afternoon. The rain has stopped falling. The air is cool and clear. The forest is interspersed with luminously green alpine meadows. Footsteps raise the scent of chamomile. The grass here, Marko tells them when they pause to rest, using florid gestures as well as words to express what the wireless operator cannot understand, would be cut three or four times a year. 'And from cows grazing such rich grass, what creamy milk we would have.'

'When I was a shepherd,' Marko tells the company, 'there was one meadow I took my sheep to that was full of wild herbs. They fed on sage, thyme and fennel. Their mutton was so good, oh my God.' He has to stop to lick his lips and swallow the saliva in his mouth. 'It needed nothing but a slow cook.'

Tom is sure it's true. They could reach out and pull the grass to eat themselves, almost. Marko is forty-three, he says;

an old peasant, rough-shaven, his jaw virtually toothless, in ragged clothes and a battered felt hat. He sports badly healed scars, his hands are cracked and swollen. He embodies a rural poverty that has been eradicated in England save for those who hang on to it.

'Look at him,' Marija tells Tom, when they walk again. 'That should be a shepherd's crook in his hand, not a Sten gun; those clips of ammunition in the pockets of his torn jacket? They should be corn for his chickens.' Marko procured the Sten gun for himself from the batch of weapons dropped for the first unit, and he holds it with a childish grip, tender and proud. Some months ago, Marija tells Tom, in a different part of Slovenia, a German Storch light reconnaissance plane was flying low. A peasant Partisan was driving his team of horses along a country lane. He pulled his Sten gun from under his seat and fired a burst at the plane. A bullet did some miraculous damage, for the Storch went into a spin and crashed. Now every Slovene Partisan wants a Sten gun, and to down a plane of his own.

Marija is often close to Tom, at his side when they pause. When she speaks to him she stands very close, and touches his arm, in a way that English women do not.

'What farm did *you* come from?' she asks.

'I was in Intelligence,' he tells her. 'We sent our agents into France, Poland, Czechoslovakia. Then suddenly we needed people in Yugoslavia; who could learn the language quickly, and had some idea of what was required. The top brass looked around the office and thought: Of course! Right here!' He smiles. 'I knew in theory all there is to know of what awaited us. In reality, everything is a surprise.'

Tom looks up. Marija is studying him, too intently. He looks away shyly. 'Why do you ask?'

'You are not a warrior,' she tells him without a pause for thought that such an accusation might wound him. 'There is something you lack.' Marija shakes her head. 'Or something you possess that warriors lack. Do not be upset, Tom. I have seen enough in this year for my lifetime. Of course we must fight, now, but when it is over what will they be good for, these brutal heroes of ours?' She looks pensive, and says, 'Me, too. What will I be good for?'

Pero walks beside the girl courier as she leads them on, eastwards. 'One more night,' she assures him, 'and we will find them.'

Day turns to night. Bats fly in veering circuits above their heads. In the meadows and open rocky wastes the fickle mountain rain soaks them. In the woods it collects on branches and falls in large drops upon their necks, slides inside shirts, down their skin.

The rain turns the surface of the world to mud. Rich black soil becomes sticky, glutinous, heavy. It cleaves to their boots. It splatters up their trousers as they walk, encrusting the fabric like mossy black mould. Their feet sink into the mud and each squelching step is more arduous than the one before.

When they stop, at dawn, there is nowhere to sit that is clean and dry, even fallen logs have become soggy and dirty. They try to wash but their hands become covered in mud. Mud gets into their food. When Tom lies down, the wet earth hugs him in an uncomfortably strong embrace.

He sleeps in mud and dreams of sinking into the earth; wakes to find this has happened, a few inches. He is shivering, damp to his bones. He shudders and hauls himself out to face another grey, sodden day, thinking, *I am alive! I, Tom Freedman, breathe again, my heart beats, blood pumps around my body.*

July 3

The others wake. The sky is a pale blue. Tom walks to the edge of the trees to take a piss. He looks out and can't understand what he sees. He stands and stares at a lake down below that hadn't been there before. Had it? They bivouaced at dawn, with a clear sight of a valley far below. Was there not pasture and meadow? Or is he confusing different days, or nights, with one another? Sunsets and daybreaks. He gazes upon the scene. A great watery riddle, which quite abruptly resolves itself. During the day, while they slept, the swollen river must have broken and flooded the valley, like Port Meadow in Oxford, where the Thames rises and spills across the flat grass.

While Tom sleeps, much can happen. It appears that Marko and Stipe had set snares this morning: the puny skinned carcasses of four rabbits are turning on wooden spits. With no salt or any other flavouring it is bland but welcome meat. As they are eating, Nikola, who is on lookout, brings two youths into their encampment. They claim to be from the second unit, near their hamlet high in the hills. After a prolonged discussion of direction and distance, and study of maps – which is not straightforward, for these boys have rarely seen such things, and cannot relate the maps' markings to what they know on the ground – Jovan decides on coordinates, and Sid taps out the request for a drop, later tonight.

*

They set off in the pale light of the afternoon. Tom walks behind the old man. When they woke from sleep on the ground Tom saw Franjo wince: rheumatism, his son explained, in his hip joints. He soon walks it out. The oldest by far but he doesn't falter. Tom's not heard him utter a word. Nikola appears to do all the talking for them both. They are from a wine-growing area, Podravje, in the north-east – 'the best wine in Yugoslavia', Nikola claims. There were two older brothers; both joined the Partisans; both have been killed. When the boy also joined, on his sixteenth birthday, his father insisted on accompanying him. The mother and a sister are at home, looking after their vineyard.

Tom has never seen a father and son so similarly featured. Both are mildly handsome. They each stand the same height, no taller than Marija; are lean; walk a little bow-legged. Franjo's hair is still light brown like his son's, from behind it is hard to tell them apart save for Franjo's slightly stockier frame. The only difference in their faces is that Nikola's is smooth. To look at Franjo is to see what Nikola will look like in twenty-five years' time; to look at Nikola is to know Franjo's appearance at the same age. How strange that must be for the father, Tom thinks: to so clearly see himself every time he regards his son. He wonders if the two dead sons bore so similar a resemblance, or whether they bore the trace of their mother. Sometimes it happens, one parent's genes pass on in their entirety to one child after another, the other parent invisible. These two, this pair, are like an allegorical painting brought to life, its meaning simple yet mysterious.

'He watches over me,' Nikola explains. 'Of course, it is I who watch over him. But I am glad he is with me. I am proud. We will build the new world together.'

In the dying light, Tom lets his gaze linger on the old man's footsteps. His boots are cracked, their soles worn down on the outside from his bandy gait.

Within moments of dusk settling, the rain begins to fall again. As if, once the light blue of the sky fades, it is the night out of which rain comes. They plod on, over great ridges that beckon one on to their summits, only for each one to turn out to be no more than another crest, the real peak yet to come. Then when, eventually, the top is attained Tom sees it is a mere foothill to another fortress of stone; further peaks corrugate the vista as far as the eye can see.

The two youths find the second unit, a knot of hard-bitten woodsmen in a moonlit clearing. One carries an axe, rather than a gun. None have uniforms; their clothes look handmade, of wool or leather. Tom imagines they'd be living in the forest, in woodcutters' cottages, even if there were no war. The two groups march in silence to the drop zone. The rain stops falling, the clouds part. Right on time, the planes come. At the noise of their engines, Tom's heart swells. He looks across and though it is dark he can see Sid Dixon grinning too. The leader of the unit assures Jovan that his men can hide everything, Jovan's *odred* should be on its way.

Pero leads them on. They tramp through damp, dark woods. Suddenly in the night a horrible sound, a long drawn-out screech, of distress or warning – What the hell is it, bird or beast? – or the anguished love call of some unknown animal rutting. It howls again, away to one side of them, off in the looming darkness. Tom stops to peer into the gloom, but he is the only one. To the others, it is of no interest.

The Third Unit

July 4

Tom wakes at midday to the smell of wood smoke. Everyone else is already up, agitated. The fire is not theirs. Stipe and Marko have gone off to find out to whom it belongs. Tom is waiting with the others, their rucksacks packed, weapons at the ready, by the time the pair return. They report to Jovan. It seems from their demeanour that there is no immediate danger.

The encampment consists of half a dozen simple tents, single sheets folded into triangular shelters open at each end, held up by rough poles and guy ropes. Their inhabitants gaze at the Partisans. They are almost all children: girls in headscarves and loose skirts that might once have been brightly coloured, now are faded and threadbare; gaunt, bare-chested boys with the grave and sombre faces of men. Older girls have babies on their skinny hips; Tom cannot tell whether they are mothers or sisters of the infants they hold. All share the same hollow-eyed expression, the same exhausted curiosity.

A small old man sits on the low branch of a tree. He seems to be looking at things now here, then there, that are not apparent to anyone else. Tom watches him, his odd behaviour compelling: he is blind, and is turning not his eye towards sights but his ear towards sounds.

There are one or two older women, with whom Jovan confers. He comes back to his group. 'We must feed these people,' he says.

Franjo and Nikola go off in one direction, Marko and Pero in another. 'Watch our cooking pot,' Marko warns Francika over his shoulder. 'And tell the Englishman to keep hold of his wireless.'

'They are starving,' she admonishes him.

Marko grins, without humour. 'A gypsy stops stealing only when he is dead,' he says. 'And even then, if you have something missing, I advise you to search his grave.'

Francika and Marija stay with the women and children, sharing their rudimentary medicine. Stipe sharpens his knife. Jovan finds a thick, low branch for him to use. He tells Tom he does not want to risk sending or receiving a radio signal.

'What happened to the men, sir?' Sid asks Tom.

'No one knows,' Tom tells him.

Shortly before dusk the hunters return. Franjo and his son have half a dozen rabbits; Marko and Pero have been more successful: each man hauls the carcass of a small deer over his shoulders. Francika has built up the gypsies' fire. The carcasses are not big. Stipe butchers them, one after the other, on the branch Jovan found. He cuts their red fur-lined skin in swatches, which one of the gypsy girls gathers and takes to a tent.

Francika sets the deer meat roasting on spits across the fire. The gypsies gather to watch. The mothers hold their children back like trained puppies, with guttural commands. The children stare at the food; their expressions suggest that the sight, or the smell, of it pains them. When it is almost ready the elder woman says a grace, and the children cross themselves. When they are permitted to eat they do not fall upon the food but consume it with a disciplined persistence, chewing their way deliberately through the meat, filling their stomachs with it, as if stashing it away to fuel them for weeks to come. The Partisans watch them: this is real hunger. The blind old man chews the meat with his gums. He looks to Tom like a runner falling ever further behind the rest of the pack. Tom looks around, and sees that the older woman is weeping. He asks Marija why. 'She is so happy,' Marija tells him. 'That is why.'

Pero and Nikola have gone to keep watch. In the light of the campfire, one of the gypsy boys steps forward and juggles with two, three, four sticks of wood. Then it is the turn of a small girl: she sings a simple song while an older boy beats the rhythm for her with two pieces of stone. They have eaten and now they take it in turns to perform. Two boys throw a smaller one between them; the tumbler has long hair and is as light as a bird, and he flies from one boy to the other. The old man sings with a child's voice. They are expressing their gratitude for the meal, Tom tells Sid. Just then Nikola and Pero come back from their watch, to be replaced by Marko and Francika. Tom notices one of the women talking to an older girl. No sooner have the guards sat down than they are each joined by one of the older gypsy girls.

Two boys dance, grinding their heels into the dirt. A girl sings a loud and fretful song. The next time Tom looks over, he sees that Pero and Nikola, and their acquaintances, have gone, vanished into the darkness away from the fire. What is happening sinks in. Aghast, Tom crosses over to where Jovan is sitting beside Marija, and tells him that the girls are giving themselves to the Partisans: they must be told that they do not need to. Jovan puts an arm around Tom's shoulders.

‘They are a proud people,’ he says. ‘Allow them their pride. They would rather give what they can than give nothing, and be beholden to us.’

‘But they’re girls,’ Tom objects. ‘Surely…’ He stops speaking.

Jovan pats him on the back. ‘We have done well today,’ he says. ‘No bridges blown, but a good day nonetheless.’

July 5

Tom falls asleep by the fire. After what feels like a few minutes he is woken: a new courier has appeared, a boy of about fourteen. They pack up speedily and leave the gypsies with brief goodbyes, and head out. The boy keeps them moving very fast: they have a long walk ahead of them, back across the Pohorje towards the main line. Within minutes their encounter with the gypsies seems to Tom as if it were a dream.

The night is dark, and there is little fear of running into German patrols, but he is aware of the Black Hand's reputation for carrying out their atrocities at night. Still, he appreciates that he is stronger than even a week ago. Becoming geared to the tempo of guerrilla life. Leg muscles, lung capacity adapting, he is growing tougher all the time, and they are walking fast, striding, at a pace he can comfortably maintain.

That day they sleep under a parachute canopy. More meat is caught, and cooked. It is salty, like pork. 'Why do the rabbits here taste better than in England?' Tom wonders.

Marko laughs, his bad teeth showing. 'It is rat!' he says. 'Even Slovene rat is better than English rabbit.'

In the afternoon, Tom writes a letter home, though there is no prospect of it being sent. Francika cuts Marija's hair. Sid, watching, requests a trim, too. When it is time for the regular scheduled wireless contact, Sid sets up his equipment. Francika sits beside him, watches how he taps the keys. Sid makes contact with HQ, another drop is agreed for midnight, in two nights' time.

As they are packing up, Nikola runs into their clearing. 'Come,' he says to Jovan, 'see what I have found.'

They drop to the edge of the forest, by an alpine meadow, and there is a wild plum tree. Pero joins Nikola clambering up: the youngsters shake the branches, purple plums cascade to the ground.

'It is a miracle to grow so high up the mountain,' Marko says. 'They will be very sour.'

Stipe bites into one. 'Madonna,' he says, and crosses himself.

They are firm, like large damsons, but as sweet as juicy plums. The soldiers eat their fill, scooping out the stones with their tongues and spitting them on the ground.

As they sit around, Pero realises that his cap is missing. Everyone helps him search for it, until Marija tells him to look up: there it is, hooked to a branch high up in the plum tree. As everyone sees it, so they become aware of Nikola trying, without success, to contain his laughter. Pero leaps at him, and the two young Partisans roll on the ground and wrestle, though it is not a fair fight since Nikola cannot stop his giggles, and Pero is soon catching them, too.

Sid Dixon watches, shaking his head. Eventually he can contain himself no longer. 'No, lads, no,' he declares. He goes over and pulls them apart. Asking Tom to translate, he explains how even wireless operators got a brief bout of training in Secret Operations martial arts.

'Dirty fighting it is, borrowed from the Japs and the Chinks,' he explains. 'If you've got to fight, you don't have a nice dance like these two lads, you get it over with as quick as you can. Aim for the most vulnerable points of your opponent's body. I'll ask our comrade here to help me demonstrate.' Sid extends a hand to Stipe, who clambers to his feet. Stipe pretends to attack him and Sid pretends to respond with an elbow in the eyes, then a knee in the groin. 'Not the Marquess of Queensberry rules, like you'd expect from us, I shouldn't doubt.' They swap parts: Sid acts out the role of villain with great gusto, and he succumbs melodramatically every time. It is very funny, not only to Tom but to the Partisans too. Sid gives Francika a stick to use as a knife and shows her how to attack some of the twenty-two parts of the human body where a lethal wound can be made.

'What if the enemy has a knife,' Jovan asks, 'but you do not?'

'There's only one answer to that, sir,' Sid tells him. He casts around, and points into the distance, to the highest mountain peak. 'Run like hell.'

Before they leave they stuff their pockets with the sweet fruit, and periodically help themselves to one as they march through the night. Tom sees Sid and Francika pass them one to the other.

July 6

Towards morning as they walk in the darkness Tom begins to sense that it must be raining again. He can hear no sound of rain falling on leaves, or on the ground, yet the dampness upon him is unmistakable. With the first faint light, the sky unblemished above, he can make out not rain but dew on his comrades, silvering their clothes, their caps, their hair.

At dawn they stop at another farmhouse; another frightened family feeds them, a good meal of wild pig, mushrooms, potatoes. This house is wealthier than any Tom has seen so far: the furniture well-made and sturdy; chests, a crib, painted with brightly coloured flowers and religious motifs.

Dead beat, they kip down all squashed together on the floor in the parlour. They go out like a light, and are sound asleep for two, three hours; thereafter each enjoys only fitful sleep. Woken by aching hip, a companion's snores, or by lice, which lay their white eggs in the seams of clothing. Tom is unaware of them while up, but trying to sleep, he can feel them squirming over his skin.

In the afternoon, as they stir, Nikola says, 'My father was afraid to lie down to sleep. He was worried that the lice would walk away with him.'

Outside, Tom finds Jovan in quiet conversation with a boy, a girl and an old woman: he is explaining the war to them, what the National Liberation Front will do for the peasants and the small farmers. It is simple-minded propaganda. Tom watches. Jovan's patience with these uneducated people, that he takes such care over them, Tom has not seen such behaviour before.

Afterwards Jovan tells Tom: 'We can't survive without the support of the people. In the towns and cities we have clandestine workers moving around: they recruit civilians into the Liberation Front, they hold secret meetings, they find informers in the local police and Home Guard. In the country everything is more dispersed, of course, but we have to know the farmhouses where we can stop. All the time we must keep explaining to the people that it is *their* revolution.'

And people were beginning to sense, now, in this summer of 1944, that the years of German occupation would not go on for ever. Not now that the Americans, the British and the Russians were on the Partisans' side. 'Every Slovene who sees you, Tom, in your British uniform, sees the end of enemy occupation come a little sooner.'

They eat bread with dandelion and vinegar; half an onion each, bitten raw like an apple. Today Jovan asks Tom if Sid is Scottish. 'Are you sure you are not from north of the English border, like Pero's mother?' he asks, waiting for Tom to translate.

'Thinks I'm a Jock, do he, sir?' the Devon farm boy says.

'I suspect it's your accent, Dixon,' Tom says. 'Or it could be your unarmed combat skills. I believe the major regards it as a compliment.'

'Every Serb village in Yugoslavia has its veterans of the Salonika front,' Jovan tells them. 'My father was one. Many men would never talk of it, but my father was one who did. He told me little of the horrors, but often of the delicious rations the English soldiers shared with him in the trenches: chocolate, and marmalade. And he told me of the Scottish nurses. Oh my God, how he loved them!' Jovan says, winking at Pero, acknowledging the young man's rare parentage. Pero blushes with pleasure.

'The nurses drove the heavy ambulances,' Jovan continues. 'They performed miracles. My father claimed that, in an emergency, one of the Scottish nurses commanded a battery of artillery.'

'In their great retreat through Albania,' Marija interjects, 'the Serbs were running so fast, who knows what they saw?'

Affecting to ignore her, Jovan continues, 'Incredible women. Warriors. Like Marija here.'

'We are all obliged to play our part,' Marija says. 'Our great army has failed us. You know what they say, Tom? That one Serb general serves under Mihailović, four joined the collaborationist government, and the other thirty are sitting out the war in the drawing-rooms of their homes in Belgrade.'

Jovan shakes his head. 'I cannot disagree with this woman,' he admits.

'He would like to,' Marija tells Tom.

Jovan and Marija speak in this way, not directly to each other but through a third person, in this case Tom. It is very odd. Jovan watches Marija intently, then looks away; Marija tosses her head like a young horse. It occurs to Tom there is something going on that he cannot quite grasp. A language, a code, he does not read.

They leave the farm as darkness falls. Linden trees in blossom smell like jasmine. After three hours they meet the third unit at the designated drop zone. There are thirty or forty soldiers. For the first time all are in some semblance of uniform; their leader is a lieutenant. He reveals that the boy who led them there is his son. 'I did not doubt he would bring you here safely,' he tells Jovan and Tom. 'I hope he did not march you too fast.'

His unit has already prepared the ground. At midnight they hear the single plane and light the fires. The canisters fall out of the sky, and the soldiers gather them up with great efficiency, four men to each item, plus two to deal with the parachute, as if this is something they do every night and is not the first such drop they have ever had.

The unit commander gives Jovan's *odred* a different boy to act as their courier up the mountain, and they climb higher. At dawn they stop to watch through binoculars as the unit they supplied attack a small bridge on the branch line that spans a narrow gorge far below. From their vantage point, panning the glasses to the left, they can see too the German barracks, a mile away. The bridge is taken, explosives attached even as vehicles full of enemy reinforcements stream out of their garrison and speed along the road.

How strange it is to watch from so far away: the landscape a model one; people, objects, miniaturised and unreal, moving surely not by their own volition but by some guiding hand. Men fall like toy soldiers. The middle of the bridge throws up a little plume of dust; a few seconds later there is a faint, muffled thud. When the dust clears Tom can see that the central span is buckled, twin tracks of the single railway line twisted like wire. He wonders if those tiny dull pinpricks of sound at the edge of his hearing are rifle shots.

'I would place our gun there,' Marija says, standing beside him, pointing to a ledge halfway down the hillside. 'I would kill many of them if Jovan would let me.'

The Partisans are on the run now, beating a retreat from the soldiers pouring from the garrison. Jovan taps Tom's arm, points to the barracks. Tom shifts the binoculars: some of the unit have skirted around the emerging Germans and are now approaching the virtually unmanned barracks. 'Hyena tactic,' Jovan says. 'One of our favourite manoeuvres.'

Now the enemy are scrambling back to their vehicles. The barracks take fire in two, three toy explosions: orange flames brighten the colourless morning. The Partisans at either end of this panorama vanish into the trees. Jovan orders his *odred* to move again. Pero embraces their courier, who sets off to rejoin his surviving comrades.

Tom and the others climb higher, out of reach. They climb where beeches no longer grow. In amongst the pines are daisies, buttercups, a profusion of wild flowers. There are so many flies and midges and bees, their buzzing is a mesh of sound in the atmosphere. Then they are up in thin air and wind where the only trees are stunted firs, they are like shrubs, standing no taller than a man with branches candelabraed in all directions. There are no mosquitoes here. A little higher even the smallest trees do not grow: the Partisans cross white rock. Here it is dangerous, exposed, the ragged line of indigent soldiers could be seen and picked off by a plane. They run and scramble towards the next cover.

The day clouds over, it is a great relief. Tom has come to share the guerrilla fighters' schizophrenic relationship with the weather. He lives outside, and longs for clement weather like a tourist. But at the time of an attack, a manoeuvre, a march, such an attitude is turned on its head. For then there is nothing worse than a clear day.

How a partisan loves the mist out of which and into which he comes and goes, a deadly ghost. How he loves the fog that muffles his approach, the dusk into which he retreats, the falling rain that covers his tracks. Then nature at her most spiteful becomes a comrade in his righteous acts. Jovan tells him that the word *partizan* came from the Russian winter of 1812, when the French troops in retreat from Moscow were picked off by marauding Cossacks in white astrakhans on white stallions, swooping with their curved sabres out of the snow.

On they go. They move every day out of necessity, yet their mobility, Tom thinks, gives them a strange conviction of superior intelligence. For they are always one step ahead – a disembodied threat the enemy cannot really grasp. Every now and then he sees where they have been and must tremble, like one who has found the footprint of a cloven hoof in the forest.

The country is large, the Partisan forces small and nimble. They strike and disappear, infuriating the occupiers, who chase after them into the wilderness. Tom is reminded of Low's cartoon in the days of the Abyssinian crisis, of Haile Selassie's troops 'provocatively retreating'. He understands how much the Germans must hate these people they regard as inferior Slavs; this place in south-eastern Europe that they'd wanted only to police with a few old *Wehrmacht* veterans.

The Fourth Unit

July 7

They loop back on themselves. They are heading not across the Pohorje range but up through its eastern foothills, to supply a unit north of the first one they supplied a week ago. As they walk, Tom thinks of their group as a single insect, a centipede of men and women wriggling across the ridges and hills, from one unit to another; from one unprotected stretch of rail track to the next.

They tramp through dark forest, walking back towards the first farm they stayed at after leaving the main body of Partisans. The sky is hidden by branches overhead. Dawn becomes apparent uncannily: tree trunks and branches dimly discernible. The walkers begin to take shape. The light that illuminates them could be coming from the ground, or from the trees themselves.

At the edge of the forest Pero waits for Jovan, who is at the back of the line. The others see Pero's worried expression. Franjo nods to Nikola, jerks his head to indicate direction; father and son fan out, one on either side. Jovan gazes across the hillside at the tiny settlement.

'What's wrong?' he asks.

'Nothing,' Pero tells him. 'I mean, something, but I can't see it.'

They all peer through the diffused early-morning light. A skein of mist draped across the hillside like a white scarf dropped by a giant in the night. There is a faint smell of burning in the air, the day after a bonfire.

'Shall we go in?' Pero asks.

'No.' Jovan tells Stipe to set up the machine gun and train it on the house. Marija kneels behind it. Marko falls back into the forest, alert, as if he'd heard something there. Jovan looks at his watch.

'What's up, sir, you reckon?' Sid Dixon asks.

'Trap, perhaps,' Tom whispers. 'Ambush. I'm not sure.'

From the barn to the side of the farmhouse a small, thin cow – one of those farting beasts of their night in the barn, no longer pregnant – emerges, udder swaying between its spindly hindlegs. It ambles across to the door of the house and stands there, a regular visitor, expected at this hour. No. It possesses a kind of docile bovine impatience, is tired of waiting to be served.

Ordering Pero and Francika to accompany him, Jovan strides out of the trees, towards the farmhouse, his gun slung over his shoulder. Midway there, under the broad branches of a pear tree, they pause, and look down upon the ground. Jovan resumes his walk towards the farm, Pero at his shoulder. Francika turns to the forest and nods before trotting after them.

Tom, Sid and the others gather their equipment and follow their comrades. At the base of the trunk of the pear tree they find the body of a boy, a youth, the son. He's been shot in the back of the head, the bullet coming out under his right ear, opening a huge wound from which his brains trickle out beside him, on the grass. The sight of his hands preoccupies Tom: they are already as large as a man's, a peasant's hands, fingernails dirty with soil from the fields.

Attached to the front door with a kitchen knife is a poster with the drawing of a hand, filled in with black ink. Inside they find the old man, wandering from one room to the other and back again, among overturned furniture and broken crockery. He seems to be looking for something, pottering about the devastated little house. He is oblivious to their presence, one after another of them pressing through to see what there is to see.

In the kitchen lies the elder daughter, the twin of the boy outside. Her skull has been crushed, her body hacked with an axe.

In the other room beside the hearth lies their mother, the old man's daughter-in-law, her throat cut. They can see the white of her gullet in the wound. She has blood smeared over her chin and face, blood smeared by the hands of one who held her. Her own small, plump hands are greasy, Tom sees, as if she has just come from milking the cows.

Then the old man becomes all of a sudden aware of them. He begins smiling, and jabbering words in a dialect Tom cannot understand, until he sees that none of the Slovenes understand either. The old man babbles, smiling, and gesturing to some place other than where they stand.

Tom steps from the house. It occurs to him to wonder what he thinks and feels, but he discovers that he has no thoughts at all. The mechanism of his mind has ground to a halt. If he feels anything, it is only that he is a little cold.

Outside, he finds Francika squatting by the ashes of a fire, stirring the ashes carefully with her knife. As Tom watches, she finds small bones, lifts them on the blade and begins to build a little pile off to one side.

Dixon stands in the doorway of the barn from which the cow had come. Tom walks up behind him. Inside, the second cow and two calves lie shot. The old woman, the old man's wife, lies curled up in the straw beside them. Her limbs, head, neck all bent at wrong angles, as if stretched in a hideous parody of sleep. Sid turns away and Tom sees tears slide down his face. 'Bastards,' Sid says. 'Fuckers,' and he wishes to curse some more but cannot do so for weeping and goes away from his colleague and officer to grieve alone.

Tom leans against the wall of the barn. Jovan comes out of the house and shoos away the cow that still hangs about, and he goes over to Francika raking about in the ashes, extracting the small child's bones with her knife.

Still Tom feels nothing, though his hands shake a little, he notices, as he lights a cigarette. But his mind is turning once more, slowly. These people have been betrayed for helping them. By a jealous neighbour with an eye on their land? Or had one of the children told a friend of the night the Partisans and foreign soldiers were given food and shelter?

While four of them keep lookout the rest dig five graves, picking and shovelling furiously, without pause, sweating and grunting with the effort. Jovan and Tom take their turn. Francika and Marija are permitted a stint, while Stipe, Pero, Franjo and Nikola reluctantly assume sentry duty. When the graves are deep enough they lower the bodies into the ground, and shovel earth upon them. Then Tom takes it upon himself to say a few words. Not prayers as such, but snatches that he remembers from his grandparents' funeral: in English, which Pero translates.

'Lord, I am a stranger, and a sojourner, as all my fathers were. Spare me a little, before I go hence, and be no more seen. For man that is born of woman has but a short time to live, and is full of misery. He comes up, and is cut down, like a flower. He flees like a shadow.'

So they bury the family who have been slaughtered, by those searching for Tom and his companions. And he would take revenge if he could, he would gladly kill those who had done this. Life is not worth living in this world while there are men who commit such atrocities. He now understands, in his guts, the meaning of occupation, and of civil war. It is a fight to the death. There is no alternative: them or us.

July 8

They walk without stopping, with insufficient food, but they endure, fuelled now by anger as well as fear. Tom forces his body up and down steep slopes, straps cutting into his shoulder, knees burning, muscles beneath the skin apparently forming themselves for the express purpose of bearing pain. Walking at night, branches swipe him in the darkness like the whips of a gauntlet they suffer, self-punishing mendicants on their endless march.

'This is nothing like the desert, sir,' Sid Dixon tells him. 'At night the sky was all alight. Tanks burned. Even when it was quiet in our sector there was always the distant rumbling of guns, and you'd look out into the desert, see these little flashes on the horizon. The enemy was in front of us: we advanced, or retreated. Here they're all around. We don't know where they are.'

At dawn they stop. Sid Dixon fetches water for Francika; he helps her roll the grey balls of *zganci* meal. Sid and Francika speak in occasional, single words, teaching each other the Slovene and the English for objects. It is their one mode of conversation; it seems sufficient for them. A word – flour, *moka;* water, *vode* – carries the meaning of other thoughts or feelings between them. Or else they do not need more than what is apparent. Solid objects, and a growing affection, a wish for the other's presence. Sid helps Francika serve the food.

They eat in silence.

'At school,' Francika announces, in time, 'we had one spoonful of cod liver oil, each day, to prevent rickets. The only animal fat we ever had.'

Tom grimaces at his own memories of such fish oil, administered for constipation.

'No, no,' Francika insists. 'Oh, it was delicious.'

'Surely you,' Tom asks, 'as country people, ate a good deal of meat?' He knows it is a conversation they have begun in order to try to take people's minds off what they dwell on.

'No,' Francika says, frowning as if this were almost too obvious to be stated. 'Maybe a sliver of chicken on a special day. But even then the adults, the men especially, not the children.'

The conversation stops, again there is silence. It will take a great effort to speak. Eventually Stipe is the one to make it.

'You know what I once saw?' he asks, in his deep growl. 'Once I saw an orange.'

Marko is sceptical, since Stipe has been to neither a city nor the sea, but Stipe will not be denied. 'A real one,' he says, with finality.

Marija throws her plate to the ground. The others' attention turns towards her. 'They are looking for us? Good! Let us go and meet them!' she demands.

There is a murmur of agreement.

'I want to kill them, German or Slovene, I don't care,' Marija says.

They wait for Jovan to say something. 'We cannot,' he says. 'We must follow our orders. We are not to engage the enemy. We must guard our British allies and their wireless.'

'Do you think they will be in a small party of ten, Marija?' Francika asks. 'They are cowards. There will be fifty of them, at least.'

There is a long silence. Then Marko says, 'In my village there were two thugs. Good for nothing but drinking and fighting.

When the Germans came, this pair rushed into Celje to join whatever bunch of killers they could. The last I heard they were in the Black Hand; they led their unit back to the village to round up communist sympathisers – or so they claimed. In reality, anyone they had a grudge against. Including my old uncle, who had no interest in politics but had once rebuked one of them for stealing milk.' Marko looks at Jovan. 'I tell you, and I don't care who hears it, if that pair survive the war I myself will track them down. I will find them, whatever hole they have crawled into. Even if they go and hide in Hitler's arse!'

There is laughter. They throw their experiences, rumours they have heard, opinions, into the circle. Someone asks Jovan what they will do about murderers and collaborators after the war.

'In Serbia,' he says, 'the Germans declared that they would carry out reprisals: for every German soldier wounded they would execute fifty inhabitants of the population; for one killed they would execute one hundred. In the towns of Kragujevac and Kraljevo they shot all the adult males. Thousands.' Jovan pauses. He removes his battered cap, runs a hand through his thick, dark hair. 'In Montenegro we attacked a column of Italian trucks. We took money, weapons, food, even good Italian wine. And we captured fifty Italian officers and men. The following day an Italian unit arrived on the scene and executed ten peasants from the nearest village. We heard this news, and knew we had to shoot our prisoners. But it was not so simple.'

'Why not?' Stipe asks.

'Yes,' Marija says. 'It could not be more simple.'

Jovan sighs. 'The soldiers had mingled with our soldiers. They had, after all, carried the booty from the road up the mountain; they had shared food, cigarettes. The officers remained aloof, in a clearing. While we discussed how to carry out the execution, the

Italian soldiers realised what was going on. They began to beg and weep for their lives, clasping our men around their knees. Our own men then begged us: "We cannot kill them. They are ordinary soldiers, not Blackshirts. How can we kill them when we have broken bread with them?"'

Jovan looks around the group. 'What would you do?' he asks. He looks from Franjo to his son Nikola; to Stipe, Marija, Tom; to Marko and Pero, to Francika, to Sid Dixon, for whom Tom translates what Jovan says.

'Some of the Montenegrin peasant leaders who fought with us against the occupiers demanded that we let them go, to forestall Italian reprisals. Others demanded immediate revenge for the peasants who had died.'

'So?' Marko asks. 'Did you shoot them?'

Jovan shakes his head. 'We agreed to let the soldiers go. But what of the officers? It seemed that we could not avoid shooting them. It had to be done. It was the right thing to do.'

'Did they beg to be released?' Marko asks.

'No,' Jovan says, shaking his head slowly at the memory. 'The officers retained their dignity. They looked shocked, but they did not cry.' He lights a cigarette. 'I still do not know if we made the correct decision. Only when this war is over will we be able to say, Yes, it was the right, or the wrong, thing to do.' He takes a drag, and exhales the smoke. 'And perhaps not even then.'

They stretch out their oilskins by the ruins of an old building. Despite his fatigue, Tom does not fall asleep, even as the day grows brighter. Did Christ come, he wonders, to remind men that they have free will, or that they do not? And if they do is it worth it, this freedom, for the acts of evil they commit? What God would think so?

July 9

They wake in the afternoon.

Somewhere in the valley below a man is slowly cutting wood, and his axe, muffled by the trees and the distance, thumps slowly, suggesting he is very old.

Marko and Nikola have caught another animal: four more small carcasses roast. Sid does not eat, saying he's not hungry. They wait to see what Tom will make of it, what his guess might be. It tastes good, though the meat is tough.

'Rabbit?' he asks.

Nikola nods. 'Good,' he says. 'Almost.'

'Nothing like,' Marko disagrees. 'This is hare.'

Sid Dixon makes his sked. There will be another drop in two days' time. 'Don't feel too good, sir,' he tells Tom.

'You reckon it was that rat we ate yesterday?' Tom says. 'Try not to think about it.'

'I've drunk enough cider out a vats where rats got in and drowned, that never bothered me. Don't see why it should now.'

Jovan is always anxious after radio communication: the Germans can pick up their signals and use triangular direction finding, will be tracking their zigzag movement around these mountains, and be close behind them.

*

They set off as soon as it is dark. Sid scurries off the track to relieve himself. Word ripples up the line to pause. Half an hour later, the same again.

'We don't stop like this,' Jovan tells Tom. 'We can't.'

'It's dysentery,' Tom says. 'It must be.'

Sid tries to walk but cannot put one foot in front of the other: he stops dead, standing. They make a stretcher out of branches and oilskin, and Stipe and Nikola carry him. They reach a peasant farmhouse. The old woman, whom they've woken, gives Dixon *rakija*, and some milk. Then she encourages them to leave.

'We have to stay,' Jovan decides. 'I'm sorry,' he tells the old woman. 'We shall leave as soon as we can.'

The woman shakes her head, mutters to herself, as if merely irritated; as if Jovan were her son who's invited a few drunken pals to stay the night.

Marko takes first watch. The rest sleep squashed all together on straw in the small byre.

So, Tom sees, do they impose themselves on families, forbid them to leave, take their food. Some are glad to see them, salute the Partisans who fight to liberate their country; others are indifferent or hostile to their aims. But all are frightened, and eager for them to go. Everywhere they stop they become guests who overstay their welcome, or their presence brings down upon their hosts the wrath of the enemy. They are pariahs. Following in their wake are soldiers, dogs, the Black Hand. The risk becomes too great. Soon they prefer to live apart from society, outcasts in the forest: they bivouac free as tramps back in England, ragged gentlemen of the woods. But it rains, and they grow hungry, or ill, and resentful of those who make no sacrifice; they long for food and shelter, and in the early morning will knock on a door.

July 10

In the afternoon they wake. The day is hot. The old woman gives them bread, and then she sends a child of the family to show them where they can find food. While Sid Dixon rests, watched by Francika, the child leads the others through the forest. Pines grow as nature has seeded them, not close together in dark regimented plantations but many yards apart, so that the ground around the trees is alpine wild-flower meadow. Here the child stops and spreads her hands. Tom looks down and sees at their feet green leaves dotted with blue-purple spots. Crawling over the springy plants, they stuff themselves with bilberries.

Back at the farmhouse they take turns on guard, or sit and lie on the grass outside, replete, dozy despite the long sleep of the night before. There is danger, yet they snooze in the sunshine. Wheeling in the blue sky, black crows caw; a sound, Tom remarks to Sid, who has been helped outside, like football rattles.

'Never 'eard one a them, sir.'

'Have you not been to a match?'

'Exeter City, that's a good ten mile away from us. Only been t'Exeter couple a times in my life. 'Fore the war, that is.'

It strikes Tom how novel this experience is for his corporal, from his narrow Devon farming valley, no less than for himself and his pre-war life of cloistered study.

Jovan and Pero are talking. Jovan is angry. It seems Pero does not know this area, they are reliant on couriers, but where is their next one? They have no contact. They have to keep moving, and hope to pick up a courier's trail and reattach themselves to the shifting, hidden network.

They sleep outside, for it is warm. Ants crawl over them and bite them where they lie. They wake, rub and shake themselves, crawl to a new spot a few yards away.

'Father,' Nikola says, 'show the Englishman your bullet.'

Franjo shrugs, reaches his thick peasant's fingers into his chest pocket and withdraws a small lump of dark metal. He gives it to his son, who passes it to Tom. The metal has no shape. Only its surprisingly heavy weight suggests its erstwhile function.

'Tell him, Father,' Nikola says. Franjo shakes his head, and looks away. Tom wonders if the old man is mute and this request is a formality, it cannot be granted but has to be made nevertheless.

'My father is shy,' Nikola says. 'I will tell you. It is a French bullet, from a long rifle, but shot by an Austrian. In the Great War.'

Franjo, still looking away, as if he has no interest in the conversation, mutters something under his breath that Tom can't hear.

'Maybe by a Hungarian,' Nikola says.

'Maybe a Muhammadan,' Marko interrupts. 'A Cossack. Or a Viking. We are peasants. Who knows who kills us?'

'A British doctor treated him. But when he came home, to his father's vineyard, my father said, "The bullet is still here. The surgeon forgot to take it out." People told him he was mad. But he said, "I can feel it inside me, moving around, it's still after me."'

Tom nods. 'But tell me, Nikola,' he says, 'how come the bullet is no longer inside your father but in my hand?'

'One day it changed its mind,' Nikola says, 'and turned around. It began to work its way out. After one year it pushed against the skin.'

Nikola looks at his father with pride. Franjo gazes into the distance. Tom cannot help being reminded of his family Labrador, who always knew when they were talking about her and would look shyly away.

'His friend,' Nikola says, 'gave him much plum brandy, while he sharpened his knife. And here it is.'

'He carries it with him?'

'When we left, my mother told him to bring it. She said it would protect him, that God would not let him be shot twice, in two great wars.'

'Does he believe this?' Tom asks.

Nikola turns to his father, who bows his head, and shrugs once again.

'He carries it for my mother, not for himself,' Nikola explains. 'She believes it.'

As they slump lazily on the dry grass, something changes: Pero looks from side to side. Marija stands up. Jovan gazes at the sky. Stipe shields his eyes and stares into the forest. Tom pricks up his ears. A sound. A far-off drumming noise. It seems to be coming from the earth: a natural occurrence perhaps, some Balkan phenomenon – earthquake, volcano. But then he notices that all the others are now gazing up into the sky. There comes that curious rough throbbing characteristic of Liberators' engines. They appear, and are followed by others.

Wave after wave, an armada of Allied bombers darken the sky. Tom is able with Jovan's binoculars to differentiate Fortresses from Liberators. When he puts them down he sees that the Partisans are waving and cheering, their voices all but lost in the overpowering drone. All they have seen of military might since the spring of 1941 has been Teutonic. Perhaps they did not really believe the Allies could match it.

July 11

They are asleep, save for Nikola on sentry duty, when a courier finds them in the early afternoon: a boy who has been looking for them for three days. He saw a German SS patrol with dogs two hours ago. Jovan decides to set off immediately, but still Sid can hardly walk and they carry him. Despite the summer warmth he shivers beneath a blanket on the stretcher. He is not the only one affected by the diet. After nothing but wild meat for days, Tom suffers griping abdominal pains, and constipation. He is even more tired than usual; his gums are swollen, and bleeding.

Marija is not surprised at Tom's condition. 'Me, too,' she tells him. 'It is mild scurvy, I suppose.'

At another peasant house Francika procures bacon fat and *rakija* for Sid, but Jovan will not let them tarry. When at dawn they stop, Marko says, 'We are passing not far from my village. I will go and get food.'

'Do not force them,' Jovan says, which seems to Tom a strange thing to say.

'They are my people,' Marko says. Stipe goes with him.

Francika feeds Sid the bacon fat and *rakija*, which seems to fix Sid's insides at last. Jovan sends the courier on ahead, after he has given Pero directions.

*

Marko and Stipe return empty-handed. Jovan asks Marko to take over sentry duty from Marija. When he has left the clearing, Stipe says, 'We could take nothing, even from his relatives. They were like a village of beggars. They said the *domobranstvo* have plundered all their stores. There was nothing, Jovan. Not even salt.'

Francika gathers blades of grass and the ends of spruce firs, their young green tender tips. She stews them in a thin soup. It is palatable, and even as he drinks it Tom can sense that it will do him good.

Franjo and Nikola produce meat, three small carcasses already caught and skinned. Francika roasts them and the pauperish companions eat their meagre portions with ravenous gratitude. There is no fat on the meat, its texture is firm but soft, and salty, and with a faint mineral taste reminiscent of gammon. But otherwise it is unlike anything Tom has ever tasted.

'*Lisica*,' Marko tells him. Fox.

Sid recovers well enough to operate the radio. British and Canadian troops have captured Caen. Sid makes contact with Italy and requests a drop tonight. The fourth unit is hiding deep in the mountains.

'We do not know them,' Jovan confides in Tom. 'Our only contact has been through the couriers. I have sent a message, told them to expect us, and supplies; ordered them to prepare an action. For some reason I am nervous.'

'A trap?' Tom asks. 'Could there be an ambush awaiting us?'

'I don't think so,' Jovan says, though he looks unconvinced. He is responsible for more than their small group of ten soldiers, for it is vital they keep the supplies coming, the sabotage repeated. Tom finds himself wondering about the nature of their mission.

Catapulted from one Partisan unit to another hiding out in the forest, they march deep into enemy territory that will be hard to withdraw from. Perhaps they are not really expected to come back: it was hoped merely that they would light fires in this southern area of the Reich, for as long as they last, and they are expendable.

Tom remembers Jack Farwell telling him, 'It is nothing for you to worry about.' What did that mean? Are they simply a decoy? Did it mean precisely that there *was* something to worry about? Jovan carries, in addition, the burden of leadership, for he alone must make decisions. Tom is struck by his loneliness.

'Do you have a wife, Jovan?' he asks suddenly. 'Children?'

Jovan looks askance at him. 'You are not a man who walks around the house looking for the back door, Tom,' he says. 'My wife was killed in the spring of nineteen forty-two. We had no children.'

'I'm so sorry,' Tom says. He didn't know he was going to ask Jovan such a question. It flew from his mouth. He had no right to.

'A mortar attack,' Jovan says quietly. 'She too was a Partisan. They told me she was in great pain. Then the pain left her, and she hummed a tune no one recognised. A simple melody, they said, though none of them could recall it for me. And then she died.'

Tom says nothing, lets Jovan lapse into his memories. But then Jovan nods to himself, as if deciding, *Enough*, and looks up. 'What of you, Tom?' he asks. 'You have a wife?'

Tom shakes his head. 'I was still a student when this war began. The day after they invaded Poland I volunteered.'

'No fiancée?'

'I haven't met the right woman,' Tom says. 'I'm still waiting. Perhaps one will appear, and when she does I will know.'

'The Platonic ideal,' Jovan says in a tone of voice that manages to suggest both agreement with and dismissal of the notion.

'Yes, perhaps my other half exists,' Tom nods, mock apologetic. 'If only we can meet, she will make me – we will make each other – whole.'

'A true romantic,' Jovan laughs. 'I had heard that Englishmen had ice where their hearts should be. Here we have one who is waiting for his Juliet.'

'When I was at Oxford,' Tom tells him, 'there were other chaps who propositioned every woman they met. It used to astonish me. And of course in the army, in wartime, even more so. Men drawn to any woman. Every woman. Womankind. Thin, fat. Tall, short. Fair, plain. Bright, dim. The only thing they have in common? What every woman has, you know? I found this very strange.' He shakes his head, and shrugs. 'I don't who is more odd: such men or myself.'

'You are not odd, Tom,' Jovan reassures him. 'You have taste. Discernment.' He laughs. 'The curse of civilisation.'

Tom wants to tell Jovan that he was not drawn to women at all. He looks at Jovan. Their eyes meet. What can Jovan see in his eyes?

July 12

They walk through the night. Tom wonders how on earth Pero is able to lead them in the darkness, following instructions from a boy, using small-scale maps, without a compass of his own. It is no wonder they get lost. Perhaps they are now. From a ridge they hear a train, then they see it, though every window is blacked-out; all that is visible are sparks, on the rails and in the plume of smoke rising from the engine.

'I want no trains to run on that track tomorrow,' Jovan tells Tom. They walk higher into the mountains. At dawn they see a milky layer of fog below them, peaks poke out like shipwrecks. Mid-morning they are met by the boy. Pero turns and bows, grinning, to those behind him, and waits for each to shake his hand.

'They are not my people,' the boy tells Jovan, very seriously, before he leads them to the fourth unit: a ragged crew more destitute and forlorn than themselves.

'Like twenty Markos, sir,' Dixon says. They do not greet Jovan's *odred* as friends but give a desultory clenched-fist salute. Unwilling comrades. One has a wounded hand wrapped in a dirty bandage, clearly swollen beneath the dressing; another sees out of only one eye; a third is lame. They have no food but roots and nuts. Their clothes are tattered and torn. Marooned in the woods, forsaken, they have few weapons: old hunting rifles, one .303-calibre Lee-Enfield. Other units have been convivial, sat down with Pero, Marko and the others to swap stories of their exploits, work out if they had mutual relatives or acquaintances.

These shrink from contact. It is as if they have been tracked down by Jovan's *odred*.

Jovan tells Tom he does not trust their guards, and posts Stipe and Nikola to keep watch. Fires are reluctantly laid. They wait for the drop that night but though there is little cloud nothing comes, no plane, no parachutes. The isolated, starveling unit are confirmed in their suspicion of the newcomers.

Tom is furious. 'They think it's a bloody picnic, Dixon. We could be on Salisbury Plain for all they know.'

'It's too bad, sir.'

'Where is your plane, Tom?' Jovan demands. 'Don't they know we are always on the move? The drop must come at the correct time and place. We cannot stay.'

'I know,' Tom tells him. 'I'm sorry.'

Sid sets up the radio. A message comes through. The drop was scrubbed due to poor weather in Italy.

They sleep in the clearing where the unit have made their camp. Tom would not be surprised to find them gone when he awakes, slunk off into the forest. Instead he is woken by voices: Jovan is arguing with their leader. Tom lies and listens.

'We are safe here.'

'You are hiding here. You have to fight.'

'We fight. One month ago we greased and soaped the track on a gradient north of here, shot up the train. Three of our men were wounded, as you see.'

'One month?' Jovan asks.

The man stares at the forest floor.

'The single-track line running north from Celje, up between the Pohorje and the Karavanken Alps – this is all you have to think about.'

'And what can we do without explosives?' The man nods towards where Tom lies. 'Where is the British dynamite?'

'We have to show these Allied soldiers that we can do something even without their help.'

Marija has been hovering close by, agitated, and now she steps forward and joins in. 'You call yourselves men?' she says.

The leader glares at her. Jovan watches her, smiling.

'You think if we ignore the fascists,' she says, 'they will be so upset that they will creep back to Germany?'

'The Americans,' the man says. 'The Russians.'

'Incredible,' Marija says. 'To have lost so much pride that you fear death like rabbits.'

'All right, Marija,' Jovan says.

'My men are tired. If we do as you ask, the Germans will be all over this mountain. We would have to leave this place. We are peasants. If we lose our lives we want at least to know that we will be buried in our own village cemetery.'

'This is how we live now,' Jovan tells him. 'We are Partisans. Gather any picks or tools that you have. You will lead us to a stretch of unguarded line. We move out in two hours. Prepare your men.'

Tom can see the mutual suspicion between the members of each group. As they climb down the mountain he realises he is doubly alert: danger might come from the enemy, or from these men around him. He's counted their number: there are twenty of them; ten in his own unit. The man with the poisoned hand walks behind Tom. Every now and then he lets out a moan of pain. The lame man limps in front.

In the forest there is always movement. Creatures that watch them from the shadows. Sunlight, dappled through the leaves or needles, always changing. If there is no movement their own ambulation creates it, the triangulation of trees and the ever-shifting perspective.

His vigilance. Senses tuned to the tightest pitch, on the verge of snapping.

Suddenly Tom notices something on the inside of his retina: scintillae dancing upon the orb of his vision, red and black motes, crawling across the bumpy grass and weeds. No. Ladybirds. Yes, that is what they are. Tens, hundreds, of ladybirds on the ground. He doesn't want to step on them with his clod-hopping size-nine boots. There would be carnage. He makes a great effort to avoid them, or as many as he can, seeing them as his booted foot comes down to earth and tripping himself to one side or the other, but the effort costs him. And the tiny lives he saves are few. He gives it up and raises his eyes so as not to see, and walks on.

Jovan posts his own soldiers as sentries along the line, Marija and Marko at one end, Francika and Franjo at the other. He doesn't trust these people, Tom can see. Using picks, shovels, poles for levers and the brute force of their combined human bodies the rest of them rip up the track for more than a hundred yards. They stack the wooden sleepers and balance the metal rails on top. Dusk. The sleepers, suffused with creosote, burn intensely. The rails, red hot, soften, and the ends bend down under their own weight. They will be no further use.

'The Todt Organisation will have a work gang out here in less than half a day,' Jovan reckons. 'They rebuild their rail lines as fast as we destroy them. Leave two snipers behind,' he orders the unit leader, 'to deter the Slovene repair crews.'

The rest leave, all together still, walking uphill for two hours until they reach a hamlet of three, four farmhouses. They sleep in different barns, breathing the pungent smell of manure.

July 13

In the morning Tom walks out from the barn to shit in the woods. On the way back he is diverted by the sound of buzzing, to a collection of half a dozen beehives above the farm. The end boards of the wooden hives are brightly decorated with peasant scenes. 'They are painted for the bees,' he hears. It is Marko. 'To help each bee locate its own hive.'

They make their way to the largest farmhouse. Franjo and Nikola stand outside, along with some members of the indigent band. No one speaks. There is something wrong. Francika and Marija come out of the house carrying rough wooden trays of food. The men follow them over to a table in the orchard. They help themselves to food. There is cornmeal boiled into a mush and cut into wedge-shaped pieces, along with raw onions, cut in half.

'What's going on?' Tom whispers to Marija.

'One of these bastards has raped a girl here,' she tells him.

'Last night?' he asks. He is incredulous. Not only has a crime been committed, and a first rule of hospitality desecrated; but Tom cannot imagine a man having the energy to do such a thing. He and his companions fell asleep exhausted last night as soon as they lay down.

'Last night?' Marija repeats. 'Of course.'

'Does anyone know which one it was?'

'He's in there now.'

'What will happen?' he wonders.

'Jovan is the commanding officer,' Marija says, as if that were all the explanation that is needed. She looks up to see Tom's puzzled frown. 'If the scum has a God to believe in, he had better be saying his prayers.'

Nothing is said, no explanation given. Twenty minutes after they have eaten Jovan and the unit leader escort a young man, the one who can only see out of one eye, out of the house. He is weeping silently from his good eye. Stipe, Marko and two members of the other unit accompany them, carrying shovels and Marko's Sten gun. None of the members of the family show themselves. The soldiers disappear around the side of the hill. Four shots are heard in quick succession.

They leave in the early afternoon, the two groups heading in opposite directions. As Jovan's *odred* walk away Franjo and Marko keep glancing back over their shoulders, wary of parting shots. To be so mistrustful of their own side makes Tom's flesh crawl. Once they are out of sight, the relief is acknowledged: Tom's gaze meets Jovan's, who shakes his head.

They walk in the afternoon, west. Some plant gives off a sharp, familiar, peppery smell. Yes, that flower, he sees, with five pink-purple petals. Some kind of cranesbill, is it? A word he has heard spoken, from his mother's mouth.

When they have stopped, and are preparing to eat, Tom sees Marko off on his own in the trees, muttering to himself. He clutches something in his fingers, is it a bracelet? He feeds it through his fingers. It is a rosary. He is praying.

'In the south,' Marija tells Tom, 'the Catholic church cooperated with the occupiers. Most priests advised their people to join the Home Guard: they hated communists more than their Italian fellow Catholics. But here in the north the Germans treat the

Church like another of their enemies. It is said that six hundred priests have been deported.'

Marko wanders back, pocketing the beads.

'Sometimes the Church is on the side of good, at others on the side of evil,' Tom reflects. 'Christianity seems able to turn its face in any direction.'

'Our Bishop of Ljubljana,' Marko says. 'He told us to defend our nation against the wolves and jackals who are poisoning our souls with their atheistic communism.'

'The Catholic Archbishop of Sarajevo went further,' Jovan tells them. 'He said that it was stupid and unworthy of Christ's disciples to think that the struggle against evil can be waged in a noble way and with gloves on. Saric is his name. We know him as the Hangman of the Serbs.'

There is a bitterness in Jovan's voice; against the bishop's cloth, or his anti-Serb, anti-Orthodox, affiliation?

'The gospel of Christ,' Tom asks Jovan, 'is it so far from your own vision? Must you reject it all?'

'History is a ruthless force,' Jovan says. 'If there was ever a possibility of a leftist, socialist Catholicism here in Slovenia, or anywhere else in Yugoslavia, it has been lost. The majority of Catholics collaborated. Those who have joined our movement have been assimilated amongst us.'

'You?' Marija asks Tom. 'Do you have religion?'

Tom considers the question for some time. 'I thought I did,' he says at length. 'Now, I am less and less sure. How about you, Marija?'

'Me?' She laughs. 'No. No. There is only this, Tom,' she says, plucking a stem of grass. 'What we can touch. And us. Men and women.' She looks at him. Their eyes meet. 'This is all there is,' she says.

*

They avoid rivers, running water no ally, muffling as it would the approach of an enemy. Even, or especially, if a good path runs beside it. But this afternoon they approach a stream. Jovan brings them to a halt. He posts lookouts up and down river and motions to the group to drink. They lie and lap like animals, sating themselves on water, filling their bellies while they can. Today there is no rush to move on. They rest by the stream, stretched out along its banks. After they have eaten, and are ready to sleep, Nikola, the youngest among them, prevails upon his father to sit on the bank. The boy steps barefoot into the stream, turns, and takes off Franjo's boots and socks. He washes his father's feet in the cold mountain water. Then he dips his fingers in a small tub and rubs what it contains into the soles of his father's feet, the heels, the toes. Some kind of grease, or fat?

Jovan has been watching this filial massage, as have all the others. He asks Nikola something, then says to the group, 'Who's next?'

One after another Jovan and Nikola wash their companions' feet, and rub the unguent into them. The cold water, then warmth rubbed into tingling skin. No one speaks as this ritual is carried out. When it is Marija's turn, Jovan spends longer than on those who have gone before. Tom's turn was pleasurable, but brisk. Now he watches Jovan massage Marija's calves with his strong hands. He rubs her feet with a slow deliberation. She closes her eyes.

And then Jovan and Nikola wash each other's feet. Dusk falls.

The Fifth Unit

July 14

A new courier leads them on a two-day slog high into the mountains, towards the fifth unit. She gives Jovan the latest information on enemy movements. Sid Dixon makes contact and gives new coordinates to base.

In the woods are thirty men and women, and youngsters. The men are well-shaven, the women clean. They have shelters constructed out of long, interwoven poles of hazel, covered with bracken. Caps, jackets, are hung on branches cut close to tree trunks, a living hat and coat stand. Ropes are strung from one tree to another, blankets hung on them to air. These Partisans seem quite at home in the forest; their clearings are like rooms in a tidy house.

'We came here two days ago. We could move at five minutes' notice,' their leader responds to Tom's admiring observation. 'Each person has his job to do.'

'You may have to move,' Jovan tells him. 'The Black Hand are not far behind us. An SS patrol was sighted to the east two days ago.'

The cook works surrounded by utensils hung from cord or branch hooks; food hangs, too, in canvas bags. A meal is served to Jovan's *odred*: a buckwheat mush, similar to but tastier than the cornmeal polenta they have sometimes been given, and a roasted meat Tom is, for a change, not the only one unable to identify.

'It is pork,' Stipe declares.

'No,' says Francika. 'This is beef. I tasted it once before. How did they get beef?'

'Young pork,' Stipe insists.

Marija shakes her head. 'These peasants,' she tells Tom, nodding at Stipe and Francika, 'eat more meat in war than in peace. This is goose. There would be more fat on pork.'

The cook of the unit reveals that they are eating badger. Jovan wrinkles his nose. Those who had not committed themselves, Marko and Nikola, nod sagely. Franjo does likewise.

'Of course,' Marija reckons, 'by October it would be much fatter.'

'My father,' Marko tells them, 'used to give our mother badgers' teeth to use as buttons.'

'Where I live,' Sid says, 'they say tis good luck if a badger crosses your path behind you. But if it crosses in front, you can bet your britches sommit bad's goin a happen.'

Tom translates for him. Francika, sitting beside Sid, nods. 'When I was a girl, my mother told us that if you hear a badger bark and an owl hoot, one after the other, it is time to ask God to make peace with your soul.'

Sid proceeds to give a demonstration of what he claims are some of the many different sounds a Devon badger makes. He begins with the wail of an infant in distress, and then a growl of warning. But as he proceeds, so the behaviour, and the sound accompanying it, become increasingly ludicrous. 'This is the sound old *jazbec* makes when he's climbing down a chimney after Santa's milk and biscuit.'

Tom translates, not sure whether what he says makes sense to them, then Sid makes a crazy sound halfway between a retch and a yelp. The Partisans enjoy his humour. By the time he has added movement to the noises, mimicking a badger's rolling gait, laughter from the two units drowns out Sid's voice.

This time the planes come, on time. The fifth unit collect the supplies. Tom gives thanks to stores. In addition to the explosives specifically requested, they have provided other useful things: weapons, food, medicine, clothing; chocolate, cigarettes. These items are invaluable to mountain guerrillas. With them everything becomes possible.

At breakfast, the unit leader briefs his soldiers: they are to attack the branch line, at a certain time and place already known to them all and closely reconnoitred. They pack up their camp. When they are ready to leave, there is little discernible evidence of their stay.

Down the mountain they trek in the morning, carrying explosives to the branch railway line. They descend through orchards groaning with fruit – apples, pears, even peaches ripening. Sid picks perfect specimens for Francika, presents each one as a princely gift. Tom teases him. 'Good to see you're doing your bit for relations between our armies, Dixon.'

Sid grins. 'She's a good soldier, sir.'

Since Sid's recovery from dysentery he and Francika are inseparable. Wasps are everywhere, devouring fermenting windfalls, buzzing with a demented, delirious greed.

Tom finds himself assailed by a memory out of the blue. His mother had made gooseberry crumble and placed it proudly on the table. 'I think you'll like this,' she told her two men. 'I found the idea in a recipe.' Tom looked at the crumble and saw she had laid sprigs of elderflower over it. The first mouthful – as the subtle taste of elderflower rose through the stringency of gooseberry – was a kind of revelation on his tongue.

What was she doing now, his dear mother, Tom wonders, back home? There is a perfume of elderflower in his nostrils. The power of the human imagination, Tom considers, is extraordinary: he has a memory, and one of his senses is awakened. Just then he glances aside and sees an elder tree close by, spread with creamy white lanterns of flowers, source of the scent that had – of course – provoked the recollection; his own madeleine, a thousand miles from his home being left further behind with every step.

'What are you thinking, Tom?' Marija asks him.

She walks beside him. 'Home,' Tom says. 'I suppose I was a little homesick. But I was also wondering what, or where, home was. My parents' house is no longer mine. I shall return to my college and probably stay there. I can't see how a college could be a real home. Perhaps home will be not a place but the realm of ideas one inhabits.' Pleased with this notion, Tom looks up and sees Marija's response. 'You think that's funny?'

'No,' she says. 'It is not funny, it is stupid. Home is where you plant a tree.'

They make their way to where the main line snakes through a valley between a river and a road that according to the unit commander is little used. Their engineers lay explosives under sleepers. Most of the plastic has been left with Jovan's group, watching from high up the hillside; Tom can see they are using only a few pounds, a fraction of what they'd been given. He wants to go down and see what they are playing at but Jovan will not allow it. The whole of their *odred* stand around him on a grassy ledge on the hill fifty feet above the track.

The engineers and escort withdraw, and they wait. After twenty minutes they hear a locomotive chugging south towards them. As it crosses the mined point, on the outside rail of a curve, the locomotive's weight sets off the detonator. Tom can just make out the rail buckle and snap: the wheels of the train, which might have jumped the gap in a straight track, spin in a void; the momentum of the train pulls it further off the bend, and off the rails. It is a goods train. One wagon after another slides gratifyingly clear of the track. It comes close to turning over; teeters but does not fall.

The train makes a tremendous sound, hissing and screeching like some beast being brought to an agonising halt. It takes Tom a moment to realise that this noise is not followed by silence but that there is another sound – which, if he had been aware of it at all, he had presumed to be an undercurrent of the train's derailment. In fact, it was separate, and indeed is now getting louder. Still he cannot identify the cause, until he receives a visual clue: a motorcycle appears on the road below them. Behind it come other vehicles: more motorcycles, then infantry-carrying trucks.

It is as if the enemy had known in advance of this sabotage. Or are they accompanying their trains now by road, so far as they are able? But while Tom is trying to make sense of events, a mine at the side of the road is blown up beside a truck. The tyres of other trucks are blown, causing them to veer and skid to ungainly stops: tyre-busters must have been spread. Did the saboteurs know of this convoy, then?

By this time the bullets of the Partisan machine guns are singing through the air. Everybody blazes away and there is a terrific racket, with the machine guns stuttering their killing clatter, and volleys of rifle fire, all of it greatly magnified by the echo from the steep rock on the other side of the valley.

The Germans try to reply, but their fire is so dispersed that they search in vain for any one spot to attack. Tom sees a Partisan boy creep down from the rocks and throw a Molotov bottle at a truck. It bursts into flames. The valley is full of smoke and the stench of burning oil. Another truck is afire, grey-uniformed soldiers leap from its floor where they had been taking shelter. Out in the open they fall like ninepins. But there are so many of them. The boy who threw the Molotov has been hit and lies in the road. It is clear from the growing impunity with which the Germans counter-attack that other Partisans are dead.

Sid Dixon nudges Tom. 'Sir.' He looks over. Marija is arguing furiously with Jovan for the right to take her LMG down the hill. Jovan tells her it is out of the question. Stipe is trying to calm her down. Marko is nodding towards Dixon and Tom, and muttering at Jovan: were it not for the Englishmen and their precious radio the others would be at liberty to rush down the hill and mete out revenge. Tom turns away.

They melt back into the woods. The Partisans' resentment, that they are no more than chaperones, forbidden to fight, is palpable in their bad tempers. They speak snappishly, and look away. They meet with the survivors of the unit, hand over the supplies they'd been guarding for them. Jovan's *odred* stand back, at a distance expressive of their shame. When it is time to part, they say nothing.

'I can see how they feel, sir,' Sid Dixon tells Tom, as they walk, east, back into the Pohorje, and south. 'I feel it too. What do they think of us?'

'I know,' Tom agrees. 'I don't like it any more than you do, Dixon.'

The afternoon is hot. They walk through the day, up and down, through woods and pasture. Jovan does not let them stop but keeps them marching in the cool of the evening and into the night, exhausting his soldiers' anger, forcing it out of them through their muscles, their endless footsteps.

When at last Jovan lets them stop, in a copse of oak trees, they do not eat but sink to the ground and fall asleep where they lie.

The Sixth Unit

July 15

Tom wakes mid-morning. Stipe is building a cooking fire. Jovan is shaving. He tells Tom that Pero and Franjo have gone to find food. The others are still sleeping.

'I could eat a horse,' Tom says. 'Which, come to think about it, is the only animal we haven't eaten here.' He follows Jovan's lead, shaving without a mirror, by feel alone.

Pero returns with a bag of potatoes on his shoulder. Franjo carries two chickens, their feet tied together. As they stand there, and Pero tells Jovan of the peasant who haggled with him over the price they should pay, Tom notices blood on the beaks of the dead chickens, and their closed eyes. Stipe takes the potatoes, places them in the embers of the fire. Franjo plucks one of the chickens. Francika stirs, and within moments is plucking the other.

After breakfast they lie on the ground, replete and still. The silence is eventually broken by Francika. 'We understand,' she tells Jovan. 'We have to do what we have been assigned to do.' She speaks on the others' behalf, to Jovan, but she is also addressing them.

'For three years, since the summer of 'forty-one,' Jovan tells them, 'we have fought this guerrilla war. Never attacking the enemy head on but always at the flank or the rear, and then retreating into the woods and hills. The enemy has chased us but we have lost them. They have gathered fifty thousand men – SS, Hungarians, Italians, Bulgarians, Chetniks – as they did last year in the mountains of Montenegro, and surrounded us with a ring of steel. They carried orders to kill every one of us, down to the last man. But we broke out, and made our way back to Bosnia.'

'Ah, Tito is the greatest general since Napoleon,' says Stipe.

'Napoleon,' says Marko. 'Our dear Napoleon.' He shakes his head. He seems to be remembering an old friend, with great affection. 'He made Ljubljana the capital of the Illyrian Provinces,' he tells Tom.

'You are wrong, Stipe,' Pero says excitedly. 'Tito is the greatest general since Alexander the Great.'

'He must be a Slovene,' Marko suggests.

'He's a Croat,' Marija tells him.

'Then his mother must be a Slovene,' Marko rejoins. This conjecture appears to be acceptable to all.

'On the trek from Montenegro,' Jovan resumes, 'we had nothing to eat but roots and horsemeat. We have made retreat into a glorious military achievement. And with every successful retreat the Germans have become more angry, and have sent more divisions to the Balkans to deal with us.' He shakes his head. 'After we broke out,' he says, 'they sent patrols to scour the mountains. They discovered the wounded we had left behind, and slaughtered them all. Along with their unarmed nurses, who had stayed beside them.'

Later, Tom sits next to Jovan. He pokes a further hole in his trouser belt. Their arms brush against each other as he twists his penknife into the leather. Jovan's body odour is tinged with a strawberry perfume.

'I have been thinking about the reprisals,' Tom says, 'that the Germans inflict after your battles with them. It must be terrible to see civilians shot for your actions.'

Jovan shakes his head. 'Some have sympathy for the Chetniks, for that reason,' he says. 'They are members of a tribe. They fight for their tribe, its protection and its freedom. If innocent members of their tribe are executed, then what is the meaning of their action? Or their identity at all? Whereas, for us communists, it is different. We educate ourselves away from our primitive attachments to a clan, or region. Our identity is international as well as national. Me? No, Tom. I have no sympathy.'

The tone of his voice causes Tom to look at Jovan. He sees hatred in his eyes.

'The reprisals are no excuse for inaction. The Chetniks have betrayed their country. They will be liquidated.' Jovan sees the quiver of alarm on Tom's countenance, and smiles. 'It is treason,' Jovan says. 'I believe you would accord it the same punishment.'

Tom lights a cigarette. 'I suppose so,' he says. But still, it seems too harsh a judgement. Perhaps there is something unbridgeable dividing them, after all.

As if reading Tom's thoughts, Jovan says, 'Do not worry, Tom. They are trying to liquidate us.'

Tom nods. 'Do you not fear death, Jovan?'

Jovan accepts the cigarette Tom offers him. 'Pain I enjoy no more than any other man,' he says. 'Women are different, their biology has made them braver. But death? No. I agree that a man's dying is more the survivors' affair than his own.'

'Did Marshal Tito say that?' Tom asks.

Jovan smiles. 'Thomas Mann,' he says.

*

Franjo carries the radio, Nikola the one battery, Marko the pedal dynamo; Stipe hauls Marija's LMG; all on top of their personal loads – except that they possess barely anything beyond their weapons.

The Englishmen have been gradually divesting themselves of their kit. Tom has given away his spare trousers, to Pero. Marko wears his spare shirt. He swapped his large rucksack for Stipe's knapsack, the gun carrier delighted to be able to fit the LMG into a backpack. Tom's own equipment has been reduced to code books, pistol, sub-machine gun and ammunition, maps, flashlight, oilskin, mountain sleeping bag, one spare pair of socks and underwear, a bottle of aspirin and another of iodine, toothbrush, soap and razor. Another good reason for minimising their possessions: they are now as poor as the Partisans, no longer the wealthy bourgeois visitors. To change into a fresh shirt when the others could not now seems unthinkable.

They stop at a small farmhouse, squeeze into the parlour to sleep. The pungent smell of dried mutton that hangs from a rafter mingles with their body odours and the smell of woollen clothes, wet with the morning dew, drying upon them as they lie.

When they wake they are given a tray of ground maize baked in milk and cut into pieces like scones. There are two boys, an old man and three women. All the men of Slovenia are gone from their homes: away with the Home Guard or the Partisans.

In the afternoon Tom sits on a plank bench leaning against the outside wall of a small stone barn, reading, and watching two women lazily scything corn in a field below the house. They appear, with their leisurely strokes, to be doing nothing at all. He has never done such work. Would forcing greater speed from the implement made the action inefficient, counterproductive?

Refocusing his awareness from such conjecture to the women in the field he finds they have each moved twenty yards, are slowly clearing great swathes.

The old man sits beneath an apple tree, sharpening fresh blades.

Marija appears. Tom gestures to her to join him. She sits beside him, gazes upon the scene. 'This is how things will change,' she says, nodding towards the harvesters, and then patting the ammunition belt slung over her own shoulder. 'Women doing what only men did before. Doing it well. Men will not be able to claim that women are not capable.'

'But you,' he says, 'could you not do what you wanted before?'

'Yes, of course,' she says impatiently. 'In the intelligentsia women here had some freedom, it is the same in England, no? But only two generations ago ninety-nine per cent of people in the Balkans were peasants.'

They bite grains of corn between their teeth, the nutty taste sticks to their tongues.

Marija smiles at some inner reflection, and when Tom catches her eye he raises his eyebrows, inviting her to share the memory.

'My Serbian father-in-law was a wealthy peasant,' she tells him. 'But a peasant still. My husband and I were married in Belgrade, with our friends. When my husband took me to visit his family, I did not join the men at meals but sat with the women in the kitchen. His mother spoke only when spoken to. She and her daughters worked like slaves. They looked after the sheep, the poultry, the dairy. They cooked, cleaned, mended clothes. They wove and spun and made blankets on hand-looms. Always they were spinning: producing yarn for the cloth. But my mother-in-law had no voice in the government of the household. She deferred on all matters to the opinion of her husband.

'In fact, her own son, my Radovan, gave his mother orders. I was furious. We had our first row as husband and wife. I should have known then that he was spineless. For all his talk of modern civilisation, after ten minutes in his tribe he had become a junior version of his father. A little dictator in his own house. It would have saved time if I had left him then. Instead...'

Marija falls silent.

'Please carry on,' Tom says.

'No,' she says. 'It is boring. I must bore you.'

'Not at all,' he says. 'I love to listen to you talk.'

'Talk?' Marija says. 'That is all?' Seeing Tom flustered, she laughs. 'And you?' she says. 'You have no wife?'

Tom shakes his head, gazing at the ground.

'You are too handsome not to have a sweetheart back in – what do you call it? – Blightsky?'

'Blighty,' Tom tells her.

'Blighty,' she repeats.

He glances up to see her sharp blue-violet eyes looking intently at him. He smiles and looks away, unable to hold her gaze.

Glancing to his left, Tom sees, too, Jovan: he is watching them, with hooded eyes.

July 16

Nikola runs into the house from his lookout post: he's sighted a German patrol, climbing the mountain. The Partisans grab their equipment and depart the house and the scything women; they leave without food.

They reach the forest and from its darkness watch, gasping, to see if they have been seen. 'No,' Jovan says. 'We cannot wait to find out, it might be too late. We must assume they are after us. Move. Go.'

They march without pause uphill, legs burning, lungs on fire. On flat stretches their speed increases, they are almost trotting. For two hours Jovan insists upon this pace. Finally he calls a halt. They collapse. Each is in his or her own cocoon of pain. But as they get their breath back they look up, smile at each other, aware of what they have just done.

Marija voices their achievement. 'Now that,' she declares, 'that is the way to retreat.'

Is the patrol still chasing them? Jovan will not let them light a fire. They sleep in a deep dell, in which pine trees grow slender and dark and straight up towards the distant sky.

They've just begun to stir when they hear and then see a little Henschel zooming overhead, buzzing and circling in the afternoon air and freezing them into immobility beneath the trees. Is the pilot looking for them? After a while he goes off, fluttering like a leaf in the currents of air that rise and fall in these mountain valleys, and disappears in the direction of Maribor.

Pero goes off in search of a courier to take them to the sixth unit who are somewhere in the hills above a town called Mislinje – close to the viaduct that was Tom's first target. They clean their weapons, rest, search for food. Sid and Marko show each other the Devon and the Slovene methods of setting snares for rabbits; they cannot risk a hunter's shot, a single gunshot would require that lookouts be sent to the four points of the compass. After a few hours they circle around to check on the traps. They are all empty.

Tom looks forward to conversation with Jovan. He speaks with his soldiers, but often the two of them find themselves together under a tree; leaning against a sun-warmed rock.

'Ah, Tom, it is good to rest,' Jovan says.

They eat a few tiny wild raspberries. To make them last, Tom locates each miniature pip in his mouth, cracks it between his teeth.

'Good to take the weight off one's feet,' Tom agrees.

'The first time I was put in prison,' Jovan says quietly, 'was in nineteen thirty-three, during student demonstrations in Belgrade against the dictatorship, confined in a cell with half a dozen other men. Twice a day, for just ten minutes, we could walk around a yard. It was all the exercise we had. I remember how the day I came out my legs, walking down the street away from Glavnjača prison, felt unfamiliar to me, my stride was so long and loose I feared I was about to fly up from the pavement.'

'Your party was already outlawed?'

Jovan nods. 'The second time they imprisoned me,' he says, 'was less cordial. For their initial method to extract information they told me to kneel down. They chained the hands and feet together, behind me. One of them pushed me, and I fell forward on to my front. Another stuffed a rag in my mouth. The third struck the soles of my feet with a pizzle. You don't know this? It's a whip made from a dried bull's penis. An instrument of torture the Serb police inherited from the Turks.'

Tom grimaces.

The expression on Jovan's face suggests pleasant reminiscence. 'On the foot, each blow is like a sharp cut. At the same instant you feel a stab in the brain. Your body wants to scream but because of the gag in your mouth you can't; instead you produce a pathetic grunt in the depths of your intestines.'

'They say any man can be broken,' Tom offers.

Jovan nods slowly. 'Perhaps. There may well be more efficient inquisitors than those Serbian agents. I was still wavering, at that time, between politics and literature. Then one day the chief interrogator put pencils between my toes, and squeezed with all his might.'

Tom realises Jovan has no more fruit. He takes Jovan's hands and makes a bowl of his palms, pouring a few of his own raspberries in.

Jovan puts a wrinkled little raspberry in his mouth, chews it, looks at Tom and smiles. He shakes his head. 'Unbelievable pain. It may not be logical, but I never wrote another story again. That day, Tom, I was not merely a communist, but became a revolutionary.' He takes a deep breath, and pats Tom on the shoulder. 'Enough rest, I think.' He climbs to his feet, and orders the resumption of their march, further on across the mountains.

July 17

They have no food, are too high now for wild berries, or a farmhouse from which to buy provisions. It rains in the night. In the morning the sky is clear and blue. A courier Pero has been waiting for appears at midday. 'We must leave now,' he tells Jovan.

'It is better to wait for darkness.'

'Sir, there is an enemy patrol just over that hill.'

Again they march at a brisk pace in the noon sun, descending through puddles. Bracken smells musky in the heat, after rain. Tom loses any sense of his surroundings. At first he concentrates on each footstep, every yard propelled forward, but this only makes the struggle more arduous. Awareness focuses on joints that cry out for respite, lungs desperate for a breather. So he tries to think of something quite different. What comes to mind are the few Union debates he attended at university. Too shy to take part himself, he half-admired and half-despised those who, imbued with an unpleasant self-confidence, swaggered forth their rhetoric. If there was one secret to it, someone told him, it was that the less you believed in something the easier it was to argue for it. He imagines now debates in the Union in which Jovan is taking part, arguing for what he believes in, for justice and dignity for all, and wipes the floor with the cynical young Ciceros and Quintilians of Oxford.

Miles go by of which he is unaware.

*

They pause, rest, while Dixon sets up the radio. Franjo and Nikola persuade some of their comrades to help them pull thistles they have found in a high alpine meadow: the root, Nikola explains, can be eaten raw, according to his father. Sometimes the plant comes out of the ground whole; at others, it snaps at ground level, and the victim curses the waste of energy.

Franjo seems able to tease each root out whole. Tom watches, unsure whether or not he is hungry enough to participate. Marija yanks at thistles, most of them break off, she grabs another.

'An incredible woman.'

Tom turns, to find Jovan beside him, shaking his head.

'My mother, when she married my father, said, "I am leading my beloved ox by his tether, so that he will not roar, throw his weight around and beat me." We have tried to move forward. My wife was my equal, in my eyes. But in her own eyes, in many ways she was still restrained by the ideas put in her head during her childhood. But this woman.' He gestures towards Marija. 'She is free.' He nods to himself. 'In her own head, she is free.'

Sid Dixon makes contact with base. News is good: in the east, Soviet armies are advancing on the Baltic states. In Italy, the Eighth Army has captured Arezzo and reached the Arno river. A drop is arranged for twelve o'clock tonight; the courier will lead them to the sixth unit.

The group descend, towards Mislinje. Tom thinks he sees black squirrels. Weren't they? They are gone. Was he dreaming? They were black as moles. The pace is too fast for conversation; he cannot ask Marija, ahead of him. It is clever, he considers, to have women in the *odred*: they keep up the pace, though it must be more difficult for them; and so the men keep up too, out of pride. But how extraordinary, really, to have been a wealthy and glamorous, upper-class Jewish intellectual, passing her time between Ljubljana and Belgrade, and now be thrust into this vagabond life.

The day is hot. They walk among trees, passing through little swarms of midges and gnats that stick to their perspiring skin. The earth, too, is sweating: odours rise from the soil and from the plants of the soil, aromas commingling into so pungent a smell that Tom imagines the forests they walk in as the armpits of the world.

As they cross high meadows the air carries the sound of cowbells. And then Tom is aware of unpleasant sensations on his neck, his arm. Something is biting him.

'Horseflies, sir,' Sid Dixon declares, with a rare vehemence. 'Can't stand the little bastards.'

There is the smell of new-mown grass. They see ahead of them an old man cutting hay. He does not pause in his rhythmic labours when they approach. It is easy to imagine, as they pass, that he is less reaping fodder for his animals than releasing this smell, this essence of grass, into the atmosphere, for the benefit of the passing Partisans.

What minute grains of dust bear the aroma? Tom wonders. How full is the atmosphere of unseen grains of soil, specks of mud, the landscape airborne; of invisible pollen and spores, nature's life-bearing seeds seeking wombs for their growth? We breathe them in, all the time, he realises. They are part of what we are. We are made by the land we are living in, and are surely altered by it.

They cross the high meadows of an alpine landscape in the evening – white isolated houses with orange tiled roofs – and then drop through the trees. When they come out of the forest they can see the lights of the town, Mislinje, and the courier is very apologetic. He tells Jovan they are going to reach the sixth unit later than he had thought. Perhaps not before midnight.

'Then we must walk faster,' Jovan tells him.

They press on into the night. When they meet the sixth unit there is little time to prepare the pasture where the drop is due to land. Jovan tells the commander – who has thirty men at his disposal – that, of course, it would be best to explain what is needed and to leave him to organise it, but there is no time. Jovan orders all the unit members to gather, with his *odred*, and takes total command, designating who will build fires, and so on. The sky is clear. The sound of engines are heard, the fires are lit, the plane drops its load. Jovan watches from a distance. The unit commander tells him he should go. The enemy are too close. He and his men know these hills, every hidden fold, every deep copse.

Before they leave, Sid cuts himself a section of parachute. Tom asks him why.

'Rather not say, sir,' Dixon answers. 'May not work at all, see.'

Tom does not push it. 'You're a riddle wrapped in a mystery, Dixon,' is all he says.

The Seventh Unit

July 18

As Tom lies in his sleeping bag, he hears a sound in the woods, an unearthly high-pitched cry. It is different from those he has heard before. He thinks it must be an owl but it is unlike any owl he has heard in England. It comes again: an almost human shriek, both anxious and threatening. It takes him a while to fall asleep.

When they wake, there is nothing to eat except for a few berries. You have to consume so many to get any goodness. Marko finds some grey mushrooms, which he gobbles up raw, but no one else is quite hungry enough to trust Marko's assurance that they are perfectly safe to eat.

Tom believed he possessed control of his appetites, and desires. He is undone by hunger after another hard day and night march. He feels weak, and has lost interest in the day ahead. The body craves fodder, like a beast.

But they gather their equipment together, shoulder their rucksacks and weapons, and move on.

'Guess we've got to go, sir,' Sid Dixon says, cajoling himself or encouraging his officer, and the others, into action. Stipe shoulders the LMG, Nikola the wireless, Franjo lifting the pack onto his son's back. Tom takes a deep breath, and sets off. And that is the thing: you come to the limit of your inner resources, you reach the end of your tether – drained, wretched, spent. And then you carry on. Each time. And gradually you get used to this recurring condition, it becomes familiar. You have nothing left, but there you are – you watch yourself, surprised – putting one foot in front of the other. You refuse to throw up the sponge; you carry on, all of you. Not one of you would quit, now, you'd be failing not only yourself but your comrades, your companions, and that would be unthinkable. He is one of a band of soldiers whose commitment to each other is total.

When they rest, rather than try to take their minds off the sorry lack of food, Jovan does the opposite.

'My grandfather, my mother's father, the head of a large Serb household in Herzegovina, liked to eat alone in the evening,' he tells them. 'His wife, my grandmother, served him, scurrying to and fro between the kitchen and his room. First she brought a little bottle of plum brandy, seventy per cent proof, as an aperitif. Then she would bring *meze*: a few slices of *pršuta* ham, *kačkavalj* – strong white cheese – and some pickled gherkins.'

Tom is surely not alone, he thinks, looking round, in salivating at the prospect of these delicacies; his stomach grumbles and aches.

'Then the main dish, *bosanski lonac*, made by his wife herself because it was too important to leave to the cook. Three different types of meat: fat spring lamb, rich pork and tender beef, cooked for eighteen hours with onions, parsnips, leeks, carrots.' Jovan recites this list of vegetables with slow relish. 'Red peppers, potatoes, tomatoes, garlic, celery and peppercorns. My grandfather ate this dish with a warm *pogača*, our rich home-made bread.'

As Jovan continues his description of this Bosnian meal, Tom notices that the pangs of hunger it has exacerbated are abating – as if perversely soothed by the memory, or imagination, of food.

After Jovan has finished, Marko asks him, 'You know why the Turks eat their meat before their soup?' He nods, as if giving himself approval to tell the story. 'When they were besieging Vienna they started to eat their dinner one night. They were just finishing their soup when the Poles came up from behind and bit them on their arses. The Turks fled, leaving the meat behind. That is why, ever since, Turks eat their meat first, just to be on the safe side.'

This anecdote brings much appreciative laughter from Marko's comrades. Marija tells Tom that despite the fact that their country has once again been annexed, it is hard for the Slovenes to shake off hundreds of years of antipathy to the Ottoman empire – or of deference to German-speaking powers to the north.

'The Germans regard the northern half of Slovenia as an integral part of their new Reich,' she says. 'All place names and family names have been Germanicised. Over the last two years Germans have been brought in to staff local government offices and to teach in the schools. Ninety per cent of the intellectual and professional classes have been sent to prison or labour camps.'

'Farms have been left uncultivated,' Stipe joins in. 'The German government has promised these to veterans of the *Wehrmacht* when the war is over.'

'I heard,' Jovan says, 'that when the Italian blackshirt battalions entered Ljubljana they were met with total hostility.'

'But it is true,' Stipe admits, 'that a few politicians, frightened old men, offered their services to Mussolini.'

'Politicians!' Marko exclaims, and spits onto the pine needles on the forest floor. He is damned if he wants anyone to rule his country except the rascals and fools who have a native right to do so. 'What do you expect?'

'Did you know, English friends,' Pero says, pausing and translating his own words for Dixon, keen that Sid be included, 'that on the birthday of our great poet Prešeren, word was passed round Ljubljana that everybody was to stay indoors? And sure enough, in the whole of our capital city, not a single Slovene stepped out of his house. And the Italians had no idea why. They thought a great plague had descended.'

They pass through an area where blood-sucking parasites, clinging to leaves and branches, attach themselves to bodies that brush against them. Now, like mothers with their children they check each other for ticks, then exchange roles, as always in the same pairs: the two women; the two officers, Tom and Jovan; father and son; Pero and Sid Dixon; Marko and Stipe.

Tom and Jovan sit a little way away from the nearest pair. Jovan takes off his shirt. He is leaner than he should be: there is a slight looseness to his skin, over wasted muscles. The privations of guerrilla warfare. Tom guesses that before the war Jovan must have been a couple of stones heavier. And it is strange how people's body odour ceases to be objectionable. Or is it only Jovan's? People smell simply as human animals. Each one is different. Jovan's odour is tinged with sweetness.

There are half a dozen of the insects attached to Jovan's torso, their bulbous little bodies filled with his blood. As he attends to them, Tom hears himself say, 'Tell me, Jovan. I understand that sex is banned. I understand why, in an army, at war. But can love be prohibited?'

'It must be ignored,' Jovan says. 'There will be time enough for that after the war.'

'Do you love Marija?' Tom asks.

Jovan pulls away. He reddens, his eyes flare. With hostility, Tom thinks, as much as embarrassment, and he regrets again speaking so openly of such things. He had no permission to. It is the liberating effect of speaking in another tongue; he would not be so indiscreet in English.

Jovan smiles, a wry and bitter smile, eyes narrowed. 'Oh, Englishman,' he says. 'Can't you see, Tom, you're the one she has feelings for?'

Tom takes a sharp breath, as if Jovan's words had administered a slap to the back of his neck. It is a shock. Yet not at all.

'There are more,' Tom says, and pulls Jovan gently back towards him. They continue the job in silence. They cannot pluck the ticks out for that would leave the insects' jaws buried in the skin: they have to unscrew them, slowly, then gently pull them free. This Tom does, and then he squeezes them, gleefully, and watches the hideous creatures perish in tiny eruptions of his companion's blood.

July 19

They walk through the night, at a steady pace. A nail in Tom's boot begins to bother him soon after they set off, but there is no question of stopping to deal with it. He can feel the blister form. He tries to ignore it, and does so for minutes at a time, but the pain keeps reasserting itself. It becomes the hot centre of his consciousness. How paltry one's will! No wonder spiritual disciplines demand mastery over the discomforts of the body: the monk kneeling on a stone floor; the yogi walking over hot coals.

He is diverted by a sound that chills him to his bones: a dog barking, not far from them in the woods. A night patrol? Does it have their scent? They have all stopped, and stand rigidly still in the darkness. There is movement behind. Tom turns, sees Marko making his way up the line, having a word with each in turn. He speaks to Francika, then comes to Tom. 'Fox,' he says. 'A lonely male. Telling the vixens he is here, if they want him.'

They resume, and within moments Tom's foot once more has his attention. How pathetic he is, he considers, unable to rise above this trivial concern, his entire existence no longer a part of this great enterprise but reduced to a tiny blister on the little toe of his left foot.

Or maybe both the pain and the reproof are ways to avoid Marija? When, at dawn, they camp, Tom keeps his distance from her. He watches her when he can do so unobserved. What a strange creature she is. Does she not reciprocate Jovan's feelings? Is Jovan right, that it is he, Tom, she prefers? How is that possible?

Jovan tells them they will spend the day here, and meet their next courier in the evening, a mile away. Sid Dixon is delighted at this news. 'Sir,' he tells Tom, 'I think this place will do.' Without further explanation he lies down and goes to sleep.

Tom wraps himself in his blanket. He looks across and sees Marija is looking in his direction. She smiles, a private communication between them, an intimate signal. He reciprocates as best he can, then closes his eyes. It seems there is a current between them now, something that for her is understood.

They wake, one after another, in the late morning, and in silence rise and walk towards the edge of the forest, fifty yards away, drawn out of the gloom of the trees to the light. It is as if a signal has alerted them though none has been given: they move like somnambulists or shades impelled by they know not what. They stop and look beyond the shadows. Out in the meadow Sid Dixon is dancing, barechested, darting about in the long grass, pouncing among the flowers, swooping upon some unseen prey. It could, Tom thinks, be a theatrical performance of a kind he's seen given by young women in student productions, of the *Bacchae* by Euripides, the *Antigone* of Sophocles. But this is a tough young English corporal, a long way from home, in hostile country, who is not acting but really has gone insane. What on earth is Tom to do with him?

Dixon brings his private performance to an end, and comes towards the forest. The skin of his torso is pale and muscular. Halfway there he pauses, and peers into the trees. Presumably he can just begin to make them out now, though they each stand embarrassed, motionless as tree trunks.

Dixon has removed his shirt, and this, Tom sees, he holds in his left hand. He's tied the cuffs and the bottom of the shirt, the buttons are done up, he clenches the collar tight. There is something inside, that is clear from its shape, something light and formless. Twigs, perhaps. Dixon enters the forest with the shirt held up like a trophy, and grins. The Yugoslavs turn, and walk back to the encampment, leaving Tom to deal with his eccentric compatriot.

The shirt, Tom sees as Sid comes closer, holds something alive: the twigs prod and poke against the material, they are confined against their will.

Dixon raises the shirt once more. 'Grasshoppers,' he says. 'Way I figures it is this, sir: the stream comes down from the mountains, then meanders through the meadow. Plenty of grasshoppers will a tried to jump it and fallen short, ended up a nice meal for many a trout. Trout used to 'em, see? Make a fine bait.'

'Bait?' Tom asks stupidly.

'Oh, got worms as well, sir, don't you worry. Dug 'em up earlier.'

The two men walk back to the bivouac. 'Found some canes yonder, reeds I should say more likely, should do us for rods.'

'Rods?' Tom says.

Dixon looks at him askance. 'I'm hoping you'll come with me, sir. You have done a bit of angling, have you?'

No, Tom Freedman has never fished before, beyond a spot of shrimping on seaside holidays, with a bucket and net. He watches what Sid does and copies him as best he can.

By the time they've tied the silk lines to the rods, and baited the bent pine that serves for hooks, the sun is high and the sky blue and cloudless. They begin in the meadow, where clear water runs over smooth stones and clean gravel. The men stand by the stream, looming hulks any fish there shrink away from, under the banks, into the shadows. They catch nothing. Stipe wanders over, observes their prowess. Marija watches them. Under their eyes Tom perceives the absurdity of such futile patience.

He and Dixon manoeuvre downstream, less by design than repetitive admissions of failure. Changes of mind. No, not here, after all. Perhaps there.

Towards noon they quit the meadow, as it gives way to undergrowth on the banks, and trees, too, birches and oaks. Here the air is soft and tinged with the smell of wet earth and standing water, breathed up from the river edge. The river is murkier, there is mud at the banks, and moss on shapeless stones. Like a dreary pungent stretch of England transplanted.

Tom comes to a bend, which makes a kind of pool. He sticks a worm on the hook, unwinds the silk off the wooden peg Dixon has fashioned for a bobbin, and drops the hook into the water. It settles slowly out of sight. There is a ripple on the surface. Tom feels a pull on the line. He strikes, and then there is a tug.

With no reel, but a makeshift rod barely longer than his own height, and the same again of line, Tom can play only the most facile of games with the fish. Yet it is small, and tired, and comes to him, and he sees its shape rising to the surface, and all the speckles of its coat. He shelves it out with his left hand. A pound, he reckons, perhaps a little more.

It is the first trout of many. He and Dixon, a little way ahead of him, move downstream, and they hang the fish that they catch on twigs and branches of the trees.

*

In a while the stream comes out of the trees, the smell of earth dissipates, Tom finds himself back in the open. The water, brown and clear as ale, babbles shallow over pebbles. Tom crunches across the gravel-bed to a little island above a deep, round pool that is stirred by a circular eddy which swings bubbles and streaks of spume into narrowing whorls, so that the pool might be polished ammonite come to liquid life.

A breeze comes up from the valley below and the day clouds over. Suddenly it is ideal: grey, with a little purl upon the water. Here is a fine spot. Tom gazes into the pool. The clear water, the turning currents, the dappled light, make for a captivating image. He sees a big trout nose out from under a ledge. So, Tom thinks: the pool belongs to this old fellow. A cannibal trout who'll eat other fish to keep his pool cleaned out. Tom's father, he recalls, told him of seeing a squirrel that had fallen in a river being carried downstream; flailing vainly to reach the bank. Brought into a pool like this, it was dragged under by the resident. A grinning pike. One of his father's stories. Was it true?

This big old trout studies the worm on Tom's hook a while, then he backs under the ledge like a submarine reversing into dock.

There'll be no joy here, it will take better tack – and a more experienced fisherman – to capture this one. Tom moves on, recasts. So this, he imagines, is what captivates the angler, this mood: in passive, hopeful expectation of a tug, and then the challenge to one's skill, and the primitive excitement of the capture of prey. A state of being on the brink. A state of imminence. The immediate past, even up until a moment ago, is forgotten; the future holds no fear. What lies beyond a few metres from him even unto the infinities of space have no relevance to anything at all.

*

A small fish rises a few yards from where he stands; then, just under the bank, another, a larger one. Tom feels a heavy tug, and the end of his rod curves into a hoop. He guesses immediately it is only a small one, a half, a quarter of a pound. It fights gamely, as Sid tells him all trout do, but he has it landed in a moment. It lies motionless on the pebbles with an open, gaping mouth, but as he bends to pick it up it flips and twists. Tense muscular spasms. He grasps the slippery body firmly in his left hand, works the hook free from its mouth. Then he bends again and strikes its head against a stone. It lies limp in his palm, its silver sides spotted with rose. It has a delicate cucumber scent he's not noticed before, with the others he'd caught. Its eyes stare, expressionless. Its slipperiness is beginning already to grow viscous against his palm.

What has he done? Smashed the delicate mechanism inside the tiny skull of the trout. The living machine, now broken.

Tom and Sid climb back up the stream in the afternoon, one on either bank, gathering the fish they've caught, so many they weave a rudimentary tray to carry them. Two dozen they bear to their disbelieving comrades, a biblical gift.

His mother used to roll trout in oatmeal, fry them and serve with melted butter. Here Francika simply grills them on the skillet as they are, but Marija garnishes the fish with a tangy herb she has found by the stream, and the Partisans and the Englishmen relish every mouthful of the crisp skin and the pale, succulent flesh.

July 21

'I don't know where we are,' Pero says. This is their second night on the move, a day in the forest without food, searching for the next courier.

'We are lost,' says Marko, spitting at the ground.

'I did not say that,' Pero objects. 'No, we are not lost. This is a lie. I am just not sure where the seventh unit is.'

The courier line has been broken. Pero thought he knew the area but it seems he was mistaken. Their maps are too small-scale to be any more than a general guide, little help with the particularities of the terrain. They march on, using Tom's compass, in an easterly direction.

They come to a tiny hamlet. No dogs bark in the night but geese cackle and hiss, hostile to their passing. Two figures are already up and going about their business. They see the travellers are Partisans and try to scurry inside and close their doors. The Partisans ask for food but they will not give them any. Their last sustenance was a brew of nettles. 'Not a bad cuppa, sir,' Dixon had pronounced. 'Could do with a spot of sugar.' The trout is already a distant memory.

'You have food,' Jovan tells the villagers.

'No, no, we have no food.'

He offers to pay but they refuse.

'It's clear this village is pro-quisling,' Tom says to Jovan. 'We are starving. I don't understand. We have to take their food.'

Jovan shakes his head.

'I don't think I get it, sir,' Sid Dixon tells Tom. 'If they're collaborating with the enemy, they're lucky not to be shot, never mind lose a bit a grub.'

Tom pursues the issue with Jovan.

'No, Tom,' Jovan insists. 'We can't take their food. We cannot give the Liberation Front a bad name.'

They leave the village unharmed. Jovan explains to Tom that Marshal Tito ordered as long ago as early 'forty-two that anyone taking food from or harming civilians will be shot.

'It purified us,' Jovan says. 'It helped to make us into a proud army. And there is a Chinese proverb. "'Partisans among the people are like fish in a river: the river can live by itself, but not the fish."'

'I admire your discipline, Jovan,' Tom assures him. 'I just wish I wasn't so damnably hungry.'

As they walk from the village the geese stretch their necks at them and hiss out hate. Sid asks Tom to order him not to run into their midst and grab one by its neck.

As dawn breaks they quench their thirst with dew droplets on fir cones. They make camp in the forest. Tom sleeps well. He wakes to find Francika has amassed a stew of boiled clover and wild spinach, birch bark and roots. It tastes good, and is greatly appreciated; though Tom would give much for a hunk of bread or meat; for tucker.

Morale is low. They are hungry, have no courier, are vulnerable.

'I don't like it, sir,' Sid tells Tom.

'Me neither.'

They lie, dozing, fearful, gazing at nothing other than sunlight playing through the tops of the trees.

Marija sits beside Tom. They pull stems of grass, and suck

them. 'I am scared,' she tells him. 'This I don't like! I don't want to be frightened. Let them kill me, let me kill them.' She turns to Tom and fixes him with her piercing gaze. 'Do you see?' she asks.

'I do,' Tom says, nodding. 'I understand.'

July 22

They pass a tiny chapel that must serve a small number of isolated settlements. They stop at a farm. Dawn is almost upon them. Jovan posts Stipe on sentry duty and the rest enter the farmhouse. Jovan tells the family that they will not be allowed to leave the house until the *odred* has departed. The mother is trembling as she prepares food. There is an old man white with fear. The emotion is so palpable that the children as they emerge pick up on it instantly, and freeze against the wall of the kitchen. Do they believe the Partisans will kill them, good Catholics as they undoubtedly are? They have a plaster figure of the Virgin Mary in a shrine in the wall of the kitchen. Are they already scared of German reprisals? Most likely the husband is with the Home Guard, and they fear that this will be found out – if the Partisans don't know already.

Jovan is friendly, talking with the children, counting out money to pay the mother for the food they take. Tom was supplied with gold sovereigns and Reichsmark notes in Italy that he keeps in a money belt around his waist, and which he doles out to Jovan.

Half of them sleep on the bench that runs around the wall of the room, the rest on the floor, on hay brought in from the barn. Tom now sleeps with his gun on one side and pack on the other so that he can grab them in the dark if needs be. He sleeps with his boots on. 'If you need to piss in the night,' Marko advises him, 'don't go out alone. You may be attacked by the dogs.'

*

They are given delicious venison stew when they awake. Like animals that hunt, they have starved; now there is food, they gorge themselves. Afterwards, Sid sets up the radio. Francika helps him. Still they communicate in single words, though the number increases daily.

'Aerial.'

'*Anten. Bunka?*'

Sid chuckles. 'Knob,' he says, raising his eyebrows.

Francika pokes him, mock-angry.

Tom goes outside. From the high farm he can look across into a lower valley, with two small farms along its ridge, and beyond the rocky peaks of mountains looming above. It is one of those late-summer days in which autumn is already present: ribbons of mist hang in the valley, there is a thin grey skin of cloud above which Tom can sense the sun waiting to burn through, and dissipate all the moisture in the air and on the ground. It will be a hot afternoon again. But for now the sky is grey and all the colours are muted, yet separate from each other, somehow drenched in their own existence: the trees are dark green, the houses are white, the fence poles around the small gardens and paddocks are a hard bleached brown.

As if by a miracle a courier appears. How did he find them? Sid Dixon makes contact with Italy. There's heavy rain in Normandy and the western front has halted, but the Russians have entered Latvia.

There will be a drop the day after tomorrow a few hours' march from here. After their initial destruction of the bridge and the tunnel, all such major targets were well guarded; even with the subsequent six units' modest actions – rocks in steep cuttings thrown onto the line here, rails blown there – enemy troops are patrolling up and down the tracks.

Jovan sends Pero, Nikola and Stipe out around the mountain to look for movement down below. They return, each reports seeing none, so Jovan decides that rather than press on to the seventh unit and wait with them for the drop, they should stay here tonight, and for a second day.

The effect is extraordinary: everyone becomes busy, doing things they have not had time to carry through – washing clothes, for there is now time to dry them. Their mood is carefree. They relax. Tom realises the tension under which they live most of the time, even when nothing is happening. Jovan has decided they are safe, for now.

The nervous old man seems to have made the decision to throw in his lot with his unwanted guests. He produces a bottle of plum brandy and pours small glasses for the Partisans. It is fumy and rough and very strong, and on empty stomachs, having not touched alcohol for weeks, the effect is immediate. It is as if their host has infused them with giddiness; a levity.

The Slovenes tease Jovan for his Serb defects; he mocks them for their national weaknesses. Defects of which he is proud; weaknesses they cherish.

'If you went to any Slovene town on a Saturday night you would find everyone reeling in the streets, they are all drunkards,' Jovan tells Tom. 'Women as well as men. In Serbia we are able to celebrate all day and all evening without losing control of our senses.'

'It is because Serbs don't work,' says Stipe. 'Yes, they lie around all day with nothing to do but eat and drink. We Slovenes work hard, like the English, and then we have but a short time to enjoy ourselves.'

'You know, Tom,' Marija says, 'even before the war, the Slovene authorities did not beat and torture our political prisoners. Instead of doing our own dirty work, Serb inquisitors were imported.' She looks towards Jovan. 'Is this not true?' she asks.

Jovan nods reluctantly. 'I was told this myself, when I was in prison,' he says.

Sid and Francika talk to each other in their conversation of single words.

'Cigarette,' Sid says, rolling her one.

'*Cigaretni*,' Francika says, accepting his proffered lighter.

'Gasper,' Sid says, and smiles.

'Gyas perr,' Francika copies him, and they chuckle at each other idiotically.

'Brandy?' Sid asks her, holding up his glass.

Francika mimes the fruit from which it's made, plucking plums from their branches. '*Slive*.'

Sid imitates her actions and becomes a juggler, not picking but throwing the invisible fruit up in the air. And then clumsily dropping them. 'Plums,' he says.

Francika manages to nod despite her laughter. '*Slivovka*.'

More brandy is produced, there is further talk and laughter. At some point Tom realises he needs some fresh air. He goes outside. It was sweaty and raucous in the smoke-filled, cramped parlour, and his head is ringing. He stumbles away from the house, and takes a piss in the field. He feels dopey, content not to think about anything. He walks halfway back to the house but then stops, and turns away from the house once more. Through a wash of blue-white nebulae the sky is alight with stars. As Tom watches, he sees one fall, over on the western edge of his vision. He closes his eyes. The silence and the cool night air are delicious. Then he becomes aware of something. Someone, beside him, did they touch his arm? He opens his eyes.

'It's very strange, isn't it?' Marija says.

'Strange?' Tom asks. 'How so?'

'What we are doing is so important. It really is. I believe this. And then we look up there and realise it's not important at all.'

Tom nods. They both gaze upward. He can sense her arm hanging beside his. He wonders how close their fingers are to each other's. Will she let hers brush against his? Will his fingers reach out, and take hers? Time passes. No, it seems they will not.

After a while Marija stirs. He thinks they are parting, to return inside, but they are held together a moment longer by some mild force – no more, perhaps, than a lull of indecision, or a slight reluctance to have a pleasant moment end – and just as he realises how close not just their arms but their whole bodies are to one another Marija kisses him in the starlit darkness. He smells the brandy on her breath at the same time as he tastes the fruit on her tongue, lingering, warm. He feels flushed with something close to embarrassment to be kissing his friend. He puts out of his mind that it is Marija kissing him, it is no one, just lips, a mouth, a warm tongue, it could be anyone, anyone at all.

Marija presses against him, surely feels his arousal. As if the merest evidence of his desire satisfies something in her, she pulls away from him. He thinks he sees a gleam of triumph in her moonlit eyes.

'No,' Marija whispers. 'No, Tom, we cannot. For myself, I do not care, but I could not stand it if they shot you too.'

Tom, urged on by the novel power of such a kiss, pulls her back to him and kisses her deeply. When eventually they pull apart both are short of breath.

'Oh, Tom,' Marija gasps. She turns and runs into the pasture, her footsteps receding into the silent darkness. Tom stands, confused and triumphant. So that is what it is, to kiss a woman. It is not unpleasant, not at all. Perhaps it would be possible, the rest of it too? Not just the cloisters of academia but also a family, a normal life?

July 23

They sleep like hibernating animals. Wake with mild and not entirely unwelcome headaches. 'Feel pretty seedy,' Tom admits to Sid. Their skin is puffy from oversleep – what greater luxury? And food – again a stew, lamb this time, with hot bread straight from the brick oven beside the stove, and thick red wine. Jovan is paying well, and the woman and the old man have found their stores for them.

Marija does not look at Tom, but he watches her. She somehow communicates, lets him know that she is aware of him. Her mind picks up his body on its radar.

Towards noon Tom is standing outside the house when he hears aircraft overhead. He looks up and sees a single Fieseler Storch dive-bomber above, at low level. He assumes it is on its way somewhere, but suddenly he sees it nose over into an almost vertical dive. Tom is dimly aware of Jovan calling him inside, but is rooted to the spot. A quarter of a mile away lies another farmhouse and barn, higher and more out in the open than the one they are in. The plane hits it with 500-pound bombs. Someone grabs Tom and pulls him in. They watch from the crowded window. Before it leaves, the plane strafes the bombed farmhouse with 20-mm-cannon fire, a gratuitous aggressive gesture.

Tom looks at Jovan, who nods. From Sid's expression he too realises: their radio transmission yesterday was monitored, their position plotted. They have been saved by two farms being unusually close together. The German pilots have picked the wrong one.

As they stand watching, they become aware of the family they are staying with. The children are crying. The old man says, 'There are ten people there.'

There is surely no one alive in the blown-up burning ruins. They are responsible for this horror. They want to stay, to bury the dead, but Jovan says they cannot: an enemy patrol will come to inspect the carnage. Tom places ten gold coins on the dresser in the kitchen. Not enough sovereigns have ever been minted for reparation. They leave hurriedly, in dazed and sombre mood. There is a faint smell of roasting meat in the air.

July 24

They walk all afternoon and all night, led by their courier towards the seventh unit. It is hot. Tom thinks of the dead family, probably much like the one they stayed with four hundred yards away: slaughtered for the sake of what? A few rail tracks?

Dawn finds them plodding grimly across the saddle of a hill. Having walked as stunned automatons they now become more alert. The world becomes visible around them. Tom sees jagged rocks of the peak that juts against the sky, the firmament attaining colour as if being slowly injected with blue dye. Wispy white clouds. Dark vegetation grows below the bare summit, it looks like moss in the distance, and gradually small individual trees become apparent scattered high up, marooned from the forest below, their brave blind seeds blown into a crevice with a little mud, taking root and growing in the thin wind-ridden air up there, stunted and alone. There is a scent of something musky, suddenly, perhaps a pine marten or a fox passed across this track a moment ago. There is the sound of a single songbird, one Tom cannot identify. An excitable cheep, cheep, cheep that runs up and down as if on a little thin rollercoaster of song. Perhaps he has never heard it before, it is native to this area of southern Europe: yet he suspects he has, and simply never noticed. Tom apprehends the world with all his senses being born afresh. This world in all its glory. This world which man sullies with his sordid deeds. Is Christ the redeemer present here? Or must we redeem it ourselves?

*

There has been no rain for days now. Sweltering nights, baking days. The earth on open ground is cracked in the form of a honeycomb. Tom looks at the sun and back at the ground and sees black bees rise from the fissures: specks on his eyes.

They walk parch-mouthed. Tom dreams of drops of water on his tongue. He walks next to Jovan, his head lolling. Suddenly Jovan speaks. 'In the house I grew up in,' he says, 'we drank rainwater from a cistern attached to the roof. In the hot weather, worms would grow in the water, and multiply quickly. A few pinches of salt was enough to kill them.'

The group pauses. Jovan tells them the story of his climbing Mount Biokovo, a white rock mountain on the Dalmatian coast, with his student friends ten years ago. They were intrigued to see peasant women in their black dresses climbing too, and followed them to a cave, so deep that winter ice was still preserved there in late summer. Some women went down on ropes and cut the ice with axes; others pulled the ice – and their companions – out. They took the ice to sell to restaurants and cafés in Makarska, the coastal town below.

'Many of the women developed pneumonia,' Jovan tells them. 'But what could they do? The ice brought them a few coins.'

*

The courier leads them to the seventh unit. It is a small band, barely larger than their own. Its members resemble one another: they are surely brothers, cousins, uncles. They nod to the members of Jovan's *odred*. Very little is said. Perhaps what happened yesterday is written clear upon them, for the other group feed them a little *zganci*, and do not ask questions or swap stories as they usually do. Even Pero is quiet.

Sid Dixon goes off on his own, he sits alone by a stream. Tom leaves him be. It is no wonder a melancholia comes over men in war: there is too much to take in, yet it hardly seems real; then reality rears up, throws itself in their faces; men became unmoored from the stable ground in themselves.

He realises that the plane strike has stopped him worrying about Marija. What happened between them took place on the other side of that event. A moment of silly innocence.

The drop comes in on time. Again they leave immediately, the same courier who brought them to the unit taking them away from it, south.

The Eighth Unit

July 25

They move by day, the couriers assuring them that, this high, they are safe from Slovene or German patrols. Still, Jovan has Pero and Nikola walk at the front, well ahead of the rest of them, the two boys with their eyes skinned, ears cocked.

The track steepens and they enter scattered patches of pine. Above and ahead of them they can see Pero, Nikola and the courier pause, and evidently greet someone. Then they see, coming over the pass out of the forest, a peasant followed by a train of horses laden with hay. A woman walks behind them. As Tom watches them, there is a drone in the air that causes an immediate sick feeling in the stomach, and loosens the joints of his knees: down from the sky the Stuka comes. It drops towards its target, at speed from high altitude, then is slowed down by letting air flow through loud sirens, the noise adding to the terror of the dive. Sighting the peasants and their animals, in a second it is firing and dropping bombs among the horses. Tom and the rest of their party run under the trees, lie down and watch. The horse train is in confusion. Tom can hear an animal yowl and whinny. It has been hit, and rolls down into a hollow. The plane has swerved away across the mountain, silence descends. Yet seconds later, the whine of the Stuka is heard again. Several of the horses have thrown off their loads, and when the peasants see the plane swooping around to return, they frantically start to lead the horses back into the forest. But the plane is over in a moment. Tom hears the shrieking of the guns and sees another horse roll down the hillside. Marko, meanwhile, unable to restrain himself, has run out from the trees with his Sten gun and is firing up at the now fast disappearing plane.

Then silence. The sun shines. They hurry up the slope and reach the scene. Two horses lie dead, and a Slovene woman sits sobbing in the grass beside her horribly still husband.

Later, after they have carried the man's body to his home, a wooden cabin a short walk away, they leave the woman grieving, and move on.

They are a band of surly and miserable vagrants, Tom thinks, cadging what they can, adding only sorrow to those who live here. They pass through and move on; the enemy chases them and they run away, but perhaps in reality they avoid each other, and both are parasites.

Marija walks beside him. She puts her hand on his shoulder. 'I know what you are thinking,' she says. 'I am glad it bothers you. There is only one answer.'

'What is that?' Tom asks.

'It is simple: we must win,' she says.

They walk into the evening. Jovan tells Tom what a shock the capitulation was to the Serbs. In 1918 they had inflicted bloody defeats on the Austrian and Bulgarian armies, and had crowned their military achievements with the epic winter retreat across Albania, and then the final advance back from Salonika to

Belgrade. Yet in 1941 – when part of the much larger state of Yugoslavia – they had been blown aside by the German blitzkrieg like an army of toy soldiers.

A low-pitched penetrating sound. It could be coming from anywhere, or everywhere, around them. It grows steadily in intensity, then the bomber formations begin to appear, high in the blue sky.

Long-range fighters accompany the bombers, weave back and forth above them like little sheepdogs, their S-shaped white vapour trails stitching patterns against the arrow-straight trails of the large bombers.

In less than an hour, Tom reckons, their bombs will fall on the industrial yards beyond Vienna. The roar fills the sky until the last wave disappears to the north. If only the great bombers could swat away the single planes wreaking havoc here.

July 26

Night. They pass through a village. The sweet pungent smell of rotting fruit, and manure. Dogs bark, but no one stirs. The inhabitants surely lie awake, aware that people they do not want to know about are passing through.

After another long night march, they prepare to sleep in the open, under a parachute canopy. Stipe and Marko tie its corners to tree trunks. Pero draws a map for Jovan and Tom, of where he thinks they are. Marija gathers wood for a fire. Sid checks the wireless. When Tom goes into the wood to relieve himself, he notices Francika in the distance, leaning with her head against a tree. She is mumbling to herself.

Franjo and Nikola return from a foraging expedition with a bag full of frogs. Francika heats up the skillet while father and son kill and slice up the amphibians' squat bodies, and long muscular legs. The old man fries the meat, his son passes it round.

Hunger overcomes Sid Dixon's reluctance to try it. He chews suspiciously, grimacing, then turns to Tom. 'They taste like chicken, sir.'

'I saw you earlier, praying,' Tom tells Francika. 'Do you mind me asking what you pray for?'

Francika shakes her head. 'The Mountain Ash is the last tree that still understands human speech,' she tells him. She shrugs, nonchalantly. 'This is what my mother told me. I don't know if it is true.'

'No, it may not be,' Tom agrees. 'Perhaps it is the oak.'

'You are right to tease me,' Francika says, smiling. 'I would prefer that Jovan did not see me as you have.'

'And what did you tell the tree?' Tom asks her.

Francika blushes, and looks down at the ground. The competent soldier is replaced by a young peasant woman. 'I was wondering,' she says, 'if I have been a widow for long enough.'

'And did the Mountain Ash give you an answer?'

'The tree cannot speak, Tom,' Francika tells him in a schoolmistress manner, regaining her balance in their conversation. 'It listens, and understands. Only I can answer this question for myself.'

Their courier passes them on to a fresh one, a wiry youth with a fuzzy moustache. The eighth unit is only four hours' march away. Sid contacts base.

July 27

They walk in daylight. The courier is nervous and keeps stopping, listening. They pass a man on a grey mule, heading downhill; perhaps following a long night guarding his flock of sheep in the high pastures. Might he inform Germans or Home Guard of their presence? Tom wonders. What should they do to protect themselves, and their mission? Shoot him and have done with it? The man rides on, slowly, hunched to make himself as small as possible, his body jolting like a sack of bones with every step the mule takes. Tom is appalled. Where did the idea come from? Did it come from outside him, like a burr snagged on his passing body, or from inside his own weak and frightened mind?

They walk around a hill covered with waist-high bracken. It smells like almonds. Marko assures them they'll each pick up some new ticks for themselves in the green sea of waving fronds. In the late morning they reach a wooded hill. Pero and the courier have stopped. Jovan, and then Tom, move up to join them. The courier announces that they have arrived. It is hard to know what he means. Then he puts his hands together in front of his mouth and blows into them, and out comes the sound of a bird. Then he starts to stroll through the wood. The others follow. They see a man emerge, to their left, then another, up ahead. It is hard to make sense of. More men appear, as if out of the ground, like the soldiers who grew from the teeth of the dragon that Cadmus slay. No, not the ground, Tom realises. It is caves they emerge from.

Their dozen members are gaunt and pale. Francika and their cook compare supplies. It seems the other group is better off. Tom is given a crust of corn bread and a piece of bacon fat.

They also have with them a New Zealand rear-gunner who bailed out on his way home from a bombing raid. He is a big, raw-boned boy. He reckons his pals bailed out too but were blown by the wind away from each other. He was picked up by a peasant who passed him on to a courier. They made him understand that he has to walk all the way out, and he has been shifted from one unit to the next in a gradual meander south. He is very glad to meet Tom and Sid and talks rapidly as he tells them of his travails. 'The thing is we were bombing way over in the east,' he tells them. 'Got a little lost on the way home? I mean like the compass must have been spinning like a bloody top.' He was in a Wellington: they flew along the Danube at two hundred feet, bombing barges carrying petrol and oil from the Ploesti oil fields in Romania.

'You should have seen it,' he says. 'The river a great orange flame. Plumes of thick black smoke. Beautiful.' He tells them that Partisan fighter crews are being trained in north Africa to fly Spitfires. Jovan's group, when this is translated for them, are very pleased, although they affect the pose of being unsurprised; it was exactly what they had been expecting.

'Slovene pilots,' says Marko, 'are the best in the Balkans. Now they fly Spitfires very well.'

Having prepared fires, they have a few hours to rest in the evening, before the drop. Marija kneels beside Tom and whispers in his ear, 'Will you join me for a smoke?'

They walk away from the clearing. They come to a beech with one low branch that has grown straight out from the trunk. They lean against it as if at the bar of an English pub.

'I am trying not to think of you,' Marija says. 'I thought you should know that. I am trying. We should both try.'

Tom nods. 'Of course. We have to.' He flicks open his trench lighter and lights their cigarettes. He passes one to Marija. 'What plans do you have for after the war?' he asks. As soon as he's said it he regrets it. What an idiotic thing to say.

'We should not think of afterwards,' Marija says. He is aware of her gaze turned upon him, but does not look her way. 'Perhaps it is superstitious of me. But we cannot.'

They smoke in silence, side by side, leaning against the limb of the beech tree. It could not be more truly perpendicular if a spirit level had been used. 'You must know,' Tom says, 'that Jovan has fallen for you. You do know that, Marija? He is in love with you.'

'You will fight him, for me?' she asks.

The idea is alarming. Before Tom can think of anything to say, Marija sighs.

'Men have always fallen for me, as you put it, Tom. It is not love. I have something I wish I did not.' She smiles ruefully. 'Men pick up a signal, they think it came from me. You did not seem to.'

Tom shakes his head, slowly, in agreement. 'We'd better go back,' he says, stubbing the fag-end on the rough bark.

'Yes,' Marija says. 'You are right. We must.'

The drop is made. Tom watches the scruffy Partisans make off into the night with their explosives. There is one unit left now. They head west for the remaining hours of the night.

The Ninth Unit

July 28

They sleep outside a friendly farmhouse, in a garden full of turkeys. The smell of the birds is pungent and they gobble loudly all night. The Partisans only get a couple of hours' sleep.

'Permission to silence the pests,' Marko pleads to Jovan from under his blanket. 'You have only to give the word and their necks will be painlessly broken.'

But they are revived by a generous breakfast: freshly baked, doughy, flat bread. It has been split, and fresh cream spread into it. They are given a mug of milk each. They can smell some kind of meat stewing: the size of the pan assures them there is a hearty lunch to come, too, and so it proves.

They spend the afternoon in the orchard of the farmhouse picking lice out of their clothes. A disgusting procedure: Jovan shows Tom how to find one and squash it between your nails: the creatures pop with a specific, pleasing *crack*.

Dixon's chest hair is crawling. Francika tells them that the little vermin spread typhus. Marija claims that typhus has been unheard of in peacetime for generations, but that it seems able to lie low and erupt in the unhygienic conditions of war.

The Partisans bemoan the lack of fresh clothes, or pest killer. In safe areas, soldiers' clothing can be deloused in steaming barrels. Allied stores are beginning to add DDT, an instant killer, to some of their supply drops. But here in the Fourth Zone lice are an ineradicable menace.

The ninth unit are in central Pohorje, back near the branch line. The *odred* set off in the evening light.

After an hour of walking up and down hill they see smoke in the sky ahead of them. They approach through a wood with foreboding, and when they come to the edge of the trees they find themselves looking down on a large village in the valley just below them, no more than two hundred metres away. Many houses are burning. Tom can see two German troop-carrying trucks, and three motorcycle combinations, parked in the square. There are two more lorries, one at each end of the village.

The soldiers in their grey uniforms move here and there.

Jovan passes him his glasses. 'In the square,' he says.

Tom pans, and alters the focus, and finds bodies strung from lamp-posts, half a dozen, hanging. The one at the end is swaying slightly. Out of the nearest side of the square, a crowd that was hidden to them is dispersing: they must be the villagers forced to gather and watch their neighbours being hanged.

Tom lowers the glasses; someone else pulls them from him for their turn. Pale grey smoke rises into the blue sky. There is no sound carried up to them, of shots or even shouts. A peaceful scene. These Germans have come down the white road along the middle of the wide valley and killed who? Men taken at random, probably, for some real or imagined crime: someone in the village had harboured a Partisan; a Partisan prisoner was shown to have come from the village. Men were taken and hanged from the lamp-posts. Butcher, baker, candlestick-maker. The sheer nihilism. The enemy seems less a human foe than a black beastly force.

Sid goes over to comfort Francika, who is kneeling on the ground, weeping: the scene, awful in itself, has stirred up dreadful memories.

Tom walks away. If free will means this, then God's experiment in creation is a botched endeavour. The end has come for him: he has no further use for God. He finds the pocket-edition New Testament in his pack and throws it down the hill.

He is brought back to sudden awareness of his environment by sound: those around Tom are shooting. Stipe has set up the light machine gun, Marko is firing his Sten, Franjo and Nikola are shooting their Mauser rifles. Tom unslings the Beretta from his shoulder and joins in, barely aware of what he is doing. He has broken cover and is firing. He has no fear, he is invulnerable. It does not occur to him that he might get hit. Enemy soldiers crumple and fall.

Then Tom realises that Jovan is yelling at his troops, ordering them to cease fire and withdraw. The Germans have realised what is happening and are beginning to shoot back. Marija does not want to stop. She is cursing and swearing as she fires, in tears of rage. When the clip she is using has finished, Stipe does not replace it but gently takes the gun from her.

They retreat into the trees and climb, cross the ridge into another valley, and stop. The hills hang heavy with smoke, but the sound of firing has ceased.

The Partisans are exultant, and so, Tom confesses, is he. A flame has been kindled and sweeps the tinder of the country, a pure and cleansing fire; now he is one of the arsonists. He is a warrior, too.

They walk on. The blood in their veins lowers in temperature. When they come to rest, Jovan tells the Slovenes to gather round and then, in a tone of calm anger, rebukes them for breaking cover when they knew their orders.

Tom, listening, understands full well: Stipe, Marko and the others are their bodyguard, or more particularly the radio set's bodyguard. They are not on any account to engage with the enemy. Because of him and Dixon they must deny their instincts. Just now, for the first time, they could not. After their commander's dressing-down the *odred* go about their tasks setting up camp in chastened silence.

But Marija is unrepentant. 'Did it not feel good?' she asks Tom. 'If you had told me ten years ago what joy there could be in killing I would have said you were mad. But it is a primitive pleasure. We must take it, no?' She looks at him, her violet eyes wide.

'Yes, I felt it,' Tom admits.

'I knew it,' she says with relish.

A new courier appears, a girl, with a message for Jovan: they are to be brought down from the mountains.

'But I thought we still have one more unit to supply,' Tom objects.

'There is no time.'

'But we must, surely,' Tom says. 'That is why we are here.'

'No,' Jovan tells him. 'We are here to do what we are told to do.' He reassures Tom that there is no bad news. He seems guarded. The courier takes them a short distance to a place she has been told to, then leaves. They are to wait.

As darkness falls they prepare to sleep.

Sid Dixon comes to Tom as he is laying out his oilskin. 'Could I have a word, sir?' he asks.

'Of course.'

'In private.'

This seems such a comical thing to say in the middle of woods that Tom bites his lip to curb a smirk. He walks away from the others. Sid follows him.

At a distance that is surely out of anyone's hearing, Tom pauses, and says, 'Fire away.'

Sid clears his throat. 'I'm soft on her, sir,' he says.

Tom says nothing.

'Francika. She's soft on me.'

When Tom looks at his corporal, Sid is grinning. 'We want to be together. We wants to get married and everything.' It comes tumbling out. 'I plan to take her back with me to Devon. As soon as possible. When you've got a farm to take on you can't never marry too young. That's what I'd like you to arrange, sir, if you could.'

This time Tom does smile. 'But it's impossible,' he says.

'Impossible?' Sid's eyes blaze. Even in the dying light Tom can see his cheeks darken. 'No, sir. You see, she's the one. That's it.'

'You know where we are, Dixon, what's going on. For God's sake. The Partisans disapprove of such relations, even within their own ranks. What can I possibly do?'

'I thought you might be able to wangle something, sir. Being as you and the commander are so close and all. I don't know what.'

Tom sighs. 'I'm not going to give you any bull's wool, Sid. Look, I'll mention it to the major. But in the meantime, be patient. And be discreet.'

As he lies on the ground, Tom hears the sounds of snores from his companions; occasional scurrying in the undergrowth beyond. He is wide awake. He remembers the story of the Sacred Band of Thebes: the army of lovers, made up of a hundred and fifty couples. The fighters, bound to each other by love and honour, 'although a mere handful, could overcome the world'. Was something similar forming in their own small unit? Perhaps it was the natural tendency of military life, among men or women.

Birds begin to screech and shriek in the darkness, their agitation further impediment to sleep. But towards midnight they calm down, and the forest is silent.

July 29

A new courier has come up into the mountains and found them. He has clearly run uphill. He wishes to speak, but Francika takes the tall, thin youth to one side, gives him water, makes him sit, until the pulse on his forehead ceases beating, and the sweat ceases pouring from him, and his gasping breath subsides. She nods to Jovan, who comes over. Tom follows.

'Heavy reinforcements in Celje,' the youth intones. 'Garrisons along the main line, in Lipoglav and Pragersko, are double or triple in size. On the single-track line, in Mislinje, too.'

'Are they coming down from the north?' Jovan asks.

'Heavy reinforcements in Celje,' the boy repeats. 'Garrisons along the main line.' Jovan stops him. They leave him to eat, and walk away.

'It's not good, of course,' Jovan says. 'But I'm surprised it hasn't happened earlier. They've had enough of us. They know we're here, floating from one place to another. Imagine how angry they must be.'

'Now what?' Tom asks.

'Now they will try to encircle us, close in on all sides and liquidate whatever they catch in the net. Every one of our fighters, but especially this group. You British and your radio.' He lays a hand on Tom's shoulder, and smiles. 'Do not look so alarmed, my friend. We will move and hide; hide and move. They don't like to stay in the mountains for long. A day or two away from their garrisons and the hearth calls them home.'

They consult maps. The youth comes over. He has something else to tell: mobile anti-guerrilla units. The *Crna roka* are coming from Kranj.

Dixon radios base to cancel their regular skeds, and to call off all drops until further notice. He passes on good news from elsewhere: in Normandy, the Germans are pulling back towards the Seine; in Italy, Pisa has been taken; Soviet troops have reached the Polish frontier. The news is greeted with a more sombre pleasure than usual. Even Pero simply nods, manages a weak smile.

CHAPTER FIVE

Off the Mountain

July 30

Tom does not sleep well. The weather is fine and warm. It does not rain. They cannot move for they do not know from where the enemy will come. They wait where they happen to be, somewhere in the middle of the Pohorje. As the afternoon drags on they begin to convince themselves the whole thing was a false alarm. The Germans have not been known to venture this high into the mountains. Over in the Karavanken Alps, yes, dreaded SS Mountain Divisions have been deployed, but that is on the border with Austrian Carinthia. Surely the SS are not here. Perhaps the movement of troops the youth reported has been misunderstood, actually it is the beginning of a mass Axis retreat from the Balkans. But in the late afternoon a new boy courier comes running. A tank has rumbled north up the rough road to Mount Rogla at the head of a body of men; a line of vehicles has come south to meet it, and cut the mountain range in two. A unit of the Home Guard has entered the village of Oplotnica, but the *odred* there slipped out through back gardens and up into the woods.

They load up and set out, away from the sound of dull petulant cracks behind them. Small-arms fire. The hunters are on the move.

July 31

The night is overcast and very dark. They stumble through the woods. Several times someone falls down; almost always Marko, identifiable by his loud curses. It is a small amusement. At first light the courier leads them to a hillside, where a hole, a *baza*, has been dug in which Partisans can hide.

They sit in the cover of a copse of growing sycamores, their leaves yellow-green and fluttering a little in the air. They can see in the night sky smoke rising from where they have come, to the west; the village of Lukanja burning, the courier tells them before he leaves. Also, infantry have been put in the woods to the east. They sit beneath the sycamores and listen: desultory silence, interspersed from far away in this direction, or that, by a brief flurry of rifle shots, as the enemy beat the woods around them.

The hole is fifty yards away, its entrance concealed by an overhang and a mask of undergrowth, in the grey-mud bank of a brook that trickles in a small canyon down off the mountain. By the time they have all crawled in to have a look, and out, headfirst, their legs kicking out behind them in the grey muddy gulley, the camouflage is tattered.

They scramble into the hole at dawn. Stipe can barely squeeze his shoulders through the entry. The *baza* has two chambers, with a passage so arranged that a grenade flung through the entry will have no effect on anyone lying in the large inner chamber. Except,

Tom reckons, to bring down earth that will lead to suffocation. Stout timbers support the roof, three feet from the floor. They lie, all ten of them, squeezed up and folded over themselves like fairy-tale babies in a giantesses womb. The air in the chamber thickens as they sleep. They wake, shift position, sink back into unconsciousness. How good it would be, it occurs to Tom, to be able to hibernate; to doze right through the coming autumn and winter, and emerge from the ground in the spring of 1945, when the war will surely be long over.

August 1

At dusk Jovan asks Pero to find out what is happening outside. He crawls out of the hole, and first refills their bottles with water from the brook. He whispers something through the entry before he leaves. His voice seems to come from far away, from another world. When he takes his head away a shaft of light pokes into their darkness. Then Pero stuffs fresh-cut branches across the entry to disguise it, and the light is green like sunlight seen through water.

Francika breaks pieces of bread and hands them round, with slices of pork fat.

They piss in a biscuit tin; all except for Francika, who is too shy.

They lie on their backs, knees doubled up, the warm air inside the hole making them drowsy. Someone farts. Marija curses Marko. 'You are a pig,' she tells him. 'A goat. A dog. Have you no idea of civilised human behaviour?'

'It was not me,' Marko complains. 'Check your facts before you make accusations, woman.'

'You're lucky it is dark,' she tells him. 'If I could see you I would slap your ugly peasant mug.'

'I would like to see you try it,' Marko says.

In the silence they hear someone giggling.

'There is your culprit!' Marko says. 'Too much of a coward to admit it.'

But then the malefactor, or another, breaks wind again, and they all groan and curse him.

The close dank smell of earth, damp clothes, stale breathing. It is best, Tom finds, to drift off to sleep.

He is woken by sounds outside, scrabbling and scrambling on the bank, then the shield of green undergrowth is pulled aside. *Damn and blast it*, he thinks. *It's come. Why here? Now?*

Sunlight floods through to the inner chamber. Pero's voice. 'It is me,' breathless. He crawls in to join them. The sunlight makes the air feel easier to breathe.

'I went east,' he says. 'It was quiet. The woods were silent. Animals were still. Nothing moved. Birds were hiding. I came over a ridge and you know what? Someone shot at me!' Pero seems both impressed and affronted. 'In the silence there was a sound. I thought, "Oh, that is a rifle shot. Oh, and that is a bullet whistling through the branches beside me." Then I turned and ran. Mary mother of God I ran like a lynx.'

'Like a wild boar squealing,' says Marko.

'You ran straight back here,' Jovan says, matter-of-factly, more sadness than anger in his voice.

'Of course not,' Pero says. 'I ran right around the hill, they will think I went north. Then I cut back here. I couldn't find this bank for a long time.'

They sit in the hole for the rest of the day. It is hot and the air is bad. The screen of branches has been relaid. They doze, and fidget, and grow resigned to their fate in the green submarine murk. Of course: what else could this be? They have crawled into their own tomb.

As if reading Tom's mind, Nikola says, 'We are going to die here, aren't we?'

Jovan does not disagree with him. Instead he tells them of when the Germans attacked Serbia in 1915. 'Belgrade was surrounded,' he says. 'One battalion of the Tenth Serbian Regiment received orders to fight to the last man, in order to slow the German advance. Before the final onslaught, the commander of the battalion spoke to his men below the Kalemegdan fortress. "My soldiers," he said, "my heroes. Our Supreme Commander has struck the name of our battalion from his list. We are to be sacrificed for the honour of our country. Do not worry about your lives, they no longer exist. Come, let us advance to death and to glory."'

'What happened?' Tom asks.

'They marched forward,' Jovan replies, 'and were slaughtered to the last man.'

'You can tell how moved he is, Tom,' Marija says. 'Oh, how the Serbs love to be defeated. If you went to his village you would find the old women all in black. Do you know why? To remind the young people of the sorrow, the great sorrow, after defeat to the Turks in the battle of Kosovo, in the Field of Blackbirds. When? In nineteen fifteen? When these women were young? No. When their mothers were young? No. Over five hundred years ago.'

Jovan smiles. He does not conceal his pleasure at being teased by Marija.

'Their finest defeat,' she says. 'Each generation since has tried to match it. Perhaps this time they will.'

Towards dusk they squeeze out, one after another. It is as if the earth herself gives birth to them. They feel immediately relieved, triumphant even: it is no bad thing, after all, to die in the open air.

There is enough light left to see the mess the ten of them are making of the bank. They pray that Jovan will not ask them to go back in the hole. They slither down to the brook, splash along the bottom of the canyon, climb out into the sycamores.

The young courier who brought them here reappears. He is clenched tight with fear, almost unable to speak. His courage emboldens them as much as his fear confirms the danger. Enemy patrols, the boy mumbles; advancing up the hillside from Zrecˇe, are beating the woods for *bazas*, and have already found three.

'They will be keen to find more,' Jovan says. 'Only a platoon of blind men could fail to find ours.' He orders the boy to lead them to a courier crossing point, to the west. Sid and Nikola crawl back inside the hole for the radio and battery, and the light machine gun.

August 2

They walk more slowly than they ever have before, each one of them listening intently, with eyes peeled for movement in the darkness. Did Pero tell Tom earlier that it was silent in the woods? It is never silent! There are sounds all around him, all the time: a broken twig hits the ground; a branch, growing under tension, suddenly snaps; two close-grown tree trunks groan against each other; a small creature scampers across pine cones; an owl hoots.

Each one of these sounds is, for a terrible second in their tight-strung attention, evidence of the enemy closing in around them. Jovan doubts that they will all settle down in an encampment tonight: some German troops, or the Black Hand, will surely be night hunting. It would be absurd were they not to.

They come at dawn to a hamlet whose name, if it has one, Tom does not hear. Two other groups of Partisans are already gathered here, and Tom's comrades fall upon them with unreserved conviviality. Perhaps they will not be cut down on this mountain in a hail of crossfire but, together, will fight their way out.

The whitewashed walls of ruined houses gleam in the darkness. One of the other groups has a pony; it grazes, cropping the weeds that grow everywhere. It is a grey cob. Tom pats it; he inhales the lovely sour tang of its sweaty hide. Sid comes over too, and blows softly into its nostrils. The animal becomes still.

'You seem to know what it likes,' Tom tells him.

'I love horses,' Sid says. 'I envy my old man, tell the truth. I mean, they say tractors is better than horses, but what I say is, it may be better for the farmer. Don't mean it's better for the farmworker.'

He scratches the cob behind the ears. It bends reluctantly from this human touch to graze again on the weeds.

There are between forty and fifty Partisans now. Jovan confers with the leaders of the other groups. He assumes overall command. They sleep where they can. Guards are posted.

August 3

Tom is woken by the slamming of a door. And then again, sending an ominous bolt through his nerves. And again. Artillery, not far away.

Francika has found wild strawberries. At first light, the big men with their rough peasants' hands pick the dainty berries and put them in their mouths.

'What do you think?' Tom asks Jovan.

'I believe this will be our last day,' Jovan says. He glances at Tom and smiles. 'No, no, my friend. Don't look at me like that. Our last day on this mountain, I mean. We have to break out tonight.'

'I thought…' says Tom. 'It was as if you knew…'

'No, no,' Jovan tells him. 'No man knows. And it is good to be afraid.'

Jovan steps forward and embraces him. Tom can feel himself trembling in Jovan's hold.

'The man without fear is not a man,' Jovan whispers in Tom's ear. Tom feels himself flooded with sudden emotion.

'Thank you,' Tom whispers, hugging his friend. They hold each other tight. 'Thank you.' They relax their embrace.

The others eat the strawberries as they pick them, for who knows when they may have to move, but Jovan patiently collects them in a piece of tree bark. Tom copies him, and when they have enough they lie on the grass.

Marija joins them. Jovan offers her his plate of berries. She shakes her head. 'I am as greedy and as nervous as all the others,' she admits. 'I have eaten my fill.'

A courier comes with news: an enemy detachment is three miles to the south. They await its arrival on full alert. There is no sign. An hour later a second courier: a German battalion, or a brigade, or maybe a platoon, of crack alpine troops has been spotted. Unless it's a bunch of old policemen. Or raw Slovene Home Guard boys. They're closing in from the north. Partisans are being picked off.

Nikola tells those around him that his father has given him some useful advice: if they are shot at, and there is a haystack nearby, they should hide behind it, for bullets do not penetrate hay.

'This is true,' Stipe avers. 'Or wool, either.'

'Hide behind a sheep,' Marko suggests. 'If you can catch one.'

All day long small-arms fire rattles round the edge of the woods. Jovan wants to wait till nightfall, but they all know they may have to take off at any moment.

Franjo walks off into the long grass to relieve himself, and Nikola frets that they might leave without his father. He keeps looking over in the direction he disappeared in, until after a while the old man returns.

A courier comes running into the ruined hamlet from the west, the direction in which Jovan wants to go. A column of German troops is heading directly towards them. No sooner has this news been absorbed than the woods are battered by artillery. Shells crash into the trees around them, ripping up branches, pulverising wood. They flinch and cower. Tom crawls towards a stout tree and curls up at its base, making his body as small as possible. But the wood is no more sturdy than balsa. The sound of living wood wrenching, splintering, falling. The air is filled with the smell of sawdust. And his body is enormous, an unmissable target, a blob of vulnerable flesh. Fear feels like something that grows suddenly inside his gut, something alien making him sweat and shiver as the shells fall into the wood. Tom cannot identify the source of the incoming fire, it could be artillery, mortar, even aircraft, he has not the faintest idea, his brain will not begin to function. Nor its direction. Only its target: himself. It must be a howitzer, those most accurate and deadly guns. Bangs, thuds, as shells land on the hillside around them, the sound of men screaming, groaning. He hears someone near him squeal like a rabbit, then stop.

Tom cannot tell if he is weeping or not. He can hear a sound close by, some kind of rapid percussion, then realises it is his own teeth chattering. He is looking at himself from outside. Are these trembling hands his own?

Jovan is beside him now, telling him something. Tom cannot hear him. He has to repeat it. 'Firing blind,' he says. 'They don't know where we are.'

Through his clenched-jaw grimace Tom forces himself to stutter, 'What is it?'

'Artillery,' Jovan says. 'Seventy-fives.'

No sooner has Tom comprehended this than it becomes clear to him that the German guns have changed direction and are now trained elsewhere: the explosions are some distance away. He comes slowly to himself.

Who are we? he wonders. What are we? That I can swing so wildly between bravado and cowardice? What did my response to danger depend on? Whatever my mood happened to be at that moment? What I had eaten, how I had slept? If the compass swings so wildly, what is the foundation of this reality? Perhaps there is none, and we are no more than brief displays of animal behaviour; we bloom into existence, then splutter and die, for no reason at all.

At a signal, presumably, though Tom does not see or hear it, others around him start to scuttle away, in a similar general direction, crouched as low as they can. In the same moment he realises that there are dead bodies left behind, and wounded: one man who cannot move is given a pistol; another has been shot in the arm and been patched up, and he runs with the others.

They jog through the trees, their rucksacks bumping against their backs. The sound of shells exploding in the woods recedes behind them. Tom hears the sound now of his and others' footsteps, of equipment bashing and chinking against bodies, of panting breaths. It strikes him that they could be running smack into a well-planned ambush. If so, so be it. He will run until he stops.

They gather in a copse of linden trees. The Slovenes take this as a bad omen, that here they may perish, beneath their country's symbolic tree, and when a plane circles overhead they are certain; but though they are terrified they do not mind, it seems to please them, Tom observes, that fate should be so thoughtful. There are forty of them now. The plane drops a few bombs into the trees, far enough away to induce laughter. Marko brandishes his Sten gun. 'I won't even bother to bring this one down,' he says. 'We are better off letting the pilot waste his ammunition.'

The plane flies away. There is silence. And then they hear a single, emphatic rap. For a second, their brains scramble to decipher the sound: it could be animal utterance; or is it a treefall? In that second Marko, standing a few feet from Tom, crumples to the ground.

The single rifle shot of a sniper.

Partisans begin firing into the wood. Stipe kneels and gathers Marko in his arms, puts his comrade's body over his shoulder, and rises. Tom picks up the light machine gun. Is he too busy to be afraid? He looks over his shoulder for a split second and sees with incredible clarity figures in the trees: wild men with hair falling on their shoulders like women and flowing black beards. Those who've sworn not to shave or cut their hair until King Peter is back in Belgrade.

He turns and follows others, once more running, bent over if they can. Snipers are setting their sights on their backs. They sprint and weave, and then they slow but they do not stop, they must keep moving, jogging, trotting along, for if they stop they will be shot. Keep going, keep going, keep going. Tom's consciousness slips its moorings and quite suddenly he is not here but in his childhood: cross-country running. His school had its own, archaic traditions, like all such places, some perpetuated not by the masters but by the boys themselves. One was to have a sixth-former run behind a pack of younger pupils, armed with a stick: he would hit the legs of the boy at the back, who would overtake the next, who would then be whacked, and so on. Tom was only ever struck once. A reasonable athlete, there were enough clumsy, uncoordinated boys behind him. But the memory of that single instance, when he was coming down with flu and should have been tucked up in the matron's wing, not out on the farm tracks they ran along, still stung the back of his calves for its cruelty. Passed on from boy to boy.

Yet the memory takes him now from this ordeal, running for his life, so that he glides, in a trance, out of his body.

After a long while they slow down, and stop to catch their breath. Tom rests the butt of the LMG on the ground. Stipe stands breathing like a bull, snorting, the bellows of his great barrel chest heaving, his shoulders rising and falling. He still carries Marko's body across his shoulders.

'Lay him down,' Jovan tells him.

Stipe shakes his head. He cannot speak for heaving breaths.

Jovan looks him in the eye and says, 'You're carrying a dead man. Lay him down, Stipe.'

They cover Marko with mulch and leaves, and press on.

In the afternoon they rest. Francika goes to the other groups. She collects all the food they have. Potatoes, some sugar, a little sheep's cheese, dry and hard and sour. One man has a shank of mutton but they do not dare roast it. Francika allocates a tiny portion to each Partisan, dividing them up on an outspread oilskin. Some watch her with a desultory, keen-eyed vigilance. When she is ready, each man and woman takes an equal share. Tom holds separate morsels on his tongue before he swallows them. He mingles the raw potato with granules of sugar, and with the sour cheese, savouring the taste. He doubts whether he has ever enjoyed such a delicious meal.

Looking around, at the members of the other groups and their leaders, he understands that it is not only himself who looks to Jovan to extricate them safely from peril, and words come to him from the Last Supper. 'I will strike the shepherd, and the sheep of the flock will be scattered.' They depend on him, they believe in him.

There are two ponies. They are unsaddled and led off into the woods to wander. The Partisans cannot take these animals with them any further for fear that a neigh or a stumble will give them away.

Sid Dixon comes to Tom. 'Sir,' he says, 'I don't know where the wireless is.'

'You must do,' Tom says.

'We've still got the battery, but not the bloody wireless. It's been lost, sir.'

Tom shakes his head. The wireless could have been exploded, or shot, or dropped off a cliff edge. But lost? He goes immediately over to Jovan, and tells him. Jovan's face colours so rapidly that for that instant Tom wonders if he is about to strike him. 'It is impossible,' Jovan spits. Then he looks at the ground, shakes his head. He sighs, and looks back at Tom.

'We cannot go back. There's nothing to be done. We shall continue on our way without it.'

It is early evening. The woods around them have been quiet for an hour. In another hour they will make their move.

'We dodge about,' Marija tells Tom. 'We are Slovenes. We are not running away. Not at all. We slip through encirclements.' She laughs her throaty laugh. Marija's bravado, and that of her comrades, is amusing. But it is more than that: thrilling, too. A form of resistance in itself.

'Let the Serbs retreat. We Slovenes infiltrate enemy lines,' she tells him, and those around them laugh too.

*

There are two couriers and, having scouted ahead, each comes back as the light is fading. One has a message for Jovan from headquarters: they are to come off the mountain range and make their way to a rendezvous point down on the plain. He tells the others in his group. Marko's death, and their own predicament, have brought them to a sombre state, but this order lightens their mood.

They wait, as the twilight thickens, for Jovan's order, but he will not be hurried. Partisans betray their nervousness and impatience, walking away from their companions to empty their bladders. Vehicles below them open up with odd shells that land behind them, where the trees grow thick. The crack of a detonation; three or four seconds later, a shell lands with a crash.

At last Jovan is ready. Quietly, they form up a column and follow the two couriers. They move across a crest and see over the tops of the trees below them the branch railway line down in the valley. Magnesium-white parachute flares are sent up into the night sky, where they hover for some trembling seconds, then die away in silence. It seems odd, to Tom, that they make no sound. As if Guy Fawkes Night were rendered mute. He can see yellow points of light along the line, enemy garrisons presumably. Night patrols will be out by now. The Partisans slip down off the crest, in amongst the trees again.

They know they must not be discovered as they descend for then the Germans encamped behind them will close in. Now and then the trees thin and Tom sees a flare shoot up, hang in the air, and vanish. He keeps close behind Jovan, himself tracking the couriers. Marija keeps close behind Tom. They march in the darkness, perhaps towards their deaths. Tom is tired, hungry.

He has been in this country little more than two months, and though he knows that his companions' struggle only coincides in part with his own, still he figures that part is enough; he feels a fierce, exhausted happiness.

They reach the far edge of the trees. Have they broken through the cordon undetected? Or does the greater danger yet lie before them? They look out across fields of sweetcorn. How fortunate it wasn't wheat sown here, Tom thinks, for then they'd be running across stubble and open ground – the sweetcorn harvest must be later. The railway lies a few hundred yards away. Every minute or so the dark night becomes brilliant with magnesium light, bluish, blinding. They go through the shoulder-high maize in a dark and silent column. When a flare goes up they drop to their knees and wait, watching the flare hover like a candle held up by a trembling hand. Then it dies and they scramble to their feet and file onward. The maize is wet with dew now and swishes against them as they go. From a village to their right an Armoured Fighting Vehicle fires bursts into the dark woods above and behind them, tracer streaking like livid red scars across the overcast.

They cross the single-track railway line unseen and carry on out of the Pohorje, trudging westward. *What fools*, Tom thinks, *what bloody fools they are, to let us out of their jaws.* He begins to laugh and realises that others are laughing too, afore and aft of him as they walk along, the line of Partisans overflowing with relief and the sheer joy of outwitting their large and brutal enemy. Tom grabs Jovan's sleeve to halt him, and wraps his arms around him. 'We did it,' he says. 'We did it.'

Jovan returns his embrace. But when they let go, he says, softly, 'For now.'

August 4

They nap in the last of the darkness then rise and walk on. They ferry the Savinja river north of Polzela, and cross the plain to the west. The maize is high and the field corn is ripe. Each of them breaks off a cob, unwraps the husk and the silky strands, and bites a mouthful of hard yellow kernels. They let their saliva soften it and though they know that it is fodder for the beasts of the field, unfit for human consumption, they chew the cud of each nutty mouthful as they walk, and are grateful.

Beyond the maize are great hop fields, phalanxes of rough brown poles and thick overhead wires, like the lines of telegraph poles but all confused together instead of strung out in a long line across the flat landscape. The thinner wires are festooned with green garlands of hops, mere weeks from picking and used to embitter the taste of beer drunk from here to deep inside the Third Reich. As they pass through the verdant avenues, the Partisans breathe the herby spicy air into their lungs. Tom breaks off some hops and rubs them in his hand, breaking open the flower, and the smell is fresh and tangy as sap from a pine tree.

They head north, back to the looping trajectory of the river, and climb into the woods to follow it, west, cresting the shoulders of hills above the Upper Savinja valley.

CHAPTER SIX

In the Valley

August 5

A two-man bodyguard escorts them into the present encampment of the Fourth Zone Headquarters. At first it is like approaching one of their own bivouacs – parachute canopies, food stewing, the muted sounds of human movement and activity. Except that the encampment continues, dreamlike, unrolling into the forest, and they walk on past many fires, military tents, horses, hundreds and hundreds of men camped out amongst the trees, dozing, smoking, cleaning weapons. It is unreal, only his stomach rumbling with each variation of aroma of food cooking feels real to Tom; but the effect of fatigue is to disconnect him from his body, and even the grumbling gut inside him could be elsewhere; belong to someone else. They walk on, into the heart of the Partisan army in the Fourth Zone. And just as they had, a month earlier, splintered off as a tiny *odred* from the main body of soldiers marching down from Mount Rogla, so now the Slovenes are reabsorbed into their army.

Tom feels his hand taken, and squeezed. He stops and turns. Marija gazes intently at him. She scans his face, his features, his eyes, as if to commit the precious sight to her memory. He nods, unsure what to say. For an awful moment he sees her blue eyes fill with tears and realises she is going to cry. But then Marija smiles, squeezes his hand, and lets go of it. She turns and joins Stipe and the others, who follow a soldier away between tents. Jovan, Tom sees, watches her go, with an infinitesimal shake of his head.

*

They walk on, until the soldier accompanying them stops and says something to Jovan, who says to Tom and Sid, 'The Allies' tents are over there. I must go this way. I shall see you later, my friends.'

It strikes Tom that perhaps this is the very opposite of the truth: they will never see each other again, each lost from the other in this army in the forest. He feels the blood drain from his face. Suddenly it seems that standing upright is not something to be taken for granted any longer, for the trees are swaying; perhaps there is a breeze but no, it is an earthquake; delirious how the ground buckles, it is shifting in waves…

'Sir!' Dixon catches him by the right arm and shoulder.

Jovan takes his other side and holds him up. Their escort brandishes a water bottle and proffers it to Tom's lips. He drinks. Held in his comrades' powerful grip, he feels the world steady on its axis. In time, its clever equilibrium returns.

'We need food,' Jovan says. 'We shall all eat soon.'

'Jack.'

Farwell is at the far end of the tent, with his back to the entrance. Flanked by two other men, all three bent over, studying whatever lies on a large table there. Farwell turns as Tom steps forward.

'Good God, man!'

Tom prepares to embrace his colleague, but is forestalled: Farwell puts his hand out towards him. Tom takes it and shakes it vigorously, grinning, unsure why he is so glad to see his senior officer, who looks just as he had when they parted a month ago: the major's pale, pasty face appears to have seen little of this hot southern summer.

'Good God!' Farwell repeats. 'What the hell have they done with you?' He scans Tom up and down, frowning.

It occurs to Tom that he has not seen his reflection for days, maybe weeks; had lost any interest in what he looks like. Now Farwell is a kind of mirror.

'Looks like your Jugs have dragged you through every thorn-bush in Slovenia,' he says, whether with approval, or disappointment, is hard to say. 'Good to have you back, Freedman. Go and get yourself cleaned up, rest if you need to. I'll have some food sent over. We'll debrief later. I'll show you what's being planned down here. Should be quite a show.'

August 7

When Tom begins to wake from a long sleep it is the smell of the canvas, warming in what mid-morning sun filters through the trees, that enters his consciousness first. Slowly it dawns on Tom that having eaten his fill, and put his head down for a nap on a brand-new camp-bed, he must have slept for some eighteen hours, in a deep dreamless oblivion.

Tom finds Jack Farwell exactly where he left him, back in the tent, neatly dressed, poring over maps. He nods at Tom, and sweeps his hand over the table.

'We've all been running like rabbits over these mountains, trying to keep ahead of the wolves, broken up into small battalions and tiny groups, like yours. Now it seems our hosts have had enough. They're gathering everyone here, we've dropped planeloads of supplies, and they're planning to take the whole of this valley. These Jugs may not look like soldiers, Freedman,' he says, 'they're a bunch of ruffians, the lot of them. They'd kill us to see if we'd gold fillings in our teeth. But by God, they're up for a scrap.'

Jack takes a pencil and points to an area on the map.

'We're here,' he says. 'The Savinja flows down from the Karavanken Alps. For ten miles it's carved itself a narrow valley, with high mountains on either side. There are German garrisons in two small towns, Luce, here, and Ljubno, here. Below Ljubno the valley opens out. They want to take these garrisons and plug the valley at either end. The idea is to set up an airfield on a nice flat field. Then we can really get supplies in here.'

'When's it go up?' Tom asks.

'Tomorrow night. I've got us seats in the circle above Ljubno. I think you'll find it's a nice spot.'

The two of them sit in folding canvas chairs. Jack tells Tom that Rennes has been taken. 'And there's an uprising in Warsaw: the Reds have reached the Vistula, they'll be kicking the Krauts out any day now.'

He then listens with impatience to Tom's debrief.

'There are ten units spread across the mountain range. We supplied seven of them before we were brought out. It would have been eight, but the planes never came.'

'How many bridges were blown?' Jack demands. 'How many days was the line out of action?'

Tom shakes his head. 'It's impossible to say. As time went on we had to leave once the planes had made their drops.'

'So you didn't even see the action? They may not even have used the explosive? Damn it, man, what's the point of intelligence if you haven't got any?'

Does Jack, who has been in the same country all this time, not realise how dangerous it was to stay in one place?

'We had no choice. The enemy were behind us all the way. Jovan had to keep us moving.'

'Ah.' Jack nods. 'I did wonder where he'd got to. They never told me he'd gone with you. Should have known.'

When Tom tells him they have lost their radio, Jack is furious. 'What the hell was Dixon doing?'

'It was hardly his fault, Jack, we were ambushed. People grabbed what they could.'

'Of course it wasn't his fault. No soldier ever lost a battle through any fault of his own. It's always someone else who's let him down.'

'We need to use your radio. I've got to tell base there were Chetniks on the mountain.'

'Chetniks? This far from Serbia? Hardly likely.'

'There's no doubt about it, and they were firing at us. They were with the enemy. Base have to stop giving them support, Jack, there's nothing annoys the Partisans more.'

'We don't get involved in politics.'

'We are involved in politics. We're here, are we not?'

'We obey orders. I've heard a lot of rumours myself, about all sorts of Balkan riff-raff fetching up in these mountains. Without material proof we say nothing.'

'I know what they look like, Jack. I saw them with my own eyes.'

Farwell shakes his head. 'Without evidence it's not intelligence, don't you realise? It's no more than a fancy. A trick of the light. Leave it, Freedman. That's a bloody order.'

August 8

During the night, assault units are moved into position. There is no artillery that Jack knows of, only men and women with their rifles, hundreds of them, making their way down through the dark woods. Tom scans the tops of the trees and knows that the woods seethe with movement, encircling the silent village of Ljubno, whose occupants sleep. A few sentries doze on their rifles. One reality snoozes in ignorance of another, a slow premeditated surge towards violence that is about to engulf it.

The attack begins with children: *bombashi*, hand-grenade men, except that they are boys or girls of twelve or thirteen. Around the outside of the town are a dozen bunkers, with walls of earth or brick. One or two have been built with reinforced concrete, like pillboxes. Tom knows what is coming, but when it comes he isn't sure he really sees it. In the first light of morning – there is not yet colour in the valley, mist has risen from the river and lies in shifting ribbons on the fields – the *bombashi* slip out like tree spirits from the cover of the woods and run crouching forward across the open ground. Two converge upon each bunker. There is a hiccuping rattle of light-machine-gun fire and one of the children stops running abruptly and lies down. His or her colleague reaches the bunker as do all the others. They throw their grenades over the top of the wall or through the gun-slits. The detonations are muffled, as if occurring deeper underground.

With the bunkers eliminated, the surviving *bombashi* withdraw, back to the shelter of the woods, while adult Partisans run past them, lugging light machine guns: they occupy the bunkers, beside the dead enemy, or if they are all caved in set up behind them, and put covering fire into the village. The pillboxes are transformed from defensive positions to offensive redoubts. A second wave of Partisans enters Ljubno from all directions.

The defenders of the village are now awake, and firing back. There is no artillery on either side and the only sounds carrying up the hill are the rattle of Stens and Brens, of Mausers and Berettas, and the crack of single rifle shots. The Partisans advance from house to house. It is like watching a gunfight in a silent western, but with the camera too far away. And field glasses render them somehow more, rather than less, distant: the figures two, three hundred yards away are not quite real, but actors playing the part of soldiers. They play it poorly when they fall, crumpling upon the impact of the bullet that hits them, dying without noise, discreetly, making no drama of their demise.

Tom lowers the binoculars. This was how generals saw battle, from a grassy knoll, at one remove. It would be much easier than he would ever have considered it to be to see your men fall and order reinforcements into the fray when they were not flesh and blood but models of men on an unreal diorama.

He becomes aware of an odd sound close by, on the ground, in the grass: it is like a disappointed teacher tut-tutting his pupils. Strange insects? Tom looks instinctively towards the village and sees two men in the steeple of the church, with rifles pointing towards him.

'Jack! Christ!' Tom exclaims. 'They're firing at us.' Ducking, swerving, he runs back into the trees behind him. He is pretty rattled. When he turns and peers from around the shelter of a beech trunk he sees Farwell still gazing at the scene below through his field glasses.

'Jack!' Tom yells. 'Come here, you bloody idiot.' He can hear the bullets still hissing in the grass that must be about as far as they can reach, perhaps they are old sporting rifles with a limited range. But Jack can't know that. He stands there unconcerned, surveying the scene. Tom feels like a fool, cowering behind the tree trunk. But Farwell is the fool, with his cynicism and bravado, and his being an idiot does not make Tom yellow. He calls out again and this time Jack does respond, turning reluctantly and walking slowly to join him.

'Why do they want to waste their ammo on me?' he asks. 'A scurvy trick to play. I'm not the one about to lead them into the abattoir. Those Jugs down there are. And the first thing they'll do,' he muses, 'will be to take the boots off the men they've killed, before they've even croaked.'

Tom swallows his rage, and turns back to peer at the village through his glasses. The snipers in the church steeple are shooting at men on the ground, though the flank of the hill they stand on partially blocks his view now that he and Jack have moved back, and he cannot see their targets. Scanning away from the village he can make out from where he stands a scrum of Partisans at the edge of the trees, poised to join the attack. With a shock he recognises amongst them Franjo and Nikola, father and son, side by side. And is that Pero, behind another man? All of a sudden he identifies others, not down there, now, but in retrospect: realises he'd seen Marija and Stipe – carrying the LMG – silhouettes running towards one of the bunkers. This recognition was there but he had not acknowledged it at the time: yet it lay buried, waiting, and now, an hour later, he's unearthed it.

'I'm going down, sir,' he says, and does not wait for a reply. 'Get a closer look,' he throws over his shoulder, and breaks into a run.

*

It seems as though he reaches them in a moment, had thought to join them and is there, in some H. G. Wells time machine, an impression exacerbated by the fact that he is neither out of breath nor sweating in his uniform on this warm August morning. They greet him warmly, telling their comrades, 'This is the Englishman. The one we told you about. This is he.'

Then Francika is there but she does not embrace him. 'I am the commander of this unit,' she says. 'You cannot come with us.'

'I must,' he says. If they are to fall he wishes to fall with them, not to watch, beside Farwell, as they advance into battle. If death is to be meted out this day he will be proud to receive it, to perish beside these peasant revolutionaries, rather than skulk on a hill behind a pine tree.

'I cannot allow you,' Francika says, but then an order comes to her and she has no option but to yell out, 'Advance!' and Tom is running.

Pero beside him says, 'You have no gun,' and he takes his hand and they run together to a fallen Partisan. Tom lifts the man's rifle from the ground. Around his head is a black halo of blood. Pero wrestles free an ammunition belt and they run on. Guns go off behind, in front, all around him. To Tom there is no logic. Bullets trace an invisible chaotic latticework of death. As they reach the first house someone beside him falls. They crouch against the wall of the house. Two Partisans drag the wounded soldier to shelter. His body is floppy. He is not wounded. He has gone from vitality to extinction in an instant, this extreme and awful mystery. Then someone turns his body and Tom recognises the dead soldier. It is Nikola. He must have been hit in the torso for his face and head are unblemished, his youthful skin is cleanly shaven, his green eyes gaze at existence and see nothing. In the shelter of the wall they lay him down. His father Franjo stands above him; the third, the last, of his boys to be killed in this war.

'My son,' he says quietly, yet Tom can hear every word. 'My son, let the sun shine on you for the last time.' Franjo's unused voice is low and gritty. 'My son, I will not weep. That will be for the widows of those whom we are about to kill.' Franjo's eyes are clear. He lifts his rifle, turns and walks around the corner of the house. The others follow him.

Explosives are laid against the walls of the large house where most of the garrison are billeted, or, rather, now trapped. The wall is breached, grenades are thrown in, among them small, red, Italian oval hand grenades. Surrender comes quickly and enemy soldiers file out, covered with dust, some with streaks of red blood oozing from beneath the white dust, arms in the air.

Some have fled to other houses and continue to fight. These houses are taken one by one, with gunpowder and fire, by the afternoon. Only the church remains, with an unknown number of enemy inside. The riflemen in the steeple have withdrawn from view. Rather than attack the church the Partisan commander in charge of the operation demands a surrender from those within, posts guards around the two doors to make sure there is no chance of a break-out, and then seems to ignore the church.

Prisoners are brought into the town square, where they stand with both arms aloft, save for one with his left arm in a sling. Partisan soldiers wander about, glancing at the German and Slovene Home Guard soldiers who look blank and hopeless, stunned by how history, which only yesterday had seemed to assure them of a secure and prosperous future, has quite suddenly turned on them. The Partisans coalesce in small clusters, break up and move on around the square, smoking, automatic rifles slung over their shoulders or clasped in their hands as if to remind both themselves and their enemy with their empty hands in the air:

Look, we have our guns, you do not have yours. You have wielded absolute power in this valley. You are powerless now.

Villagers too leave their houses and come as far as the edge of the square, clutches of wary women in tight headscarves and aprons, some with small children. They look as if they can only linger for a moment; the battle interrupted their daily chores, to which they must return. Old men in their frayed suits and hats give the opposite impression: they have little or nothing to do all day long and will be quite happy to congregate here and watch this changing of the guard for as long as it takes. Perhaps, Tom considers, the Partisans are no less strange to them than the Germans; certainly there are many more Slovene *Wehrmänner* amongst those with their hands in the air than in German uniform. Some might come from this very village. The Partisans are adorned in their customary weather-beaten motley of British, Italian, German and Yugoslav uniforms.

All occupying armies, Tom supposes, must be a dangerous nuisance to such villagers; an unwanted interruption to the more important activities of cleaning the house and tending the vegetables. What ingratitude! What dumb and wilful ignorance. Yes, this is a civil war as well as resistance against foreign occupier, a civil war that is raging across Yugoslavia. The Partisans are fighting to build a better world for all – including these peasants, trapped in their smug self-absorption. The Partisans will liberate their country from the Germans but also from the feudal past.

The prisoners are being separated, escorted in one direction or another, in what appears to be a peremptory and arbitrary manner. The armed guards look as if they are acting under orders except that, so far as Tom can tell, no one is giving them. He follows a cluster of fifteen or twenty through the village. Outside a house they are told to remove their boots and German uniforms. A number of them are old, for soldiers: in their late thirties or even early forties. A tall, skinny, trembling man; two short, tubby men in stained underwear. Not a single specimen conforms to the Aryan ideal, yet here they were fighting for the Reich. They had been sent all over Europe to enact Hitler's expansionist dream of conquest. Are these to meet their end here, in a mountain village in Slovenia?

One of the Partisans asks a comrade whether they should take the helmets. 'No,' the other replies. 'They look funnier like this. They can keep them. They *must* keep them.'

It is mid-afternoon and quiet now. Tom can hear the tall, thin prisoner's teeth chattering from yards away. None of the Germans speak to each other. They avoid each other's eyes, as well as their captors', each locked into his own torment. Some have holes in their socks. These men have become passive in the face of their imminent extinction. If Tom had been told of it he would have wondered why they did not attempt, at least, to overwhelm their three or four armed guards. Better to die trying to escape, surely, than to be led like lambs to the slaughter. Yet such a pathetic gesture is unthinkable here, now, in this quiet village, under the bright sun. Their destiny has been shaped by powerful forces that have brought them to this moment, and all are obliged to submit to that power; including the Partisans, one of whom even has to heap mocking insult upon murder, having them die in their helmets. Including, indeed, himself: there is nothing Tom can do to intervene; he is a passive observer as they are passive victims.

Two Partisans are going through the pockets of the discarded uniforms. Tom looks at what they find. A faded letter, a diary, a bottle of hair oil, some rubber protectives, a postcard of a dark-haired girl with a hand-written message scrawled across the corner; a photo of an old lady standing beside a farmhouse door. One of the Partisans finds a ripped grey canvas haversack, shovels these items into it, and hands it to the nearest German. Are they to be buried not with their weapons but these domestic mementoes, a mocking tribute, in a common grave?

The Partisan who'd decided the Germans should keep their helmets on says, 'Go!' He does not look at them but makes a dismissive sweeping gesture with his right hand. 'Go back to Celje. Enjoy the walk.'

The Germans look perplexed, almost upset, but then they become agitated. As if they'd been too cold in their underwear now suddenly the heat of the day is upon them, and they sweat as they come jerkily to life like marionettes, stopping and starting, until gradually reaching some kind of unspoken consensus and setting off on the white stone road out of the village. There is always one or another of them looking back over his shoulder – is this one last cruel trick? – but the Partisans watch them, chuckling, and all of a sudden Tom too finds the sight of them padding away in their grubby underwear risible and comic, the ones with their coal scuttle helmets the funniest of all, and he realises that is the point: for as many villagers as possible to see the fearsome Teuton soldiers traipsing home half-naked with holes in their socks.

Returning towards the square, Tom hears sounds beyond a house at the village edge, and is drawn towards them. The sounds are those of voices, two of them in conversation. One is harsh, the other wheedling, pleading, yet they talk over each other, with no apparent relation between the two. He steps around the corner, into an open field. Several men, some in German uniform, others in civilian clothes, are lined up facing a squad of Partisans. Upon orders from an officer, two Partisans raise their sub-machine guns and open fire. The line of men collapses like skittles hit by an invisible ball.

As Tom stands unmoving, petrified by what he's walked into, Partisan officers turn towards him. Their obvious embarrassment somehow clears his head. One of them advances a couple of steps towards him, and salutes.

'Lieutenant,' the man says. The other three also salute. All are dressed in new, clean, high-collared uniforms, 'in the Russian style,' according to Jack Farwell the day before.

'My friend,' the man continues, and only now does Tom recognise Jovan. Of course it is Jovan! How could he not have seen immediately? Tom finds himself walking back around the side of the house, steered towards the village square, as if Jovan had known that was where he'd been headed, only to be waylaid by this unpleasant diversion, and was being intuitively helpful.

'What happened?' Tom asks. 'Who were those men?'

'The mayor and his cronies,' Jovan says. 'The German commander and two of his men who have committed savage acts against the people.'

'But I thought you would bring law with you. What kind of trial could you possibly have carried out in so brief a time?' Tom demands. 'None. Merely summary justice.'

'Surely you have learned from our days together, Tom, that this is not a game.' Jovan takes a cigarette from a packet and passes it to Tom, then takes one for himself. The cigarette is triangular rather than round, and the packet has Cyrillic lettering. 'We have had intelligence from here for many months. We know from the people themselves who are the war criminals. To witness how swiftly we dispense justice will be a great reassurance to them.'

'And now the Germans' mayor is dead, you will install a new mayor?'

Jovan smiles. He lights their cigarettes with a lighter, the petrol smell of whose fluid Tom inhales; it is different from any he has smelled before. 'One of our own, Tom, yes, of course. Come. I have much to do. We shall have hundreds of Slovene *Wehrmänner* joining us. We have to give them a political education before trusting them with a weapon.'

'You have the job you came to Slovenia for,' Tom says. 'You are the political commissar.'

'I am,' says Jovan.

'I am so glad to see you,' Tom says. He wants to hug Jovan, but there are too many people around them.

'We shall see much of each other, I hope,' Jovan tells him, before being called away.

August 9

Using the wireless belonging to Farwell's operator, Morris, Sid Dixon taps out the code. 'Priority radios, PIAT ammo, rifles, Stens, Brens, mortars. As many planes as you can send. Future operations depend on holding this area as base. Please send planes every night till further notice. Soon have runway too.'

Six Partisans were killed in the assault on Ljubno yesterday. A collective funeral service is to be held for them. There are fresh flowers in vases on the window sills of the bare, whitewashed interior of the church. Up in the chancel vault are two paintings: of the Virgin Mary and child, and what looks like the portrait of a peasant, though it may, Tom suspects, be meant to represent a biblical figure. There are no signs of the church's occupation or siege: the enemy had apparently agreed to surrender in the afternoon, and after forfeiting their clothing followed their colleagues on the rough road back to Celje.

The cavernous nave fills up with Partisan soldiers. They stand in rows either side of the aisle, then cram into the side chapels, holding their caps. Tom and Dixon stand among them. Six rough-made deal coffins stand on trestles in a line at the opening of the chancel. The three-sided apse is filled with gilt-enamelled images and painted statues of Christ and his disciples, of the Virgin and another female saint whom Tom guesses is Elizabeth, mother of a man in ragged skins, John the Baptist.

The Catholic priest, standing beyond the coffins, reads the funeral Mass in Slovene. A boy to his left holds a small silver altar bell; a boy to the priest's right swings a censer whose aromatic smoky fumes reach Tom's nostrils as they waft gradually towards all corners of the church.

One of the coffins is smaller than the others: the *bombashi* Tom had seen fall, he assumes. He must have been little older than these servers with the bell and the censer. *Bombashi* are not chosen for their perilous role, they have to volunteer, and are treated with a special respect. From one of the other coffins blood has leaked through the planks, and drips with tiny red splashes on to the stone flags of the church floor. A man in a civilian suit comes forward and places a piece of brown paper on the spot, to blot it up.

The priest intones the Mass, reading from a black-bound prayer book. One of the acolytes rings his bell. The other boy swings the fumigator.

Blood from the coffin with the paper beneath it begins to drip from another plank. The men try not to watch it drip-drip onto the floor. Tom asks himself whether a dead body did not cease to bleed, but he doesn't know the answer, and is too timid to ask. Once or twice a soldier near the front turns round, seeking out or appealing to the old man to bring forward another piece of brown paper, but he does not do so.

People go up to receive the sacrament, including many Partisan soldiers. A month ago, Tom thinks, he would have, too.

When the service is over, bearers carry out the coffins, one after another. Pero and Stipe are among six men carrying one coffin on their shoulders, which has to be Nikola's, and Tom is pained to see that it is the one that is leaking blood. Franjo has been standing at the front of the congregation, obliged to watch. Now he follows his son's coffin out of the church and, in a short procession, to the village graveyard. Follows, too, a sporadic tiny trail of blood.

The bearers lay the coffins alongside graves freshly dug for them. Tom wonders where the enemy – executed or fallen in battle – are buried, for there is no sign of them here. Many villagers and peasants stand in the cemetery. Two of the bearers of the first coffin carried out jump down into the grave to help lift the coffin in. But then Jovan steps forward from a knot of officers whom Tom had not seen in the church and tells them that it is not yet time for this. Hiding their embarrassment by muttering complaint, they haul themselves out of the ground with the clumsy assistance of comrades.

Jovan turns to face the multitude and speaks out, in a loud, clear voice. 'These men and this boy,' he says, 'were killed yesterday in battle with the fascists. Their comrades know they were brave and steadfast soldiers.' His voice carries across the crowd, surely reaches the furthest listener, on this calm, sunny day; he might have had an actor's training in voice projection. He reads out the names of the fallen. 'We are sorry to lose them,' he says. 'They died as an example to the rest of us. Death to fascism! Freedom to the people!'

Six men in a line beside Jovan step forward and raise rifles Tom had not noticed before, resting on the ground beside them, and fire a volley into the deep blue summer sky.

The formalities are over. The crowd shifts, swells, disperses. The coffins are lowered. Soldiers assemble around particular graves, and throw soil in. Gravediggers use long-handled shovels to do the work. Leaving the cemetery, Tom looks back and sees Franjo standing still at the head of his son's grave, gazing at the mound of dark brown soil.

August 10

Youngsters from the villages have gathered kindling for the beacons and now they are burning, but silently, for the noise of the aircraft has become a steady drone that overrides other sound. The plane appears in the silvery sky, flashing the identification signal, and comes in to drop its load. Twelve big containers are released simultaneously from the bomb-racks, and Tom thinks how beautiful a sight it is to watch a dozen parachutes open all at once like a white flower bursting into bloom. And then the wind blows the petals apart.

While Partisan battalions occupy the liberated villages in the Savinja valley, the Fourth Zone Headquarters, wary of German air raids, remain in the hills above, in a hamlet that also houses the Soviet Mission. The British Mission has been given a large farmhouse a quarter of a mile away.

'The Germans will strike back at any moment,' Jovan says. 'Any day they will retake the valley. But in the meantime we hope you will be comfortable.'

Jovan leaves before they can ask him to whom the house had belonged. The two officers and their wireless operators inspect the premises. There are heavy wardrobes and chests of drawers made with dark wood; carpets and bedspreads in sombre colours. Lace curtains cover the small windows. The Englishmen feel like looters, plunderers of luxury. There are three bedrooms. Dixon and Morris will share.

'Which one do you want?' Tom asks.

'I don't give a damn,' Jack tells him. 'Wait. On second thoughts, you take the large bed. It would only make me miss my Cassie.'

They stow their luggage then troop downstairs, made uneasy by this stolid opulence. *Have we become ascetics in this short time?* Tom wonders. In the parlour, two glass-fronted cases hold books in German. Goethe. Heine. His spirits rise at the prospect of reading something other than coded signals.

In the kitchen they find a stout, matronly woman, with steely hair wound tight in a bun upon her head. Whether she is the mistress of the house or a servant is unclear: she says nothing, nor does she respond to their enquiries, in either Slovene or German.

'Could be she's a deaf mute, sir,' Sid offers. 'We had one in our village.'

The woman wears a white pinafore over black clothes that are surely signs of mourning.

The men unpack their few possessions, set up the wireless in the parlour. After an hour the woman sets four places on the table, with silver cutlery and a cut-glass decanter of white wine, and presently she serves them a delicious stew.

'Pour the wine, Dixon, there's a good chap,' Farwell says.

Sid reaches for the decanter only to find the woman has got to it first, and proceeds to fill each man's crystal glass.

'That what they call fast reflexes down in Devon, is it?' Morris asks.

'Does anyone else find something skittish about the old girl's outfit?' Farwell asks. 'Uncomfortably reminiscent of a waitress in a Lyons teashop. Raise your glasses,' he orders. 'We can be proud to be a part of this, boys. Supplies are pouring in, on top of the machine guns, rifles and ammo that were captured. The airfield should be ready for landings tomorrow. Why the Krauts haven't hit back I've no idea. Maybe they think there are more of us here than there are. But let's make hay. Our Jugs can really hit the railways and the roads. Plug the Germans up in Italy. Bring the war down here to a conclusion.'

The others murmur agreement, chink glasses together, and drink up the rough white wine.

August 11

Soldiers and peasants labour together getting the field ready: clearing away stones, levelling the ground, filling in holes. Jack Farwell oversees the enterprise with the Slovene commander. 'This is more like it,' he tells Tom Freedman. 'Our own aerodrome inside the Third Reich.'

Jovan is there too, in his impressive commissar's uniform. While they are eating lunch, he invites Tom to take a walk with him: there is something he wants to show his British friend.

They climb out of the valley, up forested slopes, in the shade of beech trees and tall pines. Beside the path moss grows, a thick and green carpet over great slabs of stone. After they have been walking for a little over an hour, climbing steadily, Jovan stops suddenly, and begins to search for something amongst small trees to their right beside the track. He pushes his way through bushes and Tom follows. Jovan covers their tracks with dead branches and then carefully turns a mossy stone over; he steps on to its exposed underside, and does the same to a further stone, and all at once Tom sees ahead of them a series of stepping-stones. He follows, crossing from one stone to the next, turning back each stone behind him so that its mossy surface is once more visible.

They advance in this way for almost fifty yards, until they are screened from the track, whereupon they find a new, narrow trail. This precautionary method of disguise is repeated a mile further on. Another mile and Jovan stops once more and searches in a nondescript clump of undergrowth. He finds two parallel tree trunks, long and thin, leading through the hidden greenery. They walk along these then step up onto an above-ground ladder – a series of tree trunks, suspended from the lower branches of trees. For over a hundred yards they cross this overhead bridge, before returning to terra firma.

Here they meet a single guard, rifle at his shoulder, who after greeting them sets to covering the trunks with moss and leaves.

Jovan leads Tom further, deeper into the forest, climbing higher in the heat of the afternoon. Sweat pours off Tom. They drink from a cold, clean-tasting stream, and hike on. 'Here we are,' Jovan whispers. He lifts an overhanging branch on the track to disclose a fallen log lying at right angles. They walk along the log and then down into a hollow between rocks, where a fresh track is visible. A little further on Tom makes out three half-buried log cabins, recently built, as evidenced by the smell of new-sawn lumber. They've been half dug into the ground, and are well hidden by the tall pines looming around and above them. The roofs are camouflaged by pine branches.

Tom is introduced to the doctor in charge, a young woman, Olga, who shows him round her wards. The wounded lie on straw pallets in wooden beds, beneath sheets. The smell of iodine, and much else, human odours: urine, sweat, a faint putrefaction. Fractures are extended on home-made frames. The doctor shows him a wounded youth whose right leg she'd had to amputate. 'I am not a surgeon,' she says apologetically. 'But there was no choice. I hope the stump will take an artificial limb.'

Tom notices Jovan unload from his backpack a parachute, and hand it to a nurse: bandages and ligatures here, even curtains at the windows, he realises, are made of silk cloth.

The doctor gives them a meal, beautifully tender venison, with a glass of *rakija*, fruit brandy. The small room she lives in could be in the middle of a great city: a rug on the floor, a shelf of books, a delicately stitched tablecloth. A picture of Mount Triglav on the walls, the highest mountain in Slovenia, Olga explains, the highest peak in the Julian Alps.

'For three weeks,' Jovan says, gesturing with his head in a general direction into the forest outside, 'German soldiers were camped less than two hundred metres away. Olga stayed here with her patients while the Germans searched every day for our hospital, with their Alsatian dogs. Our High Command presented her with the Medal for Bravery.'

Olga shakes her head, makes a face of modest dismissal, as if it were normal practice for medics to work in fear of armed attack, deep in hiding. Olga is slim, with dark rings around her brown eyes; she is certainly no older than Tom.

'When they find a hospital,' Jovan says, 'the Germans wipe out everyone. Doctors, nurses. The patients are shot in their bunks, and the hospital is burned.'

'Winter is bad, of course,' Olga says. 'The snow betrays those who cross it. It has become a Partisan skill to cover footprints with fresh snow.'

Tom asks Olga more about her work, and what her medical speciality was. She raises her dark eyebrows. 'I do not have one yet, I have not finished my medical studies,' she says. 'Now, I must learn by my mistakes.'

'Let us raise a toast to this doctor for every one of her amputations,' Jovan says, lifting his glass. 'Our soldiers use the discarded limbs to lay false trails in the forest for the German dogs. But now we will be able to take these wounded men out of the country, to fully equipped hospitals in Italy, as your commanders have promised us. This is why your planes must land.'

*

On the walk back down to the valley, in the relative, pleasant cool of the evening, Tom asks Jovan if it might be possible to allow Francika to leave, with Sid.

'If there's room in one of the planes,' Tom says. 'Not at first, when the injured must be got out, but later.'

Jovan makes no response.

'I mean,' Tom says, 'if there's room.'

'There is no problem,' Jovan says. 'No problem.'

August 12

They hear the planes. Away over the mountains to the south. They pile wood high on the fires so the pilots will be able to see their signals. The planes sound as if they are directly overhead but they sweep away unseen. On the ground hope drains from those staring avidly, blindly into the dark.

Then the Dakotas come around again, four of them in the clear mountain sky, and they sweep down, their lights turned on, like great fireflies in the night. Down, down, and in a rush they are bumping along the rough runway. Hundreds of Partisans sweep upon them like parasitic insects and in minutes the planes have been gutted, their precious innards spilled and piled in heaps on the grass.

As each plane is emptied so the wounded embark: survivors of the battle, and others who have been brought down from hidden hospitals by stretcher and ox-cart; when the planes are full they taxi around and take off again the way they had come in.

Tom keeps expecting the operation to be interrupted by a screaming Stuka, a firing Messerschmitt, but it does not happen. What are the enemy waiting for? This impunity is inexplicable.

Stumbling back to their isolated farmhouse, Tom and Jack can hear the whisper of distant artillery, and feel minute tremors in the ground beneath them.

'Where the hell's that coming from?' Jack mutters. Tom does not know.

Returning, exhausted, to his bed in the strange house, Tom sinks into the horsehair mattress. For a moment as he is falling asleep he is jarred back awake by the sensation that the ground upon which he lies has become suddenly, hazardously, soft: it is about to swallow him. Then he recalls where he is, no longer on the forest floor but in a soft farm bed; and lets himself fall.

Breakfast is served by their silent matron. Hard-boiled eggs and thin strips of cold meat, with a hot black drink that smells like an ill-remembered vegetable and tastes like something pretending, poorly, to be coffee.

Sid Dixon sets up the new radio that has been delivered in one of the night's planes. He sings as he busies himself, checking and fitting the valves and the batteries. *It won't be a stylish marriage. We can't afford a carriage*. Tom asks how he's getting on.

'Relieved to have this wireless, sir, I don't mind tellin 'e. An I spent time with Francika yesterday.'

'Have you got beyond single words yet?'

'She's doing better with English than I am with theirs. An if she can understand me she should have no problem back ome.'

Tom tells Sid that he has requested a new radio operator, in the hope that both he and Francika can be taken out along with the wounded.

'She was a bit funny yesterday, to be honest,' Sid admits. 'Scared. I couldn't tell you if it was a fear of flying, what she's never done before, or summat else. I told her not to worry. Not to be afeared a nothing with me there.'

Tom gives Sid the enciphered signals to Base Operations in Italy. Sid makes contact, and when he is finished finds the BBC. The news is not so good. Fighting on the western front is going slowly, with the Germans putting up incredible resistance, just as they are in Italy: there, they've evacuated Florence but are defending a line a little north. It's not clear what's going on in Poland.

Tom goes to the valley to liaise with the Partisan ground crews. He returns at midday, arriving at the same time as Jack Farwell, back from a meeting with the commander of the Fourth Zone over targets to be attacked and the gathering of intelligence. Jack slaps his cap on the table in the hall. 'Tomorrow!' he exclaims, his nose thoroughly out of joint. 'It's still bloody well tomorrow when they're going to hit the railway depots in Zidani Most. Never, *Today, we've done it, bravo!* The fact of the matter is, Freedman, I have no idea where our supplies are going. They disappear into the hills. The Jugs have a pretty dashing sense of accounting. They're supposed to be attacking the roads and railways but I'm convinced they're storing the stuff up for future use.'

'What future use?' Tom asks. The men hang up their coats and go through to the parlour.

'They can see the end of hostilities in sight, and they're saving their strength.'

'But for what?'

Jack frowns. 'To sort out their internal enemies and their external borders, of course. You must have picked up at least a gleaning of reality on the ground while you were sitting out the war with those pansies in Baker Street.' He looks askance at Tom. 'Or one of those country houses you commandeered.' He lights a cigarette, inhales, makes a face of disapproval. 'I've requested that they place train watchers along the lines, and they say, "Yes, of course," but I'm getting no more gen from them at all. Is there nothing to drink around here?'

Tom fetches their hostess from the kitchen and, having become accustomed to the senior officer's requirements, she pours Jack and Tom each a shot of brandy. Jack inhales the fumy scent with distaste, before he takes a sip.

'Good God, Freedman, what I'd give for something decent.'

Sid Dixon appears, back from some trip with an air of subterfuge. He salutes the officers formally. 'Permission to report delivery of essential supplies, sir.'

'What the devil are you talking about, Corporal?' Jack demands.

From his knapsack Sid flourishes, like a conjuror, two hundred packs of Player's, and three bottles of single malt whisky. 'They was in one a the parachute containers.'

'The Jugs gave them to you?'

'I did a little persuading, sir. They're a good bunch a lads.'

Tom wonders how Sid bargained and chaffered using only the isolated Slovene words he knows.

'Well done.' Jack beams, slapping Sid on the back. His mood switches as his attention flips from one thing to the next. 'I say, Freedman, you're damned fortunate being able to speak the lingo. They invited us to a cultural evening for the villagers tonight. I've told them you'll be honoured to represent His Majesty's Government and to give a speech.'

'Thanks, Jack.'

'Pleasure, old chap. And while you're there chucking back their rough brandy we'll make a start on this Scotch for you.'

The room is large, but it is no hall. Perhaps it was the mayor's office, Tom surmises. There must be two hundred people packed in, sitting on the floor, most of them cross-legged. To judge by their uniforms, some were among those who'd been garrisoned here, with the Germans. Many are civilians. There is a black, battered Bechstein; scratched and splintered, it looks like it has been the target of an attack all of its own. A soldier plays Chopin, and though some of the keys are off, and wander, he wrings a disfigured beauty from the instrument: he coaxes the piano into summoning up its last reserves of musical strength for one final performance.

A drama is staged, with acting that is little more than a read-through of dialogue theatrically overblown, about an elderly Slovene woman and her courageous granddaughters saved from death and worse by heroes of the Soviet Red Army.

Jovan takes to the platform and speaks of the Slavic bond with mother Russia. He receives a loud yet clearly dutiful reception; Tom suspects that he cannot shake off his Serb background, that he still feels a mystic attachment that these Catholic Slovenes do not. The Soviet commissar then talks in a monotone, recounting the sacrifices on the eastern front, in the great cities of the Soviet Union, and urging the Yugoslavs to greater effort. He takes his seat apparently oblivious to the lukewarm response from all but the few Partisan soldiers present, some of whom yell, '*Zivio Marechal Stalin*,' and '*Zivio Rdeča Armada*.'

Jovan returns to the stage to introduce his Allied comrade. Tom gives his speech, in which he expresses his and his colleagues' pride at sharing this great struggle with the National Liberation Front. The applause is loud and generous. As he returns to his seat by the wall, Tom finds questions hurled at him: what did he think of the play? Was the acting not marvellous? Could a play of such quality be found in London?

A choir of crippled soldiers make their determined way to the front. They sing songs that rise and fall as boats on a swelling sea, an accordion creating the waves, lifting the audience with them. There are Partisan songs that start slow and melodious then leap into rousing choruses that make Tom's heart soar. A dozen soldiers, men and women, form in front of the singers an interweaving line, a latticework of arms, and dance from side to side of the room. They rest, briefly, when someone takes advantage of a break between songs to cry out, '*Nasa je Trst!*' and immediately the call is taken up, first by a few of those surrounding the initiator, and then by the whole room. '*Nasa je Trst! Nasa je Trst!*' People stamp their feet to the beat of the chant.

Eventually a member of the choir lifts one of his crutches and waves it to indicate, Enough. The chant subsides, voices fall to silence, and the choir begins again.

There is a mood of jubilation and defiance in the room. Tom is cheered, but his mind wanders, and his stomach crawls with anxiety – when will the German planes come? And the army behind, flooding into the valley?

The choir end with a song that within seconds of its opening words has everyone rising to their feet. It is '*Hej Slavenia*', hymn to the Slavic spirit that Tom's neighbour tells him has become the de facto Yugoslav national anthem. Soldiers throw their caps in the air. Suddenly there is Marija, working her way through the crowd towards him. Tom's heart beats faster. Damn, damn! He wonders if it would be possible to avoid her, to slip backwards, away from her. No, he cannot. He shoulders between singing men and meets her. Their hands clasp, unseen amongst the jostling bodies. Each of them gazes into the other's eyes. Tom plays his part. Until, at the end of the song, they are bumped apart in the crowd.

August 13

Four more planes are expected in the night. Two hidden hospitals have been cleared. Now Olga's patients are brought down the wooded slopes to the road beside the Savinja river, where they are put onto ox-wagons and rolled along the bumpy road. The hospital lies beyond Luce, the village north of Ljubno, and the journey is five bone-shaking miles. Tom is at the landing field. He can hear the groans of the wounded as they trundle past him.

Shortly before the appointed time Dixon receives a signal informing them that, due to poor weather, the Dakotas will not arrive. Containing his fury and dismay as best he can, Tom relays the bad news to the ground crews and to Olga and her staff. The ox-carts are turned around, the groaning injured begin the painful return journey to their hidden hospital.

Over breakfast, a bowl of maize porridge, with warm milk, Tom tells his colleagues about the cabaret. Jack is incensed. 'The Jugs never acknowledge Allied support in public. It's shabby behaviour.'

'But the people aren't fooled,' Tom points out. 'They see British planes dropping British supplies.'

'Yes, and they're told that the Russians have paid for it. You know what else they're told? That we're going to make the Slovenes pay us back at the end of the war. That bowler-hatted gents will appear with a pile of chits itemising all they owe us.'

*

The British are informed by a junior staff officer that they are to be given a liaison interpreter, and that from now on all communication with headquarters is to be channelled through him. Appointments must be made to see the Partisan commander or the commissar through the interpreter. 'How the hell can I do my job?' Farwell demands. 'I'll sort this out. And I'll bet you, Freedman, the Soviets don't need to make bloody appointments.' He storms off.

When the interpreter arrives it is none other than Pero. He and Tom share a smoke and catch up. Pero appears older; his voice is half an octave deeper than that of the youth Tom had met in Semic. Tom asks him about the new recruits, those captured in Ljubno who have changed sides and joined the Partisans.

'They all claim that they were conscripted against their will,' Pero tells him. 'In action against us, they say, they always shot over our heads.'

Pero also says that German reinforcements have been seen amassing in Celje. 'They will be very keen to come back here,' he says. 'There is nothing fascists like less than to be laughed at.'

When he leaves, Pero nods with great formality and shakes Tom's hand. It strikes Tom as odd, for they have never done so before, until he feels not skin but paper in his palm.

Some time after Pero has gone, Tom is preparing that day's message to transmit to the firm, when Sid comes in to their house. He looks glum. There's clearly something wrong.

'You feeling all right?' Tom asks him.

Dixon doesn't answer at first. It is as if there is a time delay between his brain receiving the sound of Tom's voice and responding to it. Slowly he looks up. 'I can't find her, sir. Looked all over.'

'Francika?'

'Tracked down our old buddies; none a them'll tell me nothing. Every one a them shrugs his shoulders. I don't get it.'

'I'll look into it,' Tom promises. 'In the meantime, don't brood on it. Here's the message to send.'

In the early evening, after their caretaker has given them a heavy stew for their meal, with suety dumplings, Tom goes into the orchard outside the farmhouse. The sky is clear, the world is quiet. He would be happy to spend the evening inside, grappling with the high German of *Elective Affinities*, with a glass of damson brandy. This would not be a bad place to sit out the war. If only the war would stay away. He rereads the note Pero passed him. All it says, in dark pencil on a scrap of pale paper, in a flamboyant yet legible, upright script, is *Do not despair. We shall be together*. He studies the writing, as if the shape of the letters written in Marija's hand might hold more meaning than the words themselves.

Tom checks his watch, fetches his greatcoat, and makes for the valley. He trots down an incline through the woods. The night is cool and the air smells less of the resin of the pine trees than of the earth they grow from: peaty and sour.

August 14

The night sky is clear, and cool. Piles of wood are ready to be lit. Soldiers stand around the field, prepared to run forward to unload the planes. They have ox-drawn carts, wheelbarrows. Behind them are the wounded: in a few hours each one will be in an Allied hospital in southern Italy, receiving treatment that will save many of their lives. But what an ordeal it is for them to reach safety: passage down the mountain, the flight; every movement, for many, an agony.

Jack Farwell is in a better mood, having extracted the assurance of a meeting tomorrow to discuss the British Mission's position. 'Look at that, Freedman,' he says, leaning back. 'The Jugs should have the finest astronomers on the planet.' Tom gazes upwards. 'Endlessly expanding, so they say,' Jack continues. 'No end and no beginning either.' Tom looks at his colleague: Jack wears a grave expression as he considers these cosmological mysteries. 'A lot of nonsense, of course,' he decides.

Tom is unable to suppress a chuckle. 'In what particular way, Jack?' he asks.

Jack turns and looks at him, frowning, rather like a parent whose child's intellect has developed, worryingly, overnight. 'Science is all very well, Freedman,' he says. 'One day it will answer every question. Apart from the most difficult ones. Those we have to answer ourselves.'

Before Tom can respond, there is a yell. A courier runs towards them. He has come from the British Mission, with a note from

Sid Dixon. Jack snatches it from the courier. Tom can guess its content. The weight of the stew in his stomach makes him want to sit on the ground. The flights are cancelled. Poor weather in Italy. How can this be true?

It is his job to pass on this news to the Slovenes. He tells the senior staff officer, who salutes Tom with what feels like contemptuous formality. Word is passed around. Soldiers disperse. The wounded are ferried back. A figure approaches in the starlight. A tall, slim woman. Olga, the doctor.

'I must protest in the strongest possible terms,' she says.

Jack Farwell, discerning her mood, does not step forward for a translation but lets his junior officer deal with the confrontation.

'I cannot allow my patients to be dragged up and down the mountain. Is this the British sense of humour? You think this is funny? Why do you not tell us before?'

'I'm so sorry,' is all Tom can muster. 'It's a *débâcle*. I'm so sorry.'

Olga turns and stalks off. Jack joins Tom. 'Good show,' he says. 'You said a few anodyne words, I assume. The best one could do in the circumstances. It's a sorry business, Freedman.'

They walk back to the farmhouse. Tom feels an unpleasant mixture of impotence and shame. He cannot sleep.

August 15

Sid is plunged in gloom. There is no word of Francika. Pero makes his daily visit, but cannot help. He knows nothing of her whereabouts. Tom sits over the scheduled wireless contact: despite his recriminations, there is no apology for the late message last night. Further flights are planned for the night ahead.

The Partisan headquarters is in a large farmhouse surrounded by trees, close to a rockface: shelter to be reached in the event of an attack. The Englishmen are invited to sit at a table on the terrace. The first floor of the house is constructed from large stones; everything above is made of wood, from the thick rough-cut floor beams to the roof-shingles. There are window boxes in which bright red begonias bloom from their profusion of dull green leaves. A single bee buzzes dozily from one flower to another.

They wait a long time. Jack, to Tom's surprise, is calm. Patience, standard requirement for a soldier, had not appeared to be one of his attributes. The British army runs to a schedule; that schedule may be perpetually delayed or abandoned, but is always, immediately, redrawn. The Yugoslavs are less bothered about time-keeping – one of the reasons those British officers Tom had been briefed by in Bari affected a contempt for them.

The afternoon is hot. Tom loosens another button of his shirt. He took off his tie some weeks ago, to secure a bivouac in the rain one night, and has not worn one since. His peaked cap, which caught in the branches, gave way long ago to a beret. But

Jack's khaki uniform looks as it did the day they arrived, as if a batman were pressing it daily.

There is a good deal of coming and going. Everyone wears a red star in his or her side-cap. Some have silk shirts, sewn from Allied parachutes. They come with written or spoken reports, most of which cause uproar, and must be dealt with immediately.

A long while after the time of the Englishmen's appointment a door opens in the house, releasing what sounds like a recording of laughter. A moment later the Soviet liaison officer, a short, pugnacious-looking man, emerges on the terrace. He smiles at the Englishmen, revealing steel teeth. Then he trots down the steps and is gone.

A further five minutes go by before they are summoned to the commander's office. They find Jovan sitting beside him, on the other side of a trestle table that acts as a desk. The two men rise, and salute the British officers. No apology is given for their being kept waiting.

'Now look here,' Jack exclaims. 'We're pouring supplies for your army into this valley, and I'm told I have to make appointments to see you through an interpreter who's not even an officer?'

Tom begins to translate, but the commander raises his hand. 'Please,' he says, gesturing towards two wooden chairs. 'Wait a moment. Let us not discuss these issues before we have offered you our hospitality.'

He says nothing more, and so they sit in uncomfortable silence, waiting a little longer. Tom glances across at Jovan, offering the opportunity for eye contact, but there is no response. Jovan stares at the door, which eventually opens, and in comes a young, uniformed woman with a tray that she lays on the table. On the tray is a glass decanter filled with a pale liquid and four small glasses, and two plates: one with a loaf of bread, the other half a dozen sausages. The bread and a couple of the sausages have been cut into slices.

Jovan pours the liquor, and gestures to the food. 'Please help yourself: this is good pork. Engels regretted the idiocy of rural life, but the farmers here know what to do with their pigs.'

The commander has thick black hair and eyebrows, and thin crooked lips. 'How can we work with you,' he asks, 'when you support our enemy? Even after all the evidence of their collaboration.'

Jack is at a loss to understand. Jovan flourishes what he calls a Chetnik press release: it praises the American president and people, now that a senior army officer has joined General Draža Mihailović in Serbia.

Jack shakes his head. 'I find this hard to believe,' he says. 'The British government withdrew its liaison officers and ceased support of Mihailović more than two months ago.'

Hearing these words, Tom has to restrain himself from staring, incredulous, at his senior officer. Instead he focuses on a dark grain in a wooden floorboard, as he wonders why Jack didn't tell him this before? When he ordered Tom not to report seeing Chetniks in Slovenia.

'The Yanks have their own ideas, but still…' Jack protests, frowning at the piece of paper in his hand.

'All right,' Jovan says. 'Forget the Americans. Let us talk only about the British. Tell us: what are you doing in Istria?'

'Istria? Our army's a million miles from there,' Jack tells him. 'Still bogged down in Italy.'

'But you are planning an invasion, are you not?' Jovan continues. With a wave of his hand he dismisses any forthcoming objection. 'It is no secret, Major: Mr Churchill has told Marshal Tito. It is a good idea. But we ask you: for what, exactly?'

'I know nothing about it,' Farwell blusters. 'All I know is that we are supplying you with the means to attack the Hun.'

Tom translates. The commander watches. Perhaps he will keep his thin lips closed, let Jovan do all the talking.

'The question is, Major, to what end?' Jovan asks.

As soon as Tom has translated, the commander says with calm politeness, 'Please, have some more bread and sausage.'

Tom chews the heavy bread. Jovan pours more *slivovka*. The sausage is tough, and spicy.

'One day you want us to stop the German troops coming into our country,' Jovan says. 'The next day you want us to stop them leaving.'

Jovan is sweating. The commander's grim suspicious gaze is fixed on Jack Farwell. There is an atmosphere of paranoia in the room. It occurs to Tom that the lighting is all wrong, on this summer afternoon. The scene should take place in darkness; in black and white, like *The Maltese Falcon*.

'We want evidence that you're using the weapons we give you,' Jack says. 'And we want information on trains. It doesn't seem so much to ask.'

'Ah, but why? That is the question: why do you want this information? The same question that must always be asked of British intelligence in the Balkans.'

'So we can bomb the Hun from the air.'

'And then what, Major?' Jovan enquires.

Jack falters. 'There's a war to be won. It's not won yet.'

'Don't think we don't know,' Jovan says, nodding. The commander's lips are still sealed and crooked, but they surely betray a smile. As if Jovan has just played his trump in a four-handed game of cards. Outfoxing the British representative.

*

They walk slowly back around the curved hillsides of the valley to their farmhouse. Tom stumbles. He wonders how many shots he drank in the end, and how much alcohol was really soaked up by the bread and sausage. His thoughts do not cohere. Surely it is still the afternoon, yet the sun is not shining. The sky is grey. Drinking always renders Tom thuddingly stupid.

'What was all that about?' he asks.

'Leave it to the grown-ups,' Jack says, striding ahead. 'Don't worry your little head about it.' He stops abruptly, and waits for Tom to catch up. 'I'm sorry, Freedman, but you need to face one or two realities about our friends here. Remember, above all, that they do what their Uncle Joe tells them.'

All Tom can think of is that he needs a tall glass of cool well-water and a few hours' sleep before leaving for the airfield tonight. 'But a landing in Istria? Is that true?'

'Of course,' Jack says. They walk on, side by side. 'As your commissar friend said, it's no secret. The Dalmatian islands, while they've been occupied by the Germans, have been a chain of defensive spikes,' he tells Tom. 'But the Partisans are contesting them now. If and when the islands are taken from the Germans, they'll become perfect dropping-off points. We could come up around Trieste and attack the German army in Italy from behind.' Unlike Tom, Jack is one of those whose brain cells are enlivened by fermented fruit. 'The Jugs want to snatch Trieste for themselves. And what's more, I'll wager they want not just Trieste but a part of southern Austria. That's what happens in war: the border moves in one direction, and when the tide turns the victors shift it in the other.'

Content with his diagnosis, Farwell strides along. 'I'll prepare a report and give it to Morris to send,' he announces.

*

There is confusion around the airfield. The doctor, Olga, has refused to bring her patients down to the landing field until the planes arrive. Tom explains to Pero, to pass on to the senior staff officer, that Allied rules do not allow for any plane to stay on the ground for more than thirty minutes. If the Slovenes wait until the first plane lands, there will not be enough time to get the injured down from the hospital. Messages shuttle to and fro. Olga does not yield.

The first plane lands. A message is sent to the hospital. Supplies are unloaded and they do indeed, Tom sees, disappear into the night. Word comes from the hospital: the patients are on their way. One or two wounded men who were already in the valley board the first plane, but there is no sign of the hospital patients. The thirty minutes tick by. One after another propellers whirr, the Dakotas' thick black tyres bounce and rumble over the field and the planes take off into the dark sky, empty.

Tom returns to the Mission farmhouse. He knows the mile-long route by heart, and is so tired he is practically asleep on his feet, but he moves fast. It seems that he remembers someone calling his name, and wonders dimly who it was. Halfway home he crosses a glade and realises that someone – or something – is following him. He stops, turns. A figure trots towards him. 'I was calling you,' the man gasps. 'Did you not hear?' It is Jovan. 'How fast you stride, Tom,' he says, drawing close. A foot away Tom can just about see his face in the starlight. Jovan is smiling. 'Have you time to talk with an old friend?'

They lie on the grass, the fresh dew seeping through their coats. 'I am sorry, Tom,' Jovan says. 'For my behaviour.'

'It's been hard,' Tom tells him.

'For me, too. But I have had a greater responsibility than mere friendship. I can only hope that you understand.'

'It's good to see you,' Tom says. 'I mean you, as you were, the Jovan I know.' He is no longer tired. They smoke, and drink *slivovka* from a bottle Jovan has with him.

'You know,' Tom says, 'in Bari, in the officers' mess, Churchill was broadcast, giving one of his great speeches. A thousand miles away the Nazis were banging on the door of my country, bombing it daily. And my companions turned from the wireless and resumed their game of cards without a trace of emotion. Their cynicism made me sick. Yet I felt stupid for being moved.' He takes a slug of liquor. 'And now I'm here, where liberty is not taken for granted but fought for, dreamed of, seized.'

Jovan nods. 'Do you trust your own commanding officer?'

'Trust?' Tom asks, shocked. 'Yes, of course. With my life.'

'Even though you do not like him? Are there not things he does not tell you? He is more interested in *our* troop movements than in the enemy's.'

Tom wonders quite how much Jack has not told him. 'Do you trust *your* commander?' he asks.

'I am obedient to our revolution,' Jovan tells him.

'Yes, and we have a common enemy. Why do you deny us?' Tom says. 'Your Allies. Me.'

'Study your history, Tom. Your Civil War was so long ago, it has become myth for you.' Jovan speaks quietly, his voice warm, neither arguing nor preaching. 'Here our new country is being born, and pain is inevitable. The intolerance of nature in producing a healthy child sometimes gravely damages the mother, does it not?'

They talk, and smoke. Tom waits for Jovan to mention Marija, but he does not, so Tom asks if he has seen her.

'Once. Twice.' Jovan gestures over his shoulder. 'She is in the woods there, somewhere. I think, my friend, that I will wait until you have gone before I speak to her again.'

Tom shakes his head. Dawn breaks so slowly that Tom is unaware of it, he only finds Jovan's face becoming clearer, as if illuminated not by light but the renewed pleasure of his own gaze upon it. Tom asks him of the future. When Jovan smiles, his handsome face creases. He must be as tired as Tom. His face and hair are damp with dew.

'Our Partisan Army is how big, exactly, I'm not sure – three hundred thousand? In a population across Yugoslavia of sixteen million. So what of the Chetniks, the Ustasha, and their sympathisers? What of the peasants, who keep their weapons oiled, hidden, and ready to hand? What of those who stayed safe in the occupied cities and towns? They say that in Zagreb the well-heeled women have kept pace with the fashions of Paris. Those generals strolling in their gardens in Belgrade: will they welcome us? No, I do not think they will.'

'But they will not fight you?'

Jovan smiles grimly. 'There are others enough for that. This is where it will end, Tom, do you see? Here in Slovenia. It will be hell on earth, very soon. All the dregs will end up here, fighting for their rotten lives. Chetniks, Ljotic's treasonous Serbs. Croatian fascist Ustashi and Muhammadan Bosniaks of the Waffen SS Mountain Division, whose savagery is beyond description. White Russians, Cossacks, Swabians from the Banat who joined the Prinz Eugen Division and have hunted us without mercy for the last two years. They'll all be washed up here, the detritus of war, along with anti-communist civilians tagging along behind them like rats.' Jovan shakes his head. When their eyes meet, Tom sees the hatred and resolve that fatigue cannot extinguish. 'We must be strong,' Jovan says, 'and build our new country.'

'And are you strong?' Tom asks.

'We are.' Jovan laughs. 'Of course we are.' He gets up, offers a hand, pulls Tom to his feet. They embrace. Jovan steps back. 'If tomorrow,' he says, 'once again I am only the commissar, forgive me.'

How odd: in the forest, on the hard ground, with strange noises, shifting light and temperature, Tom often slept deeply. In a thick-walled farmhouse, under sheet and blanket on a soft mattress, sleep is fitful; he springs wide awake with his mind fretting. Trust curdles. Is there nothing he can do to restore it?

August 16

In the morning they eat their breakfast in sombre mood. Sid Dixon is preoccupied. Jack Farwell has Tom encipher his long report to base.

'I can't agree with you, Jack,' Tom tells him. 'Stopping the provision of weapons?'

'Until we can be sure what they're being used for.'

Tom tells Jack what happened last night: that Allied planes took off without waiting for the wounded. 'They already feel furious, that we don't understand how much store they set by saving their wounded. Refusing to take their patients to Italy will make it much worse.'

'Threats are the only thing they'll understand,' Jack avers. 'These are all we have to bargain with. Send the report as written.'

There is a knock on the door. Their housekeeper opens it. It is Pero, but he does not come in; he would prefer that one of the British officers step outside. When the housekeeper tells them, Tom does not bother to translate but goes out himself.

There are two Partisan soldiers. Each of them is tough looking, as brawny as Stipe. 'These are your bodyguards,' Pero says. He is embarrassed, his eyes do not meet Tom's. 'They have been assigned to you for your own protection.'

'Thank you,' Tom says. 'Please, pass on our thanks to the commander.' He salutes each of the soldiers. Whatever is going on, he will remain formal and polite in his manners.

Pero's discomfort is painful. He is half-turned away, shifts from one foot to the other: though he must stay, he does not want conversation. Tom looks up. Clouds are like grey rags fluttering in the high mountains. There will soon be rain here in the valley.

Tom returns inside, drinks the dregs of the coffee substitute they are served.

'Shall we put him on the next plane?'

Tom frowns at Jack. 'Pero?' He wants to send Pero to Italy?

'Dixon. Is he any use to you? Doesn't look like it.'

'The Partisan woman he's fallen in love with,' Tom says. 'There's no word of her.'

'Nor will there be. Not now. Look, you remember they told us there's only so long you can last in the field. Dixon's licked. He needs to be got out.'

Tom listens, and nods agreement.

After Sid has wired the report, Farwell asks Tom to send Pero to request an interview with the commander, so that he can be informed of the report and what it contains. The relief – that he can leave, if only temporarily – is evident in Pero's open smile. He trots off towards the wood.

Pero returns an hour later. 'It is not possible today.'

When Tom relays this to Jack, Farwell decides he will go and sit on the terrace of the National Liberation Front Headquarters until it becomes possible.

His way is blocked by the two Partisans outside. Their bodyguard has become an armed guard.

While Jack fumes and blusters, Tom withdraws to his room. He has a headache: the sky is closing in on the earth, the atmospheric pressure compresses his skull. He writes a note to Marija. He's not sure why. He feels he ought to, yet with a pen in his hand he doesn't know what to write. If he does not pursue her, who knows whether the chance of love, of marriage, will arise again. Nothing can come of it, anyhow: look at Dixon and his Francika, it will not be allowed – which only renders the prospect more romantic. Or should he say what he believes to be true? He is not the man for her.

Tom writes the note, but can he now trust Pero to deliver it? He folds it away in a pocket of his jacket.

In the evening the storm comes, first the sound: a delicate roll like the tympanum in Sibelius' Finlandia Suite. Then a silence, a stillness, as the light fades, before it falls like a herd of wild horses, thundering past them, rain crashing to the ground.

August 17

The planes have stopped coming. The Englishmen are under virtual house arrest. Sid Dixon stirs himself when it's time for a sked, to send messages that state: 'No change.' Pero tells Tom that Slovene Home Guard forces seem by all accounts to be growing stronger, despite the fact that the Germans, their patrons, are clearly facing ultimate defeat.

'Further proof of the Partisans' passivity,' Jack exclaims when Tom shares the rumour at breakfast. The house is gloomy. Their hostess has lit lamps though it is a morning in August.

But Jack is in bullish mood. 'They'll buckle before we do,' he insists. 'We've been playing liar dice for centuries.'

'They really think we're up to something?'

'If we weren't, we'd hardly be doing our job, would we?'

Tom frowns. 'What job?' he asks.

'Of course it's good to derail a few trains,' Jack says, in a voice he must think is meant to sound reassuring. 'Look, Freedman,' he says, and begins to shift the cups and bowls, plates, cutlery, glasses, pots of jam and of honey, around the table. 'Yes, the PM wants a landing in Istria. Not to send our troops round the corner and down into Italy but to send them straight up here, through the middle of Slovenia and up through the Ljubljana Gap.'

'A southern front,' Tom says. He stares at the rearranged utensils in amazement.

'Brooke's behind it,' Jack continues. 'Alexander's been behind it all along. He's even prepared to take troops from the impasse in Italy, as well as new divisions, send them through the Gap and into the plains of the Danube.' Jack picks up a knife and makes as if to stab someone. 'Churchill wants to "thrust a dagger under Germany's armpit", as he puts it. The problem, naturally, is the Americans. Clark's amenable, but Marshall's dead against it. And Roosevelt, I'm afraid, is as naive as he's honourable. He wants to please Stalin, to keep to what they agreed in Tehran; he doesn't understand that there's no point in winning the war on the battlefield and then losing it at the conference table.'

Tom struggles to take it all in. Jack smiles. It seems to please him inordinately to know more than his junior officer. He calls for their hostess, and hands her the coffee jug for a refill.

'Are you saying,' Tom begins, 'that you've been gathering gen about the Partisans, while I've been scarpering about the hills of Slovenia as a cover? A decoy?'

'Certainly not!' Jack tells him. 'Good God, no. What you boys have been doing is vital. But I've had other things to do as well. The point is, we want to reach Vienna before the Russians.'

'While Stalin,' Tom nods, 'is desperate to get as far south and east as possible, never mind beat us to Berlin.'

Jack grins. 'You're getting it. Not quite as stupid as you look, Freedman,' he says. 'The Allies have to block Soviet expansion in southern Europe. The fact is,' he says, lighting a cigarette, 'you and I are pawns, Freedman, as we always knew we were. It's just that the game we're in is rather larger than you realised.'

The chicory coffee is poured. Jack takes a sip and says, 'I do believe I'm finding this less revolting by the day.'

'So we're more duplicitous than they are,' Tom says. 'And always have been? At least it's their bloody country. We've not been playing a straight hand from day one?'

Jack Farwell peers through the smoke at Tom, shakes his head. 'Don't go native on me, there's a good chap,' he says. 'You'd be no use to anyone.'

Throughout the morning the rain roars and crashes upon the roof and the ground. Tom peers out of the window, through the falling rain, is just able to make out the two bodyguards sheltering under the beech tree a few yards from the house, huddled inside inadequate oilskins. Needlessly miserable. The weather's enough to keep the British under house arrest anyhow. It will also deter an enemy attack on the valley.

August 18

'Do not worry, we are going to give you handouts, with all the information you need.'

Jack and Tom have been summoned to the Partisan Headquarters. After two days the rain has eased to a drizzle, and they have trudged through mud. Jovan hands them each a piece of paper with German positions, and movements, typed out on it.

'We can't verify this.' Jack shakes his head. 'It's meaningless. We need to see for ourselves.'

When this has been translated, the commander nods, with a broad, knowing smile that reminds Tom of the bad acting in the Partisan play he saw: yes, the smile says, it is just as we suspected. 'Before you take out our wounded, you have demanded information. We give it to you. You are not happy. Why? Because it is *other* information you want. *Our* troop numbers and positions.'

'Why would we give a damn about your forces?'

The commander smiles again. His behaviour suggests an odd mixture of Machiavellian statecraft and peasant cunning. 'You and your American friends want to take Austria,' he says.

While Tom translates, so he anticipates Jack's reaction. The procedure is comical.

'What the hell do we want with Austria?' Jack responds, his hackles rising; the Englishman's acting is of a slightly higher standard than the Slovene's. Tom watches with acute embarrassment. And shame. For how can Jovan suspect what Jack is up to, yet believe Tom knows nothing of it? 'We want to get off this damned continent and go home,' Jack continues. 'But of course we'll stay and administer disputed border areas; and the frontiers will be determined by post-war peace negotiation, and treaties.'

The commander rises to his feet. 'You think we should trust you to sort out our borders?' he asks. He gestures to Jovan, who passes fresh sheets of paper to the Englishmen. 'German troops are reinforcing north of here, as you can see,' the commander says, pointing at the paper. He smiles again, and sits down, begins to write in a ledger.

The meeting is over.

Jack and Tom return to their Mission house in a gloomy, paranoid mood, only to find Dixon and Morris eager with news from Brigadier Maclean, head of the British Mission to Yugoslavia: an order from Marshal Tito, via the British, to his Fourth Zone command to launch a major attack against rail and road targets in Slovenia in the first week of September. It is to be coordinated with other such offensives throughout the Yugoslav territories, in order to impede the withdrawal of German forces from the Balkans, and their redeployment against the Allies on the western and eastern fronts.

This is the first time a Partisan order has been transmitted to a British liaison officer, to be delivered by him to the Partisans. 'The Germans must have broken the Jug signals,' Jack tells Tom. He can hardly contain his glee. There is a further message, stating that there should be no mention of the attacks in Partisan radio messages. Jack takes Morris with him to deliver the order. At first the bodyguard will not let them leave the house, but Tom translates until they understand that an order from their supreme commander is the issue, whereupon they escort Farwell and Morris at a fast pace.

August 23

The sun is shining once again, summer has returned to the valley. The ground has dried out, exuding the humid odours of damp earth as it does so. And the mood everywhere is changed: the Partisans' heavy mask of distrust has lifted, while the Englishmen's resentment has dissipated as their freedom of movement is restored. News from elsewhere is good: the Soviets have attacked Romania. The liberation of Paris seems imminent.

Ratweek is the codename given to the operation: the major target in the Fourth Zone is the railway bridge across the Sava at Litija, close to where Tom and his party crossed the river when they travelled north three months ago. The Partisans' Seventh Corps will approach from the south; the Brigades in the Fourth Zone, including most of the soldiers in this valley, will attack from the north.

Tom works without sleeping now, running between Dixon's wireless, the Partisan HQ and the airfield, coordinating drops not only here in the valley but across the north of the country. Explosives are needed for the attack on the bridge, and for a number of smaller operations against rail lines and roads. Sid Dixon's melancholia is put aside as he is caught up in the endless job of sending and receiving messages.

Brigadier Maclean has also sent word of a promotion: Jack is to be Colonel Farwell, which will give him greater authority with the Partisan command. There is no word on any such promotion for Tom, but he cares little.

*

After a week of breakneck preparations, in the middle of the day Tom tells Sid to grab a couple of towels. Tom is tired, and sweaty; dust has got under his clothes and stuck to his skin; he has smoked too many cigarettes. They walk down to the river in the valley, find a spot that is quiet and lined with trees, and strip off. The river is clear, gliding over blue stones. Sid's face and neck, hands and forearms, are dark brown; but his torso is white; like some strange piebald human animal. Tom knows he must look the same.

The river is not deep, it barely covers their knees, and they slide on the stones underfoot and, laughing, stumble with a splash. Sid sits in the shallows and throws stones into the middle of the river. Tom floats on his back in a channel towards the far bank, letting the sluggish current take him, feet first, slowly downstream. He hopes there are no leeches. The water is cool. It feels satiny on his skin. He closes his eyes. The sun is warm on his face. He is not moving fast enough to be hurt if he hits a boulder. He spreads his arms wide, and drifts. His mind empties...

Tom wakes. It takes a moment for his situation to make sense. He has drifted towards the bank, is in shadow. He looks upriver: has probably floated no more than a hundred yards, been asleep a minute, or two at most. He hears voices, looks through the trees, and sees two figures. It is too far away to make out what they are saying, but it is clear that they are arguing. The woman turns and walks away. The man calls after her, something Tom cannot decipher, but he recognises the voice, and immediately the figure: it is Jovan. The woman is Marija.

Turning onto his front, Tom swims a silent breaststroke towards them. Marija has stopped, or at least paused. Jovan watches her. She turns, slowly, shaking her head.

'Don't say no,' Jovan says. 'Give me hope, that is all I ask.'

Tom reaches the bank, and watches. Jovan is no more than twenty yards away.

'I don't ask for any more, not now, not yet, how could I?'

Without really looking in his direction, speaking instead as she turns from him, Marija says, 'All right,' and strolls away.

Tom waits until Jovan lights himself a cigarette, stands and walks purposefully off in a different direction than Marija. Tom swims silently back upstream, or, when the water is too shallow, pulls himself along by the smooth stones on the riverbed. So, he thinks: Jovan has not waited for Tom to leave. He knows what he wants, and goes after it.

Now information, opinions, rumours, all the spoken stuff of everyday life, is once again shared between the Partisans and all their allies. The British are told that even as this nest of operations is being planned, so the Germans are massing for their attack on the valley, despite news of their losses in Italy and Greece. 'The problem with the Krauts is they don't know when they're licked,' Jack reckons.

August 25

Tom walks from the airfield back to the Mission house. Explosives, rifles, PIATS have been delivered. The last of the hospital's heavily wounded have been taken away, to Italy.

Tom trudges the final half-mile back to the house. Birdsong mocks his tiredness. His hand reaches into the pocket where he put the note he'd written to Marija. He discovers with a shock that the pocket is empty. How can that be? Did he give it to Pero? Surely not. But he is so tired. Perhaps he did.

Sleep is brief but deep. At breakfast, while Tom drinks the ersatz coffee and pretends it will revive him, Farwell holds forth. 'No more silly pranks,' he declares. 'The Jugs are going to have at them. It's neck or nothing now.' He has persuaded base to send six fighter planes from Mediterranean Command to lead the attack on the bridge and soften up the German positions.

'And the best news of all,' he tells Tom, 'is that you are going with them.' He claps Tom on the shoulder. 'I'm only sorry to miss the hullabaloo myself.'

Tom hopes that his dislike of Jack is masked by the excitement he feels. 'Does Jovan know?' he asks.

'The commissar is in full agreement,' Jack assures him. 'You go and see the job's done, Freedman,' he says. 'Blow the bastards to perdition.'

CHAPTER SEVEN

Attack on the Bridge

September 2

Jack is still snoring when Tom slips out of the house. Their housekeeper got up before dawn to cook him ham and eggs. He wipes his plate with black bread; swallows the last of the coffee, brown and sweet.

Sid Dixon shakes Tom's hand. 'Wish I were coming with you, sir,' he says. Then, remembering what has not been mentioned these last frantic days, adds, 'If you see her, sir…'

Tom nods. 'I will.'

They set off in the early morning, trudging the sleepy stiffness out of their bones, *odred*s and companies coalescing bit by bit into a brigade of soldiers snaking through the woods. Few know where they are going. Each soldier follows the one in front. Company commanders were only given the location at dawn, couriers fanning out in the night from headquarters with battle plans.

The soldiers travel light, each with a rifle or sub-machine gun over one shoulder, and ammunition. A small canvas bag or knapsack over the other: inside it a canteen, knife, spoon perhaps. At least all are now armed, Tom reckons, many bearing British weapons. They walk in single file along forest paths. No one speaks. The rustling and clinking of their clothes and arms, the tread of their footsteps, amount to little more than a murmur in the trees. It's impossible to determine how many of them there are in front of and behind him.

*

The pace is familiar: fast and unrelenting. Tom is galled to find it tough to keep up. It is a month since the last *pokret* – but he's hardly been sedentary during these weeks. Yet he is breathing hard. He considers stepping aside from the path, the bustling pedestrian convoy, to take a rest. The mere notion shames him: from the next level of his character he detects, as if it has physical properties, determination rising. He will not yield. The exertion of will-power is also a familiar sensation from the forced marches, and it is soon followed by a corresponding response in his body: a second wind, his lungs becoming accustomed to the burden. Muscles loosen. Joints are oiled. Dependable mechanisms of a human animal.

Pero marches in front of him, assigned to the role of interpreter for the Allied officer. He does not walk up on his toes any more, bouncing up off each tread; his stride is settled, and steadier.

After a few hours they pause to rest on a hillside. Below them is a vineyard. The ripe green and yellow grapes hang in swollen bunches, tantalising the hungry foot soldiers. Tom is having a smoke with the company commander when a sergeant comes over with a request.

'Permission to eat grapes, sir.'

The commander looks lazily over towards his men, the vineyard, and around the surrounding hills. He nods. 'Permission granted. Take necessary precautions.'

Lookouts are posted along the ridge. The sergeant gives a signal. The soldiers place their weapons on the ground and rush down to the vines. They stuff themselves with grapes, handfuls at a time, the juice flowing down their jaws.

*

The human snake of soldiers crosses open meadows. Peasants work in the fields, horse-drawn ploughs rattle along uneven furrows, the air is filled with the smell of freshly turned earth. The Partisans glance anxiously at the sky, prick up their ears, unprotected by the canopy of trees.

They pass by a village. Two bullocks are requisitioned: the owner of one is recompensed with a promissory note at which he stares morosely as his beast is led away; whether he distrusts the promise or is simply illiterate Tom cannot tell. He glances back and sees more of the line behind him, before they re-enter the woods.

The sun is still high when they come to rest in the fields and orchards of a hamlet. Great vats – of aluminium and copper – are boiling on open fires. A stew of beef, with little seasoning but herbs thrown in; potatoes, carrots. The bullocks that have come with them these last few miles are led away to have their throats cut. In an open barn, on a wooden table made of rough-hewn planks nailed together, a butcher divides a carcass ready for the vat. Small circles of men peel potatoes.

A stout pair carry one of the vats, with a pole stuck through its two handles, into an orchard. The soldiers lying there rise from the grass like dead men. Holding their jerrycans they form a chow line. A cook doles out the stew. It is rich with meat. They know that a serious battle lies ahead.

Tom comes across Marija and Stipe in the afternoon, in the corner of a field at one side of the village, a little removed from the main body of soldiers. He approaches slowly. Stipe sees him, and nudges Marija. She glances towards him, and a look of hatred flashes in her eyes. She stands. Tom feels for a moment a spasm of physical fear. He has seen her anger and knows it is beyond her control. Will she draw a pistol or a knife? She turns away.

Tom collects himself, swallows, stiffens his weak resolve, steps towards her. 'Marija.'

She does not look at him.

'Can we talk?' he asks. 'It is good to see you.'

Marija lights herself a cigarette. She grasps the hand that holds a match, using one hand to stop the other shaking. When finally she looks at Tom her fury has been succeeded by contempt. 'Talk, yes,' she says. 'Why not?'

Tom cannot fathom what is going on, but Marija shakes her head, and enlightens him. 'Do not worry. I am not some sweet young *ingénue*. I am a once-married woman, Tom. I am older than you. It is not your fault that when I opened your note I hoped you had written to invite me to your home in England. To share the life of a poor scholar in Oxford or a schoolteacher in some quiet market town. Of course you would be wrong to offer me this. Of course Jovan is a more appropriate man for me. Yes, he loves me. You think I do not know? What does it matter what I feel? Or that I met you?'

So, she has read the note. 'Marija—'

'No, Tom, please.' She drops the cigarette, half-smoked, to the ground, and stubs it out with the toe of her boot. There is a crack in the leather along the side, just above the sole. She glances up at him, then turns and looks into the distance, where two ponies are grazing by a pear tree. 'Your honesty,' Marija says, 'is admirable. I do not care for it, that is all.'

Marija turns, and walks away. Watching her, Tom finds himself overcome by a great sorrow. He is aware of a pressure in his throat, pricking behind his eyes, not known since childhood, the urge to cry. For Marija? For Jovan? For himself, in his confusion?

Tom walks away from the village, hoping that movement might shift this sadness, this need to weep, from his body. There must be a ring of sentries to stop him wandering too far. What if an enemy plane flies overhead and spots all this activity? he wonders. He sees a team of soldiers. One looks as if he is kneading dough. Another is tying string around a finished loaf, as if wrapping a gift. As Tom comes closer he is struck by a sickeningly sweet smell, which he recognises as that of plastic explosives. They have been delivered shaped like black sausages: each soldier rolls eight or ten of these together, and then a length of fuse is attached.

Back at the headquarters Pero is chatting with couriers who wait to be sent ahead. Tom takes him aside. 'Did you give Marija my note?' he asks. 'Was it you?'

Pero looks around, fearful that someone might overhear them. And understand English. 'I should not have.' He grins, is boyish once more. 'One of the guards took it from your pocket, and passed it to me. I should have handed it to our intelligence chief. But I knew it had nothing to do with politics, or war. We could all see how Marija felt. She cannot hide her feelings.' Pero smiles, is glad to have played the role of go-between. How can Tom be cross with him? Did he himself not want the note delivered?

'Suppose you were found out?' he asks. 'I dread to think what punishment you would have received.'

Pero nods, and then his eyes widen for a moment, as if he had not considered the consequences. Perhaps he really hadn't. 'You and Marija are my friends,' he says, and he seems to Tom to become even younger again. He speaks like a child, his voice almost a whine, as if he is justifying what he did to a parent, or teacher; yet what he says has the moral authority of a man.

*

In the late afternoon Tom tries to count the soldiers scattered in the grass, around the houses and barns. There are perhaps a thousand. Few will have eaten as well as this for a long time. They have slept, they doze, a long, lazy siesta. Some are delousing each other. A man sits on a tree stump and receives a shave from his unit's barber. The barber wipes the lather off his cut-throat razor with a leaf. In one of the orchards a girl is singing. Others, unable to sleep, perhaps, unable to still their contemplation of what might lie ahead, clean their weapons; some roll green tobacco in strips of paper and smoke, passing the cigarettes to their companions. Tom loops his arm through the sling of his Beretta, lowers his head to the grass, closes his eyes and in moments sleep switches off his consciousness.

They receive their orders at dusk and leave the hamlet, each soldier with two or three plastic charges in his knapsack. Tom watches them assemble in the meadow, take their place in line, move forward unquestioningly, dumb pilgrims to battle. He thinks, watching them, that surely every infantry in the world is and always has been composed of tough young men. But this one is augmented by schoolgirls; boys whose voices have not yet broken; bow-legged old men; peasants, some with their broad-beamed, heavy-bosomed wives beside them. Their smallholding and what little they owned burned in a moment of spiteful destruction by some enemy patrol on a Slovenian hillside. There are farm girls with big red hands; a tailor from Maribor; urban intellectuals and artists toughened in the fresh air; pretty women like Marija, cartridge belt slung across her chest, followed by Stipe carrying their light machine gun.

The uniforms in the crocodile line have a comic variety of colour: the khaki of British battle-dress, *Wehrmacht* dark grey,

Alpini light green, one man in the tight-fitting black britches of the *Gestapo*, camouflage canvas, tailored blankets. Many wear their own, civilian clothes, with only the *Titovka* cap on their heads the one binding, identifying mark they have in common.

Weapons too are motley: Berettas, P38s, long-barrelled French Lebel rifles dating back to the early 1900s, Brens and Lee-Enfields, lobster-shaped Schmeissers. The occasional pistol: German lugers and American 45s. An army of amateurs; a revolutionary army.

September 3

They march through the dark in single file. The exact route is known only to couriers at the front, runners at the rear. In spite of the chilly air Tom sweats profusely. In the woods there is little light and at times he holds the tail of Pero's jacket; the man behind him grasps his. When they pass through fields and orchards the stars illuminate their passage. Beneath fruit trees Tom stretches up his arms, his fingers groping for apples, but though he is tall the branches have already been stripped.

Back in the forest it is as if they burrow through a black tunnel, their faces brushed and whipped by branches. The pace quickens. Tom stumbles, is yanked forward, he trots to keep up with Pero, and understands they are going downhill. In the darkness he knows they are ascending when his legs have to work harder and his lungs gulp for oxygen.

'*Stoj!*' They stop, clumsily, then wait. Sit down. Tom chews on a lump of black bread he'd stowed in his pocket, passes a piece to Pero.

'*Tisina.*' The word is passed along – 'Silence' – and they listen to the drone of vehicles on some road not far away that seem to be going in the direction from which they have come. Another order: '*Naprej.*' They rise, and move forward.

Despite the pace, they do not reach their destination before dawn. Tom realises that the trees amongst which he passes are differentiating themselves one from another, and trunks from branches, leaves, in shades of silvery grey. He has that uncanny feeling of light coming not from the sky but from the ground. As a child he loved adventure stories that involved journeys to the centre of the earth; folk tales set in underground worlds. The question of how light reached those kingdoms was essential to their wonder. So, too, there is magic at dawn in the forest.

Once more the order for silence comes down the line. There is another German garrison to clear. Will it be the last? They climb a hill and look behind them on a fog-filled valley, the tops of trees emerging like stalagmites. The sun tinges the green hills a pale pink. The soldiers crest the ridge and reach a village that they learn is their destination: from here the attack will be launched. Forest stretches out below. Through it flows the Sava river. The Litija bridge is down there, two miles away.

The men and women flop down, in barns where there is space, or in the open, and sleep. When Tom is woken, he and Pero go and find the headquarters staff. They chew on lumps of boiled meat and bread, while the company commanders speculate on when the air attack will come off. The Allied planes are due any time after four.

At two o'clock the commanders return to their companies, detachments are sent to take up their positions. Tom and Pero move forward. Soldiers lean against tree trunks, crouch by the path, lie on the forest floor. Some smoke, others doze. One or two look anxious, troubled by the violence that awaits. As he passes her, Tom notices one young woman give an involuntary shudder: her body is trying to shake off the morbid prospects conjured by her mind. Yet most are lost in thought, gazing at nothing visible, in a state of narcoleptic vacancy, or acceptance.

*

Tom and Pero reach the divisional commander. 'How far are we from the bridge?' Tom asks.

The commander is a young man, much the same age as Tom. He removes his *Titovka*, to reveal a shaven head. Perhaps he had bad lice? It gives him a menacing appearance. 'One kilometre.'

Tom shakes his head. 'The bomb line is one mile.'

The commander shrugs his shoulders, and laughs. 'One kilometre, one mile.'

Tom wanders away. He would like to see Marija, and Stipe. Not to speak with them but just to see her, on the eve of battle, summoning within herself – he is certain she must perform such a ritual – martial energy; a brooding malevolence. But he cannot find them. He is struck, indeed, by how few soldiers there seem to be. Whether this is because they are now dispersed across the forested hill above the bridge, or because as the time of the attack draws near so however many there are do not seem to him to be enough, Tom is not sure. He returns to the shaven-headed commander. Tom offers him a cigarette.

The commander inhales deeply, and exhales through his nose. 'I thought he was your interpreter,' he says, nodding to Pero.

'He is not supposed to speak our language so well,' Pero protests. 'It is not my fault, sir. I did not teach him.'

As they talk, Tom and the commander find out they were born in the same month, April, 1918. Both were studying when war called them out, one at Oxford, the other in Budapest.

'Will you return, do you think, when this is over?' Tom asks. He wonders if the man shaves his head to disguise his education.

'I studied history. Now I am one of those making it. I suppose afterwards I shall have to teach it.'

They cease their conversation, and wait. The Partisans await the Allied air attack like a runner the starting pistol. How vital the planes are! Sound takes on that anticipatory quality familiar, from all the midnight drops, of an emptiness, a silence in which noise is imminent. The airwaves, it seems, are themselves taut with expectation.

Shortly before four thirty they hear the faint sound of the planes. The commander leaps up, grabbing his Schmeisser, and runs to his lookout point. Tom follows, with his binoculars. Far above, six fighters fly over, very high. Tom looks around. Every soldier peers through the canopy of leaves above him. The enemy's guns are still silent, for he is unaware who is overhead and what is about to befall him.

The first of the six Mustangs comes back, diving, and now the ack-ack opens up. Tom sees from the plane's wings two black shapes detach themselves and drop down. The crunch of the explosion mingles with the flak, as the second plane comes in. Under the trees the Partisans now are laughing and slapping each other on the back, yelling encouragement to the pilots as one Mustang after the other dives, unloads its bombs, and is gone. There are the final bursts of anti-aircraft fire that chase the last plane from the valley like a terrier yapping after a visitor. The silence that follows the departure of the last plane is eerie. It is terribly strange, for it cannot last. Tom is suspended from existence, he hovers above it, time holds its breath.

And then suddenly there is gunfire everywhere. On the far side of the river the brigade that has come up from the free territory in the south – tracing perhaps the same route Tom and the others took three months ago – is making its attack.

The commander waves his Schmeisser in the air and yells to his men, '*Juris, hura!*' He rushes forward through the trees, followed by soldiers, including Tom and Pero. They scurry down the steep hillside, grabbing saplings and branches to slow their helter-skelter headlong progress.

In a gap between trees Tom sees the bridge laid across the wide river, high sides a latticework of metal. On the far bank a farmhouse is consumed by yellow flames. The bridge is untouched. The Mustangs with their small bombs were enough merely to inspire the Partisans, demoralise the enemy.

As the slope of the hill flattens out, Tom and Pero sprint through the trees. They come to a road which runs straight for a hundred yards then curves gradually out of sight. Partisans ahead of them are moving forward carefully. Then others come back the other way, carrying the wounded. As Tom walks along the road, he hears the whistle of German mortar shells. He flings himself down. Others hug either side of the road. Some have not taken cover. The commander walks slowly towards the bend in the road: the communist officers pride themselves on meeting danger head on. Tom is glad that Pero crouches beside him – even if only, perhaps, because these are his orders. They lie low, and Tom passes a cigarette to Pero, and another to a boy behind him. If this is the only road to the bridge, he wonders, then where is everyone? Suddenly he is rocked back. Pero, a couple of yards ahead, looks at him, as surprised as Tom is. Something has happened but no one knows what. But of course: a mortar shell landed, close by. Tom turns to the boy. The boy's eyes widen as his shirt and jacket bloom with blood. Tom crawls across and grasps his shoulders, and lowers him gently to the grass. The boy moans. Blood trickles from his lips, his nose. His face is otherwise pale. He still looks surprised. He gulps sounds that are like words, faintly, then he gasps and the life is gone from him. Tom reaches over and closes the boy's eyes. He turns and sees that mortars are still coming in, landing in puffs of black smoke.

A young woman stalks up the road carrying a sub-machine gun. Reaching the bend in the road she stops, leans back and fires her gun from the hip. A crouching figure tries to pull her down to cover, grabbing one of her trouser legs, but she kicks herself free and runs on, disappearing from sight.

She is the last one Tom sees go on towards the bridge. Others come the other way, retreating; some wounded, many not. They come back with the air of people who have changed their minds about something.

Tom runs past them. He has a compulsion to see the bridge, or the attack, or simply what lies around the bend in the road. The view of a battlefield is rarely clear. Even the few who are able to think clearly can make little sense of the chaos when they are in the midst of it. When he turns the corner, Tom can see the bridge two to three hundred yards ahead. Figures are running in all directions. Mortar fire comes from German positions; there is a tank in front of the bridge. Small-arms fire rattles around them, past them. A disorientating din. Tom feels a tug on his sleeve and lets himself be dragged by Pero towards the frail shelter of some thin trees at the side of the road.

There are many Partisans sheltering amongst the trees. Some lean out from behind a trunk, fire from their carbines, then duck back. Tom becomes aware of a strong, sweet smell. Peering deeper into the wood he makes out Partisan sappers preparing their explosive devices from the plastic loaves brought in in twos and threes. First a path has to be cleared to the bridge.

Tom and Pero work their way through the wood, closer towards the river. There are many soldiers but it is hard to tell if they are massing here for a full-frontal assault or hiding, having retreated from the perilous road. They come across the young commander. A girl is beside him. She cuts off the sleeve of the right arm of his jacket.

'What's happening?' Tom asks him.

Now the girl removes the sleeve of the commander's shirt. 'We took them by surprise,' he says, with some vehemence, though this may be due to the pain he must be feeling. His arm is covered in blood. It pours from a wound above his elbow. 'But they were expecting us,' he says, with equal anger.

The young woman dresses the wound with a bandage. 'Come back,' she tells him. 'Come to the rear.'

'No,' he replies. 'The bone is not broken. Our people on the other side,' he says, turning to Tom, 'they have artillery. Anti-tank guns. They have ox-carts to carry the wounded home! We must wait for them to break through and clear the bridge, before we can mine it.'

'But German reinforcements might come while you are waiting...' Tom ventures.

The commander frowns, as if Tom has reminded him of something he'd considered, but then tried to ignore. 'Yes, yes. But if we hold them off till nightfall.' He shakes his head, as if disagreeing with himself.

The young woman ties the bandage and the commander rises without a word to her, or to Tom, and walks through the trees towards the bridge, calling out to his soldiers to accompany him. They obey, getting stiffly to their feet. Within moments, it seems, the wood around Tom and Pero has emptied. Even the young nurse has disappeared. Tom realises with dismay that a few stupid words he uttered to the commander have prompted a proud and reckless response. The forces at his disposal are clearly inadequate to the task in hand. But why? Why are there not more Partisans? What is going on? He saw the orders sent from Marshal Tito, via British signals, for major attacks across Yugoslavia, of which this is one. And then it occurs to him: something unthinkable which, as soon as it is thought, becomes obvious: that original order was followed by other orders, separate from the Allies, for the Partisans themselves. *Do not commit large numbers of men, weapons or explosives. We shall need these for later. Make an effort, for those who provide for us. A little effort.*

It strikes Tom, too, that Jovan knows. The truth washes through him, like a wave of nausea. So why then let the command send Tom? Did Jovan think he was the simplest British officer? The one most easily duped? But there is no time to ponder now.

Tom runs after the departed Partisans, Pero with him. He reaches the edge of the wood much sooner than he had expected. There is a large, mostly open area between the wood and the river. The Partisans are storming the bridge with little covering fire, and few places to hide. They fall, stumble, are dragged and carried back.

There is a yell, a few yards away, to their left. Tom turns. Pero is already moving. It is Stipe who cried out. Tom rushes over. It is not Stipe who has been hit, but Marija, collapsed over her gun.

'Come,' Tom says. 'Quick.' Stipe lifts her shoulders, Pero her legs, and they carry her back through the trees.

'The gun,' Pero says.

'Leave it,' Tom tells him.

When they have passed beyond the line of fire they lay Marija down. Tom opens her shirt. A bullet has entered just above her left breast, and passed out below the shoulder blade, leaving a jagged hole. She is bleeding profusely. Tom takes off his shirt, dirty and sweat-soaked as it is, and they bind her as best they can.

'There is a first-aid station in the village where we stayed this morning,' Pero says.

'Good,' Tom says. 'We will carry her back.' Stipe cuts two ash saplings, lashing them together with smaller branches. Pero is gone and reappears with a blanket, with which they fashion a stretcher. Tom picks up the end opposite Stipe and they follow Pero back through the trees and up the hill away from the river. Marija is unconscious. The sounds of battle grow fainter.

The stretcher is jerry-built, and Marija's weight is awkward. Tom stumbles, and they almost drop her, so they stop and find flexible tendrils of a climbing plant and tie her to the stretcher.

It seems to take twice as long to trace the journey back from the bridge to the village, and it is dark by the time they find the small farmhouse at the end of a gloomy lane and carry Marija in. There are two low-ceilinged rooms. A Partisan follows the doctor around with a kerosene lamp. The floors are covered with hay and crowded with wounded men. They lay Marija down. An aide removes Tom's blood-soaked shirt from her. The doctor takes off his spectacles and wipes them carefully, before kneeling down and washing the wound in Marija's back. Her flesh is very white and delicate. The wound does not stop bleeding. He cleans it with sulphonamide powder and bandages it with fresh linen, then turns her over and does the same for the little entry wound above her small, pale breast. It is only as he finishes dressing the wounds that Marija wakes up. The first thing she does is to grimace and groan with pain. Tom wishes she could return to unconsciousness.

'It is all right,' the doctor says. 'We still have a little morphine.' He gives Marija an injection, and though she does not open her eyes, she stops moaning.

When the doctor stands up he looks at Tom, at his uniform, and says in English, 'May I have a cigarette?'

'How is she?' Tom asks, snapping open his lighter.

The doctor exhales the smoke. 'There is nothing I can do for her here,' he says. 'Perhaps there is nothing anyone can do.'

He smokes some more. 'I would prefer not to move her, but we shall all have to move out during the night. The Germans will be keen, as always, to kill our wounded.' He leaves them, to deal with another patient who has been brought in.

Stipe kneels beside Marija, holding her hand. She is sleeping once more.

'Could you follow the route we took?' Tom asks Pero. 'Back to the valley?'

Pero considers the question, then slowly nods. 'Yes,' he says, 'I believe I could.'

'Come on,' Tom says. 'We're leaving.'

September 4

They walk through the dark night. Stipe holds the front of the stretcher, Tom is at the back. In the depths of the forest Pero ties a plait of bindweed around his waist and Stipe's, and leads him forward. In the darkness Tom could almost forget he is a stretcher-bearer; can imagine the poles are in his hands to guide him.

Tom is in a mulish frame of mind. He has set his shoulder to this task: to get Marija home. Their temporary home in the liberated valley, and one of the hospitals there. The doctor, Olga. If she can be saved, Olga will save her.

How does Pero know the way? He is like a homing pigeon. Perhaps couriers have awakened in themselves some dormant animal instinct, some internal compass tuned to the magnetic fields of the earth.

Crossing a hilltop meadow, Tom notices a faint warm glow in the darkness ahead, intermittently visible past Stipe's solid body. As they come closer, the outline of a small wayside shrine begins to take form. The yellow light is from a tiny altar lamp. They pause for a rest. 'It is safe here,' Pero says. 'The people light the lamps in the shrines only when an area is free of German patrols.'

Marija sleeps. Pero goes to the nearby farmhouse and comes back with a loaf of bread, and some apples. The men consume half the food, then set off again.

*

The weight of the stretcher is not great, and Stipe has the heavier end, but Tom's shoulders burn. He can feel a soreness in his palms where blisters are forming, for though the bark of the ash poles is smooth it is constantly shifting, rubbing his skin, as they walk.

He is dimly aware of people following behind him.

Soon after dawn they rest in a clearing. There are twenty or thirty other Partisans with them now. Some are wounded, with bandages tied over their heads, or with sticks to help their limping gait, two more on makeshift stretchers carried by comrades. Marija is still unconscious. Stipe feeds her water, and apple mush, like a baby. She swallows it in her sleep. *Do not wake up*, Tom pleads. Then he himself puts his head to the ground, and falls asleep.

They wake very soon and walk on, having shared the last of the bread and apples. Stipe will not let the other two carry the stretcher. Pero takes over from Tom, but Stipe turns the stretcher around, with Marija carried feet first now, so that he still bears the heavier end. Tom trudges after him. The others straggle behind Tom.

The day is baking hot. They move at a slow but steady pace. Every now and again Tom hears motorised vehicles – one, or two; at other times a whole column – thundering close or rumbling in the distance along a road. There is no consistency to the vehicles' direction.

Late in the morning they stop. Tom climbs with Pero to a ridge from where they can see the way ahead. They must cross a river. Through his field glasses Tom can see small clusters of soldiers in German uniforms on the meadows above the canyon. They have red and white chequerboard insignia on the arms of their jackets: Ustasha, the Croatian fascists.

When Tom and Pero return to their comrades, Stipe waves

them frantically over: Marija is conscious. Her eyes seem to have withdrawn, are hooded and grey. Stipe tells them that she feels no pain. She smiles when she recognises Tom, kneeling beside her, taking her right hand in his.

'You are here,' she says, her voice faint.

Tom nods. 'We're going to get you back,' he tells her. 'To a hospital.'

'You are here,' she whispers. Tom feels a slight sensation, a pulse, in his bloody palm, realises it is Marija's attempt to squeeze his hand. He squeezes hers, lets it go, and stands. Around him, it is clear, are many more Partisans than there were earlier. Pero is their courier and Tom their leader. He gives the order to move out. He and Stipe carry Marija's stretcher; it occurs to Tom to appoint two able-bodied men to carry a corner each; but he cannot persuade Stipe to share a handle, and so nor does he. It is their cross to bear, together.

Pero leads the way. They descend towards the river. The trees thin out. In front of them is a clearing where the trees have been felled by loggers. A huddle of half a dozen Partisans whom they have caught up with are ahead of them, sheltering behind the last trees. They explain that a battery of howitzers are shelling the clearing, but there is no way round it, for there are cliffs above and below.

'We run,' Tom tells them. His order is passed back down the line. 'If the shells begin to sound, fall flat, then start again in the next lull.'

The soldiers wait for Pero to set off, Tom and Stipe running clumsily behind, along a little path amid boulders, over corpses of men and horses who have tried to go before them. Tom understands that his party is merely one of many in the middle of a great retreat. Shells explode around them, but not close, and they do not stop but run with their burden at a frantic pace.

Soon they reach the river. The small suspension bridge across it is undamaged, though the surrounding banks are freshly gouged, and covered with corpses. The steep meadow on the far side is also strewn with bodies. They cross the bridge at their awkward trot. Artillery begins to resound. They reach the meadow and begin to climb, moving from sparse tree to bush to mound. They put Marija on her stretcher down on the ground and lie around her. Tom looks through his binoculars: the enemy operating the mortars are dressed in Italian helmets and grey tattered uniforms, some remnant band left behind at the capitulation, marooned in a war in which they have no allegiance, but they fight on, for killing and dying is all they know.

'*Naprej*,' Tom says. They scuttle forward.

It takes so long to cross the meadow, lurching from one pathetic cover to the next: time stops and though they stagger as fast as they can they make no progress, none at all, and Tom knows they are in a dream, his dream, and this will never end. The canyon rumbles with explosions. They will spend eternity here, struggling on up the steep slope, going nowhere, comrades falling around them, until a shell hits them too. A plane roars overhead. Before they reach the relative safety of the trees it flies over them again, much lower this time, spraying the field.

The survivors congregate in the forest. Stipe tends to Marija, tries to give her water. Tom scans the group. It doesn't make sense: many must have been killed crossing the steep meadow yet there appear to be more now than when they set off across the clearing on the far side of the river. It is as if the dead have risen, and joined them.

Pero takes Tom to the highest point on the hill, from where they can see smoke rising from burning villages, to the east and to the west. Machine-gun fire echoes across the hills. From ahead of them, north-west, comes the all too frequent roar of bombs.

They walk on in the afternoon. The sun is lost in a grey sky. Droplets of rain slip through the trees and fall lightly upon them. There is a distinctive scent, that made by a mild autumn rain on fallen leaves. Tom's mind is transported: even in the midst of this inferno a sense of dread in his stomach, of going back to school after the long summer holiday. For half an hour the light drizzle refreshes them. They must find food.

They walk through a village where yellow houses on each side of the street are blackened shells, with gaping windows and roofs that have fallen in, but they do not stop.

For an hour they hear the enemy without meeting him. Once they halt and crouch and watch one, two, three, four lorries driving along a lane no more than fifty yards away. One is full of German soldiers. Another bears the insignia of the Slovene flag, with the Carniolan eagle upon it. Heading in which direction? To the bridge? To the valley? Going to, or returning from, battle?

They rise and move on, as fast as they can. But a boy runs up to Tom and tells him, 'They are not far behind us.' Tom orders a small unit to cover the retreat. He waits with them long enough to see through his binoculars a number of the enemy come over a rise not in their footsteps but off to the side, as if following a parallel course. They are dressed in greenish-grey and faded brown uniforms and wear peaked caps, but some wear scarlet fezzes with black tassels that flow behind them like the pony-tails of young girls as they run, and they have an emblem of a scimitar on their collar patches.

*

They rest in a beech grove. Tom orders the most severely wounded to be left where they are. There are not enough able-bodied men to prop up and carry them. Yet he knows he will not leave Marija behind. A score of men accept the reality of their predicament. One, whose right leg has been blown off at the knee, asks only that they be allowed to keep their weapons. A young woman, a nurse, volunteers to stay with them. Tom tells her she does not need to, it is futile, but she insists, and he does not argue in the face of her courage. A futile death is what she chooses. He looks at her. She turns shyly away. She is blond, moon-faced and plain, with freckles on her cheeks.

The beech grove is in a natural bowl on the slope of a hill. The combination of the sculpted earth and the stately trees is naturally theatrical. As they pull out Tom looks back. The soldier without a leg and one or two of his lame companions take up positions facing the way they have come, ready for their pursuers. The nurse tends to a groaning man.

They pass a farmhouse, whose peasants give them eggs and cider. Marija is once more conscious, though her eyes have sunk deeper into their sockets and her skin is grey, and she does not seem to recognise Tom this time. She whispers something but when he lowers his ear to her lips he hears nothing but her faint breathing. After they set off, an old man cries out from the farm: he limps after them, with a bottle of *rakija*.

Pero and Stipe carry the stretcher. They hear shots in the distance behind them. Tom steps aside from the column, raises his glasses. The Partisans hurry past him. He looks into the trees, changes focus, suddenly sees men in camouflage uniform, clutching sub-machine guns, crouching low and weaving through the wood.

Have they seen him? He turns and runs after his companions.

By evening their ragged column is once more longer than when the wounded were left, replenished along the way by scattered troops and stragglers. Here the rain must have fallen more heavily: they stumble along a muddy path and into the wet forest. At once they come across dead bodies scattered by a track and the thunder of shells ahead. Tom turns, raises his arm and cries, '*Naprej!*' They dash forward, towards the booming shells, with the others bunching behind Tom. They run not away from but towards each explosion, for the next round of shells should land elsewhere.

Beyond the explosions they carry on through the forest and come across half a dozen Partisans skinning a horse beside a crackling fire. Their hunger makes them unreasonable. They are drooling from the smell, impatient with hunger. It is difficult to persuade anyone to stand guard. As the flesh is roasting a woman becomes hysterical and an old man, as if infected by her, begins to scream. A female Partisan slaps the woman, who is stunned into quiescence. She slaps the old man too but this has no effect, so she takes his gun off him and swings it at his head so hard that the rifle butt breaks, and the man falls to the ground.

They eat their fill of barely cooked horsemeat. Stipe chews and spits morsels into his hand, then feeds them to Marija like a bird regurgitating food for its young. He pours drops of *rakija* onto her lips. They sleep.

After Tom has fallen fast asleep, something seems to awaken him. In his mind Christ appears: the figure from Piero della Francesca's *Baptism* in the National Gallery; yet one also from a book of his father's on the Northern Renaissance; and one too from the fresco in their local church, fourteenth century, faded. This Christ is stern, sad, understanding. Tom has rejected this saviour; he tries consciously to dispel the image, but in vain. It only melts into a still sadder, sterner gentleness. Tom opens his eyes. Around him are the trees and his slumbering companions. And silence, endless and lasting, as if there have been no planes or guns, no explosions or screams. He closes his eyes, and there is Christ again – tangible, close enough to touch. Tom begins to speak to Him: why are you here? Do you not know that I have lost my faith in you? My schoolboy religion has been dispelled by what I have seen. What hope I have I put in the hands of men: we shall make heaven on earth or we shall not, there is no help for it.

Yet the figure looks on, His expression unchanged. He is sad that Tom has lost his faith but He understands. More than that: He knows that such faith as Tom had *should* be lost. He is severe, unrelenting. Forgiveness is not the easy option, but the hardest.

'No,' Tom says. 'Do not abandon us.' He stops resisting, and the image fades as sleep absorbs him.

September 5

They wake in the forest, covered in dew. A fog has settled amongst the trees. From a nearby spring two boys ferry water, and Stipe moistens Marija's lips. She is breathing so faintly they can hardly be certain that she is alive. Her skin is clear, unlined, yet it has the pallor of an old woman. A man has died during the night.

Tom gives Pero his compass. 'It is yours,' he says. 'You may need it.' Pero studies it. He nods in gratitude.

There are about a hundred troops with them now, from various units and staffs. They are loaded down with ammunition. No one has any food. Three wounded, in great pain, choose to stay where they are and cover the rear of the ragged band, who set off, leaving behind one large cooking pot, the dead, and the wounded. They have barely begun when they hear the faint yelp of a bloodhound, and then a horse whinnying, some way behind them.

Pero walks in front, Tom and Stipe carry Marija, just the two of them again, for their fellow stretcher-bearers have disappeared and Tom lacks the will to recruit two more. He has wrapped his blistered palms in leaves. A rocket flashes in their direction from somewhere to the east. Soon mortars begin to tear up the ground and undergrowth around them, but they do not stop. They stagger blindly forward through the fog, now with two Partisans on either side of Pero, sub-machine guns at the ready should they stumble into the enemy. They are terrified but Pero strides forward. Planes fly overhead, the sound of their engines muffled.

After an hour of walking they realise the fog is thinning, and lifting, they are visible, and vulnerable, and wish that it would wrap them once more in its embrace. Pero takes over Tom's end of the stretcher. They cross a meadow in which sheep hustle away from them on their spindly legs. There is movement off to one side and Tom sees through his glasses more of the Chetniks who'd chased them off the mountain, with their black beards and long hair and silver metal skull and crossbones. Panning the glasses, he sees a band of Cossacks in their Astrakhan hats, moving along parallel to his column, as if to overtake them.

Above, planes fly about, and the convoy of straggling combatants are in full view, but it no longer seems worthy of the pilots' attention. Tom glances back and sees that on Stipe's broad peasant face tears are sliding over his cheekbones, but he does not stop.

They walk on, through forest, back into the valley. Through a break in the trees they see an enemy column down below moving slowly out along the main road. They walk through the woods in which until a few days ago two thousand soldiers were billeted. Their imprint is slight: in clearings, the ashes of camp fires; bones of chewed meat; the odd piece of metal or scrap of fabric. A Partisan lookout sees them approach but turns away as they pass. Half a dozen men dismantle a field kitchen, strapping pots and ladles to the panniers of two ponies standing patiently by.

When they reach headquarters the two men on guard let them by without a word. For a second Tom sees, in their eyes, what he and his companions must look like. Haggard men returned from battle with a comrade on a stretcher. Tom with no shirt beneath his battledress jacket. Pero all muddied. The big man bedraggled. Tom glances back, past Stipe. They are now alone. The soldiers behind them have disappeared as discreetly as they'd joined. As if they were an illusion, a band of dead men escorting them on their journey home.

Pero stops. They lay the stretcher down upon the grass. The headquarters is being emptied. One could believe the ox-carts are this region's rustic equivalents of English removals lorries. A printing press is being tied down. Archives are carried out. An officer on the wooden veranda signs a piece of paper and bends over the banister to hand it to a courier, who takes off at a jog. The officer, as he pulls himself back up to his full, familiar height, makes a quick visual sweep of what lies before him. His gaze rests on the three men. Tom detaches himself from the others and walks towards the balcony. When he reaches it he becomes aware of himself saluting his fellow officer. A fatuous gesture Jovan does not return. He looks past Tom.

'You are moving out,' Tom says.

Jovan refocuses on Tom, below him. 'It is no longer safe here,' he says. He glances back at the others, and at the body on the stretcher, then once more at Tom. 'Though the whole world knows that Germany will be defeated, the Home Guard are fighting us as never before, ferociously. It is hard to understand.' He shakes his head. 'And they are being joined by all the rabble and scum.'

Jovan looks away again, and asks the question that he must ask. 'Who is that?'

Tom slowly takes a breath; exhales it. 'Marija,' he says.

The muscles in Jovan's hard-set jaw work visibly beneath the skin, tiny tremors, intimate spasms that reveal the effort he is making to suppress any greater movement. With his mouth barely open he asks, 'Is she dead?'

'Yes.'

Jovan nods slowly. His eyes narrow, his face darkens. 'You

have brought her here,' he declares flatly. He looks down at Tom. 'Have you brought the gun?'

'The gun?' Tom asks. 'No.'

Now Jovan's face twists with confused feelings. Anger triumphs. 'Why not?' he demands. 'What use is a body?' His lips are flecked with spittle. 'A machine gun is worth five live men, and five hundred dead ones.' Jovan's face is red, his eyes blaze, he looks ready to explode.

Tom turns away.

'If it had been anyone else,' Jovan says, and Tom turns back. 'If it had been one of my men, anyone but you, I would have him shot.'

Tom shakes his head. He has nothing to say. His feelings have made Jovan into someone other than what and who he is. And he was wrong to bring Marija here.

'Is Colonel Farwell still here?' Tom asks.

'They left two days ago,' Jovan says. 'For the south. You will follow.'

Tom looks up at Jovan. Whom he thought he loved; but he did not know him.

As if reading Tom's mind, as he had often seemed to do, Jovan says, 'How could she have preferred you?' There is hatred in his eyes. 'Look at you. What do you look like? A peasant Partisan! Yes. You have achieved your metamorphosis, Tom, your rebirth. You think you are one of us now? You will always be a liberal capitalist enemy, but you are a sentimental one. I prefer Farwell. He knows what he is made of. He knows we are opposed to each other. It is me or him in the world to come.' Jovan turns away, his resolve faltering for a moment. When he turns back the hatred has gone from his face. 'Do you not see, Tom?' he says.

Tom nods. He is weak and exhausted, his stomach is empty. His mind is blank, there is no point in words. He turns away. Jovan says after him, 'The bridge has not been blown.'

Tom does not respond. He returns to the others.

They are very tired. They have eaten nothing but scraps for twenty-four hours. Pero finds a spade, and they carry the stretcher deep into the woods. Under a tall beech tree Stipe digs a hole. Tom lifts Marija. Her dead body seems much lighter than it was when he held her that night in his arms; as if her vitality had physical substance. Stipe wraps her head in the blanket they'd used for the stretcher. He says he cannot bear to think of her with dirt in her hair. They lower her into the grave, and Pero covers her with soil. The hole is filled. They bury their fallen warrior.

They leave Stipe at the grave. The one of us, Tom thinks, who truly loved her. Tom tells Pero he is going to the British Mission house to wash, eat, put on fresh clothes, before leaving.

The house is a charred ruin. The woman who had looked after the Englishmen is sifting through the still-warm ashes for metal utensils. A man of the same age recovers nails. He puts them in a little pile. A child collects shards of pottery bowls. Another finds the blade of a knife; new handles will need to be carved. They work methodically, without undue haste or excitement, as if it is something these people are used to, their home burned down at least once in every century.

Tom leaves them to their labour. The afternoon draws towards evening. He can hear occasional shots, down in the valley. He makes his way to the Soviet Mission house. It stands unscathed. The Soviets have gone, but the family who have moved back in now feed Tom. They give him hot water to wash. A boy disappears and returns with a shirt that almost fits him. Tom sleeps on a straw pallet, a deep and dreamless oblivion.

September 7

When Tom wakes it is late morning.

The woman of the house gives him bread and honey, and milk. He goes outside and finds Pero, studying the compass Tom gave him. Pero looks up, and nods.

'I have been waiting,' Pero says. 'It is time to leave.'

Tom puts a hand on Pero's shoulder. 'Let us go,' he says.

They climb through the forest. Although Tom was asleep he knows, somehow, he can sense perhaps by a moisture in the atmosphere, that it was misty earlier this morning. The sky is washed clean, and is a wonderfully pale yet bright eggshell blue. When they walk through a patch where the trees grow sparsely the glare of the sun is dazzling. They cross the first ridge, a high pasture, out of the valley. Tom pauses for breath. He looks across the grass to the wood ahead, and realises that amongst the beech and elm and birch, and odd coniferous trees, not a single one is the same colour as its neighbour. His eyes can see in the canopy of leaves every shade of green, though he lacks the words to name them. Some are flecked with brown as they begin to turn, in these first days of autumn. From pale silver birch to dark pine, they stand in their mute variety, growing slowly, even as he watches, so slowly, as if planted there just for him to gaze on.

Tom turns and looks back to the valley they are leaving, and beyond. He can see – across fifty or more miles of trees, pasture, crops, small towns, with here and there thin columns of smoke rising in the sunshine – towards distant peaks. The morning is unimprovable. He turns, and resumes their march.

Pero walks ahead. Tom strides behind him. They are young, and strong. But the young and strong fall at random, at fate's careless whim. Those who survive must remake the man-made world.

End

Bibliography

This author is indebted to the following books, particularly those by Basil Davidson, F.W.D. Deakin and Franklin Lindsay: remarkable accounts by Allied soldiers of their wartime experience:

Martin Armstrong: *The Fisherman*, a short story, 1927.

Roderick Bailey: *Forgotten Voices of the Secret War*, Ebury Press, 2008.

Stephen Clissold: *Djilas, The Progress of a Revolutionary*, Maurice Temple Smith, 1983.

Geoffrey Cox: *The Race for Trieste*, William Kimber & Co, 1977.

Terry Crowdy & Steve Noon: *S.O.E. Agent, Churchill's Secret Warriors*, Osprey Publishing, 2008.

Basil Davidson: *Partisan Picture*, Bedford Books Ltd, 1946.

F.W.D. Deakin: *The Embattled Mountain*, Oxford University Press, 1971.

Vladimir Dedijer: *The Beloved Land*, MacGibbon & Kee, 1961.

Vladimir Dedijer: *The War Diaries*, University of Michigan,1990.

Milovan Djilas: *Wartime*, Harcourt Brace Jovanovich, 1977.

Christie Lawrence: *Irregular Adventure*, Faber & Faber, 1946.

Franklin Lindsay: *Beacons in the Night – With the OSS and Tito's Partisans in Wartime Yugoslavia*, Stanford University Press, 1993.

Michael McConville: *A Small War in the Balkans, British Military involvement in wartime Yugoslavia 1941–1945*, MacMillan (and 2007 The Naval & Military Press Ltd), 1986.

Stevan K. Pavlowitch: *Hitler's New Disorder, The Second World War in Yugoslavia*, Hurst & Co., 2008.

John Phillips: *Yugoslav Story*, Jugoslovenska Revija, Belgrade, and Mladost, Zagreb, 1981.

Sebastian Ritchie: *Our Man in Yugoslavia, The Story of a Secret Service Operative*, Frank Cass, 2004.

Lindsay Rogers: *Guerrilla Surgeon*, Doubleday, 1957.

N. Thomas, K. Mikulan & D. Pavelic: *Axis Forces in Yugoslavia 1941–45*, Osprey Publishing, 1995.

Zvonimir Vuckovich: *A Balkan Tragedy, Yugoslavia 1941–1946: Memoirs of a Guerrilla Fighter*, East European Monographs, Boulder, 2004.

Velimir Vuksic: *Tito's Partisans 1941–45*, Osprey Publishing, 2003.

Peter Wilkinson: *Foreign Fields, The Story of an SOE Operative*, I.B. Tauris, 1997.

Thanks to internet resources www.historyplace.com, www.worldwar-2.net, and Wikipedia.

Acknowledgements

Many thanks to the Authors Foundation for a travel grant which enabled the author to make a visit to Slovenia.

Very special thanks to Alenka Snoj, Drago Mohar and Božo Vidmar for their hospitality and help during that trip. Thank you Bojana Kozul for making the connection.

Thanks to Monika Kokalj Kočevar, MA, at the National Museum of Contemporary History, Ljubljana.

Heartfelt thanks to editor Jason Arthur, Tom Avery, Stephanie Sweeney and all at William Heinemann and Windmill; to agent Victoria Hobbs; to map-maker Jane Randfield; and to Hania Porucznik and Reb Gowers.